Age-Dec

AGE-DECODED

First edition. March 15, 2021.

ISBN: 978-1393839491

Written by Mark P Ryall.

To my dear wife Lynne, who embraces me with her love and artistic spirit

CHAPTER 1

AGE-DECODED

IN THE YEAR 2053 ZONE1 buzzed with air and land traffic, Clap Music, café book readings, and free public seminars such as *How to Be Younger with Dignity, Demystifying Superintelligence,* and *Straightedge and Loving it.* Cities stood as tall and grand as ever, but the virtual technologies also drew entrepreneurs, new-fashioned enviros, and artisans to the vast, quaint, pseudo-rural areas. Climate change action, nuclear fusion, organic architecture, artificial superintelligence, quantum computing, flying cars, robotics, and virtual reality were all ripe and raging.

Yet the singular amazing feature of this world was its newfound luxury of limitless time, which fundamentally changed everything and everyone. In discovering *age-decoding* – the elimination of aging – UCLA genomicist Dr. Frieda Sengmeuller was awarded the 2053 Nobel Prize in Medicine.

A giddying upheaval, age-decoding meant growing old would never again drag humans inexorably, year by year, towards death. The age of agelessness had supplanted Nature's human design. Age-decoding enabled middle-aged and older people to cease growing older, lending them a leg-up on mortality. Younger people also shared the treasure, allowed to age-decode when they turned twenty-five years old, so the fresh blood of relative youth could ever flow through their veins and arteries.

For decades there had been reports of advancements in anti-aging research, with many scientific groups claiming progress. But most people viewed aging as *unsolvable,* just part of being human. Countless fanciful science fiction novels framed future worlds of immortality, but that was the domain of speculative fiction. However, when the highly regarded Dr. Frieda Sengmeuller announced her definitive breakthrough, the public was euphoric, and their long-held skepticism vanished like the fog with a late morning breeze.

Late on Saturday morning, Frieda lay next to her 10-year-old daughter Ximena on her King-sized bed. Together they were reading to each other from the ebook *Friendships: An Introduction*, which hovered as a holographic image optimally located about one meter from the edge of the bed for both to view.

Ximena took her turn reading out loud, "With empathy for your friend, comes respect from your friend. Empathy must be given, respect must be earned..."

Frieda could not concentrate on the book. She gazed out the window across the many rooftops rising up and beyond the hill; not focusing on New Orleans, just contemplating. Despite her recent fame over the past few months, all was not well with her. She asked herself, how could it come to this? My key undertaking as Director of the Authority's Ethical, Legal and Social Issues Committee (ELSI) is doomed. Now, twelve years of ELSI work is being shoved aside, practically blackballed. It infuriates me! The primary question of our mandate, *Who controls the implementation of age-decoding technology?*, we analyzed from every conceivable angle. We surveyed lawyers, philosophers, geneticists, epistemologists, sociologists, and business leaders. I felt I was at the helm of a scientific ship with a cargo so valuable that the world couldn't wait for it to come ashore. How did it crash and sink? I missed the signs. The less obvious signs: whispers in the hallways, disconnected conversations, and slightly awkward glances. The more obvious omens: ELSI content excluded from Authority Science Council meetings and National Institutes of Health briefings. Without ELSI, I fear, governments and corporations will reap the dividends of my discovery, but with no moral compass.

"Should I keep reading, Mom?"

"Yes Xi, you're doing great."

Her daughter went on, "There is a natural limit to the number of friends one person can have. By this we do not mean social media friends, but ..."

Frieda turned her mind away again, this time to her husband, Ahmed Iftikhar. She contemplated: he's the only serious love I've known. If ever I need an ear, he pulls up a chair and listens. He once explained to me how his Yarsani Iranian religious roots ingrained the respect for the equality of all living forms, so he naturally cared for others. The fact that Yarsanis were persecuted from the time of the Islamic Revolution also made him sensitive, almost defensive, at times. But that's something I never looked down upon him for. I remember when we first met, in Philadelphia, at one of my first ELSI conferences. I had just finished a keynote address on the morality of privately funded genetics research, and he chatted with me afterward in the refreshment lineup, offering congratulations. He said mine was the best speech he'd heard since working at ELSI. We ended up talking – mostly I talked and he listened – for the rest of the evening. Though he was not attractive – rapidly receding hair, a puffy chin, and somewhat disheveled nose – I found him charming, quick, and, most gratifyingly, an excellent listener.

Ximena was still reading, "A friendship never stays the same. Like a flower, it starts as a seed, then grows and blooms ..."

Frieda shifted her thoughts back to her work. Is there a way out? I'm not optimistic. Age-decoding has captured *everyone's* imagination. Immortality is on the march. I cannot slow its inertia. True, some scientists stand by me, including some ELSI members, but we're an insignificant group compared to lobbyists, business people, and politicians pushing it forward. I would gladly return my Nobel to start all over again.

Frieda glanced at her daughter, whose handsome face was partly covered by her long, wavy dark hair. She had stopped reading.

"Mom," said Ximena, "You weren't paying much attention to the reading tonight."

"You're right, Xi. I'm sorry. I've just had so much on my mind with all of this discovery stuff. Believe me, I do like reading with you. Maybe just not tonight."

"OK, but promise we can finish the book together soon."

"I promise, dear."

With that, the ebook holographic dissolved away and Frieda got up from the bed and walked into the family room.

She decided to message Ahmed rather than talking to him. Taking a seat in her favorite rocking chair, she sent him the following:

Dear Ahmed: Your daughter is here with me as we enjoy some downtime together. You should have seen her devour the new book you gave her about friendship. The life cycle of learning awes me. In the two weeks you've been gone she has read and learned so much.

But I'm afraid to say my work relating to ELSI has become impossible. I can't bear it. As of late, I know you've felt much disdain in my voice and a certain distance in my love. You must think I've overstretched your patience and ignored you these past few months, but please don't misconstrue. I'm as devoted as ever to you. Unfortunately, my work mission, my life's most important work, overwhelms me. I also feel guilty not being with Ximena during the day. I can't do my best at home, and I don't do my best at work.

The forces surrounding age-decoding have now aligned in a way that's making ELSI a sideshow in a much bigger political arena. The most powerful people seem blinded, or ignorant. At one time I counted some of them as ardent

ELSI supporters, but as events unfolded it became clear that my genetic discovery was losing control to people whose values do not align with ELSI protocol.

I can only conclude that those shaping the emerging Authority believe that ethical, legal, and social issues are too "soft" compared to the "tour de force" economic and political benefits of age-decoding. The U.S. government is losing patience with me, and the Chinese seem bent on forging an agreement with the Americans and other key countries.

When the Authority Science Council originally agreed to my request for ELSI funding, my pledge was supported by hundreds of leading scientists from both the U.S. and China, not to mention other nations such as Great Britain, France, and Canada. We felt understood and respected. I was convinced that the biggest threat to our world was not a nuclear holocaust or some grand military intrusion, but the phenomenon of unbridled genetic engineering.

You know I committed myself wholeheartedly to ELSI. It was tough work, messier than anything I've ever experienced. Ethical questions are naturally debatable. I'll never forget those years leading and pushing ELSI, and your support and love. Everything seemed in sync. It was no coincidence, Ahmed, that I met and began to love you during that important phase of my life.

You remain the only person who truly understands me. You never stopped loving me, and I never stopped loving you.

How ignorant are these individuals in control? How minimal is their capacity to learn, to truly explore the implications of genetic engineering? President Reubers is especially intolerable. How could a man like him rise to the highest levels of leadership? Political acumen, I suppose.

As you know, they have offered age-decoding to everyone older than twenty-five, free of charge, as a public entitlement. This is the unadulterated scenario I feared.

I'm now desperate. Last week I thought of releasing the ELSI draft report through non-official channels. Going to the media. You should have seen the shenanigans in our final meeting. It was both comical and tragic! If the public ever knew what was buried, they'd be terrified. I even threatened to blow the whistle at the last Authority Science Council meeting

Here I am, Nobel winner, but feeling "persona non grata" in my scientific sphere – isolated and dreading the future. I find it impossible to live with myself. I'm suffering inner poverty and can't see a way out. As you know, I've battled depression during my adult life, but please know that this is different: it's a malaise related more to external forces than internal demons. You're a naturally positive and empathic person, Ahmed, and when you get home we can talk about this more. I could use level-headed support.

Ximena sends her love and says you better get home soon so she can beat you at chess!

All my love, Frieda.

"What are you doing, Mom?" Ximena asked, curious as usual.

"I was messaging your dad. He's going to be away for a few more days so I thought he'd appreciate an update about my work."

Ximena asked Frieda for permission to take a walk in Prospect Park, which was safely located within their apartment complex.

Frieda gave her a pat on the head and a nod. "Sure, but please be back before lunch, dear."

"Okay," said Ximena, as she trotted away.

Soon after Ximena left, Frieda went to the kitchen to pour herself a cup of coffee. What a beautiful young person Ximena is, she said to herself, outwardly smiling.

Suddenly, she glimpsed two Authority security guards in the hallway, who she knew on a first-name basis.

Never would she have guessed what the guards did next, for they were meant to protect her. They walked straight towards her, without the usual pleasantries.

In a reflex, she lunged to protect her daughter, forgetting Ximena was not there. One guard tackled her and, before she could scream, shoved a foul-smelling cloth over her mouth. In her last conscious few seconds, she witnessed the second guard cleaning up the coffee which had spilled onto the white linoleum flooring.

CHAPTER 2

AGE-DECODED

THE NEWS BROKE FIRST on CNN, on November 12, 2053, at noon. The announcer bore that overwrought look of news people who are about to reveal a remarkable story. He adjusted his spectacles, hesitated, then said, "The greatest scientist of our time, Nobel laureate Dr. Frieda Sengmeuller, the inventor of age-decoding, took her own life late this morning." The announcement jolted Zone1. It was bigger than the assassination of John F. Kennedy in 1963, the terrorist attacks on the World Trade Centre in 2001, or the murder-suicide of Chinese Premier Ran Mu-Rui and his wife in 2039. "According to the Authority, Dr. Sengmeuller overdosed sometime last evening. After not reporting to work this morning, two co-workers found her on the floor in her kitchen at 11:00 am. Unfortunately, there was no hope of reviving her. Her only daughter, ten-year-old Ximena Sengmeuller, was not present at the time of the suicide. She was found, unharmed."

The funeral visitation was especially difficult for Ahmed Iftikhar. Although he was aware of her depression, he had not come to terms with Frieda killing herself. Perhaps, he thought, this funeral wasn't happening?

As Ximena mingled with some cousins, Ahmed and Jesus moved about in tandem, supporting each other. One had lost a wife, the other a daughter. They had grown close over the past five years, and Ahmed often thought Jesus was the best father-in-law in the world. They immersed themselves in the perfunctory statements and polite offerings from relatives and friends: "She was the smartest person I ever knew", "We'll miss her so much," "Let me know if I can do anything for you," and "It's such a loss for you both." During this time Ahmed experienced delusionary episodes. She's not dead. This is just a bad dream. His were normal reactions to the loss of a loved one, especially in the case of suicide.

Standing outside the church after the visitation, Ahmed was approached by a tall, thin, middle-aged woman with red hair and excessive make-up.

"Hi Ahmed, don't know if you remember me."

"Hello, I ...," he said, but he could not place her.

"It's been a long time. I'm Shirley. Shirley Whitfield, an old college friend of Frieda's. She and I were roommates. You and I met at a party a long time ago. Anyway, I'm so sorry for your loss."

He remembered her now. The fun and energetic roommate. Life of the party.

"Yes, thanks for coming Shirley."

"I can't believe this happened."

She moved toward Ahmed with outstretched arms and they briefly embraced.

"I hadn't kept contact with her," she said, "but when I heard about what happened I just had to come down. Frieda was one-of-a-kind. I'll never forget her work ethic. She had the dedication of a thousand scientists."

"She certainly did," said Ahmed.

"And she was also one of the kindest persons I ever met. Well, I guess it's time for the service. I'll see you in there."

"Thanks for coming today."

Ximena was back by now and she extended one hand to Ahmed and one to Jesus. The three of them proceeded into the main church and, using the outer aisle, worked their way up to the front of the church while stations of the cross images beckoned from the cold stone walls. As they took their place in the first pew, Ahmed spied the final station, *Christ is laid in the tomb*, which seemed to stare back mockingly. He then nodded to his parents and sister who were seated behind them and had made the trip from Iran.

A traditional Catholic ceremony it was, for the death of a loved one.

Ahmed fought back emotions. How could Frieda, who committed herself to eternalizing life for every human, cut her own life so short?

The priest focused his eyes on Frieda's funerary urn, positioned at the front edge of the primary altar. Onto it he sprinkled holy water while reciting *De Profundis*:

> *"Out of the depths have I cried unto Thee, O Lord: Lord hear my voice. Let Thine ears be attentive to the voice of my supplication.*
>
> *If Thou, Lord, shouldst mark iniquities, O Lord, who shall stand?*
>
> *But there is forgiveness with Thee: because of Thy law I wait for Thee, O Lord. My soul waiteth on His word: my soul hopeth in the Lord."*

When the time came for the eulogy, the priest nodded in the direction of Jesus. The old man pulled himself up from the pew. His drawn-out amble to the podium at the front of the packed church heightened the anticipation for his talk. He appeared scrawny and older than his age of seventy-four. Yet he was the type of man who exuded a calm sagacity that put those around him at ease – sometimes in awe. At this moment it served him well.

When he reached the podium, he steadied himself by clutching both of its elaborate wooden sides, peered out across the faces of the congregation, scratched his chin, and reached into his vest pocket for what most assumed would be his notes. He withdrew a simple white handkerchief and placed it beside the microphone.

"Frieda was my gem," he began. "An amazing daughter. She gave wholeheartedly to the world. She pushed science to the limit. I remember when she was eight years old, she worked that chemistry set in the basement extremely hard. I thought she was too young to have one, but she insisted. I worried that she'd blow us all up, but she never quite did." That drew some chuckles. He went on. "In every stage of her life, Frieda played out that same theme. As a graduate student, she pushed her advisor so aggressively on the conceptual level that she jeopardized their collaboration and her thesis. But she got it done and graduated at the top of her class. In her postdoctoral program, she revitalized the stalled UCLA project on the anti-aging proteome and garnered much-needed new funding. And when she finally set up her genome research team, she pushed the frontiers of anti-aging research so far that the U.S. government had to play catch-up in figuring out economic and political ramifications. That was Frieda: pushing ever hard. The hardest working scientist I have ever known. But it was never a blind fervor. She always knew where she was headed, though it was not always easy for the rest of us to figure out ... she was too far ahead ..."

As he continued, tears welled up for many in the crowd. They were aware that eulogies usually shed the softest of lights on their subjects, out of respect for the families. But Jesus's words, they knew, were true.

Listening to his father-in-law, Ahmed was overcome by a sense of fortuity for having known and loved such an amazing woman.

Jesus's eulogy ensued for about five more minutes. "There's a saying: *death always comes too early or too late*. In my daughter's case, it was much too early. Frieda is survived by her wonderful spouse, Dr. Ahmed Iftikhar, and her beautiful daughter, Ximena." Jesus paused and looked over to see Ahmed comforting Ximena, who was quietly sobbing. "I know that being a mother gave Frieda the utmost joy. She told me more than once that raising Xi was the most important thing she had ever done, and she only wished she could find more time for that, for being a good mother. She struggled with the dual responsibilities of scientist and mother. Her maternity leave was just two weeks, and I don't think she even took that. She was relentless on the scientific front. She would not sacrifice work, but I know she did sacrifice a lot of sleep to be with her daughter. For me, Frieda was a loving daughter, and I'm so proud to stand here before you today as her father..."

Jesus momentarily lost his power to speak and used the handkerchief for the first time to wipe below his eyes. Many others did the same.

He finished, "I and Ahmed and Xi will miss you dearly, Frieda. I urge everyone to pray for us in this time of sorrow. It's no exaggeration to say the world has lost a legend."

As Jesus worked his way back to his seat, the priest took over, "Please stand ..."

That evening, Ahmed dined with his sister and parents, whom he had not seen for about a year and a half. The plaque outside the historical Court of Two Sisters restaurant in the French Quarter read:

The two sisters, Emma and Bertha Camors, born 1858 and 1860 respectively, belonged to a proud and aristocratic Creole family ... It has also been rumored that the outrageous Marquis de Vaudreuil, the colonial royal governor who transformed New Orleans from a marshland village into a "petit Paris," was once a resident of 613 Rue Royale.

They ordered hors d'oeuvres: Creole seafood gumbo and turtle soup au sherry, and various cocktails. "Jesus's eulogy was very touching," said Ahmed's mother.

"One of the most dignified I've ever seen, and I've been to a few," added his father. "He's such a bright and well-spoken man. I'm reading his book, *Biodiversity Unplugged*. It's tremendous."

Ahmed gulped his Stella draft. He then stunned them all by stating, "I'm thinking I won't stay on looking after Ximena."

"What? Are you kidding us?" his father asked sternly. He looked at his wife, who had raised one eyebrow, then over to his daughter, who sat straight-faced. After reflecting for a few seconds, he subdued himself and whispered into Ahmed's ear, "I think you've gone through too much. Give it some time. Don't do anything rash. You're her father, Ahmed."

Ahmed responded loud enough for them all to hear, "I don't need time. I need to be on my own, as far away as I can get from any connection with Frieda. Xi reminds me of Frieda, of our relationship, and I can't deal with it, at least not right now. I'm going to ask Jesus to look after her for the time being. If I can't deal with it, that's bad for Xi."

"Let's put an end to this talk," his mother said tersely. "Just let it be. We can discuss it later."

Ahmed's sister suddenly stood up and said, "I can't imagine leaving my own child! How can you be so selfish? Really. What the hell's wrong with you?" She tossed her napkin onto her bread plate and walked stiffly in the direction of the washroom.

The background clinking of Court of Two Sisters cutlery took over, then the conversations from other tables.

Ahmed sat paralyzed and stone-faced.

"She'll calm down. She always does," said his mother.

As awkward as the situation was, his sister did return to the table a few minutes later. But before sitting down, she sternly implored Ahmed, "Promise me you'll at least re-think your plan. Please... at least promise that. Xi needs you."

Ahmed nodded, though he had no intention of changing his position.

As soon as his sister sat down, his father offered, "I'm going to order some wine, would people like white – or red?"

The wine eventually flowed in both colors for Ahmed's family. His father, who was seventy-two years old and completely bald, suggested that age-decoding would enable him to avoid death and return to work long enough to become a multi-millionaire; then, when they discovered a way of *reverse-aging*, he would regrow his hair and become a movie star. That brought laughter around the table. But they steered away from any talk about Frieda or Ximena. It was the only way Ahmed and his family could outlast the evening.

CHAPTER 3

AGE-DECODED

THE INTERVIEW PROCESS Ahmed endured with the Authority's Statistical Verification Agency the week before Frieda's funeral had been rigorous, especially the last two meetings. But he figured he had a good shot at the job. The government needed statisticians with his credentials, and his record at Celera Incorporated was impeccable.

Two days after the funeral, he was called in again and they made him an offer of employment. As he listened to the main recruiter, Ahmed's hands tremored with excitement and his mind raced. He had always worked in the private sector, most recently as part of Celera's Bioinformatics and Computational Biology Team, so a move to the Authority, into the public sector, would be a tremendous change. He wanted to do something different, to lose himself in some new action, and this seemed like a wonderful opportunity to break out. Frieda's suicide made the *status quo* unthinkable.

Then it hit him, a sudden wave of grief for her. Pent-up emotion swept through him. Never would he share with her, or love her, again. He steadied himself to respond to their offer, like a person operated by forces from a distance.

"I'd be pleased to accept your offer of employment with the Statistical Verification Agency. When would you like me to start?"

Thus, Ahmed launched a new career for himself at the Authority. He could not have imagined this would lead to a two-century commitment. Then again, with age-decoding, time recalibration was in the offing.

But Ahmed was making other changes. He had arranged to meet Jesus tomorrow, to ask him to care for Ximena.

Later that evening he found himself lazily surfing TV channels. He lay almost horizontal on the leather recliner, his bones and muscles worn out. He turned off his smartphone. The last thing he wanted was for someone to call to talk him into changing his

19

mind about Ximena. Viscerally, he compelled himself to trust that it would all work out.

The next day Ahmed met Jesus for lunch at the Beluga Café, a quaint, informal eatery specializing in eco-sustainable food. A lineup of about a dozen stretched out the doorway to the sidewalk, blocking passersby. People were striving on with life, Ahmed mused. But this vast experiment had just begun, and he wondered if people might start excusing themselves for lesser efforts because they knew their lifespans were limitless.

They both ordered avocado soup, garden salad, and the red guava juice imported from Thailand. Their conversation was polite and rational, but they knew their meeting would have serious repercussions.

As he sat across from Ahmed, Jesus wondered: Why would he be asking me to look after Ximena for an unspecified period? Was it simply the shock of Frieda's suicide that was driving him away from his daughter? Just a grief reaction? I have a tough time believing it's that simple. Yet I won't ask Ahmed to explain himself, knowing he may be in an irrational state. The odds have always been in my favor in this world, so it behooves me to step in and do my duty, to give something back. I should help without passing judgment. I know I can be a good surrogate father.

So he made an offer, "OK, Ahmed, I'll help you out. I'm seventy-four years old, but at least I won't be getting any older with age-decoding, so I'm up to the challenge. If I was eighty-four, I wouldn't dare try this. So I'm in, for the time being, until you're accustomed to your new job. You need time and space for yourself, and I respect that. I assume you'll change your mind and come to your senses eventually. She's a beautiful child. Though the law places no burden on me to accept her, I will. After all, she's in my blood."

Awestruck by his father-in-law, Ahmed fought back the impulse to break down. "You're a terrific man, Jesus ... better than me. Thank you."

"You don't need to say such a thing. Look, you've been hit hard by extraordinary circumstances. Time will help. Believe me. Time will help."

"I hope you're right. All I know is that I've got to do this."

"Yes ... and I wish you all the best with the new job."

"I know you'll take special care of Xi. I know you'll do what I can't do right now."

"I'll manage, with lots of help from a nanny or two," said Jesus. "In time you'll come around. You will always be her father."

Later that evening Ahmed dropped some of Ximena's belongings off at Jesus's apartment. Ximena lay asleep in her new room. Ahmed was feeling uncomfortable and eager to leave, and Jesus did not deter him. A strange sensation hit Ahmed as it dawned on him that he was separating from his only daughter. With one sheepish nod to Jesus, he was out the door.

Jesus walked to the doorway of Ximena's bedroom and glanced inside. Her eyes were closed and her delicate head was enveloped by two large white pillows. It was his first moment of fathering her.

Jesus contemplated how luck was sometimes a double-edged sword. Xi had great early luck as a child. Born of two fine parents: a famous mother and a highly-regarded father. Both intelligent, successful scientists. But over the past week, her mother's tragic suicide and her father's decision to leave had completely vanquished Xi's good fortune. She, so young, was now dealt these horrible cards.

Jesus had been an excellent father to Frieda, and he would try his best to do the same for Ximena, to bring back her good fortune. He fixed his eyes on her once more. He adored the sound of her name: *Ximena*. It had that three-syllable rhythmic beauty. What did it mean? Oh yes, *Listening*.

That's perfect, he thought. No doubt she was listening to everything in her dreams right now, taking it all in.

CHAPTER 4

IN THE YEAR 2254, A full two centuries after Dr. Frieda Sengmeuller unveiled age-decoding to the world, the young man Jason Smith emerged from the encasement – which looked like the hull of a small sailboat – unsure of where he had been or where he was going. His last conscious thought had been two centuries ago, as a breezy teenager.

Jason had just "thawed out" from *cryopreservation*. He stood dazed, sore, and jittery. Just get away from this thing, he thought, and figure out what's going on. Usually, when he awoke, he tried to decipher his dreams, a fanciful idea he picked up from a newspaper article he read three years ago when he was sixteen. But this time he couldn't remember dreaming. Just a long, continuous sleep.

"Don't be afraid, Jason. Come forward please... come forward," a voice whispered from a distance.

Jason peered in the direction of the voice, but only silence hung in the air. Above, he noticed an array of dimly lit orange lights, hundreds of feet high, suspended from a silvery, scaled ceiling. To his right was a vast arrangement of aisles and stacks, like a large library. To his left was a small office, rectangular in shape, with sunlight shining through its one large window. Jason decided to proceed in that direction, to find the source of the voice. Catching his jacket briefly on the jagged edge of the shell, he managed to dislodge himself, then stepped forward along the tile floor.

"Who's there?" Jason whispered, "Who are you?"

There came no reply. Jason walked slowly forward, though his legs ached deep down in his ligaments and joints, not because of age – biologically, he was nineteen years old – but because he had been frozen for so long after that faraway event in the year 2050.

He yearned to meet the person behind the whispering voice. "Who's there?" he asked. His mind packed questions and fired out endless possibilities, fully loaded and invigorated. Not so his legs. He had to force them forward one step at a time. "You still there?"

"Yes – over here". Jason altered his course slightly and forced his legs to transport him many more steps.

Presently, a hand pressed softly upon his shoulder. "This way," implored a person who guided him forward and into the office. Jason turned to see a man, who pointed to a chair and said, "Please, sit down here,". He lowered himself onto it and studied the man, who appeared middle-aged, stout, and clean-cut.

"Hi Jason, my name is Tom Stephenson," he said, slowly pacing back and forth and appearing to want to say more. Jason sat and readied to listen. He shifted his eyes away for a moment to scan the room. It was a simple office with one window, a desk, but no desk chair, just the one he was sitting in. The ceiling and floor were off-white. On the wall opposite him was an LED sign which read *Sphygmomanometer: Non-Eubeing Compatible*. Below it was a mounted blood pressure device, like the one his doctor had used on him during his checkup last year. The wall behind the desk was embedded with several tiny LEDs.

Tom finally spoke again, "Son, I'm going to say some things you won't understand, but trust me, I'm here to help you. I only have a couple of minutes, so please listen carefully. First, you're now in Zone1, and you're not like most others in Zone1. They're *eubeings*, and you're not."

"Eubeings?" Jason asked.

"People who are *age-decoded*. A method discovered about two centuries ago, in 2053, by Dr. Frieda Sengmeuller of UCLA–"

"You mean it's 2253 now?" asked Jason, flabbergasted.

"It's 2254 now, to be exact," he said. "You've been dormant for two hundred years." He continued, "Age-decoding was a brilliant breakthrough in genetic engineering, a method to stop aging in its tracks, to freeze any person in their current biological age. Nobel prize winner she was, Dr. Frieda," he added, grinning slightly. "This caused major changes in the world, as you might imagine. The many and profound effects are still unfolding today. The word *human* is pretty much eradicated from our Zone1 lexicon. *Eubeings* is now the standard term for age-decoded people, who represent the vast majority of people."

Jason could not believe what he had just heard. But he appreciated that Tom had a straightforward way of explaining things.

"Second, you should be extremely careful about *etalk*."

Jason looked at him and asked, "Etalk? What's that?"

"Etalk is simply personal digital communication of any type using an NIT. That's an acronym for *neurointegrated transponders*. Etalk was popularized more than two centuries ago, around the year 2000, first with Blackberrys and Nokia, then Apple, Samsung, Huawei, and various more complex smartphones. Of course, you know about all of that. But what you don't know about is the current form of etalk, the NIT, invented about a century ago. An NIT is positioned inside the brain of almost every single human in Zone1." He began pacing again, more slowly this time. "If you communicate using your NIT, that's etalk. I advise you to be cautious in using it. Many people get lazy and just etalk even when they're conversing face-to-face. Saves them from moving their mouth, tongue, or lips. But you never know to what extent it's monitored by the government. Nobody knows. If you play it safe and converse without the NIT, that's called *talking naturally*. Of course, you don't have an NIT yet, so until you get one you don't need to bother with what I'm saying."

"Very interesting," said Jason. "Can the government use an NIT to detect people talking to themselves, too? Or is communication only detectable when it takes place between the NITs of two people?"

"Ah, great question," said Tom. "It's only detectable for person-to-person communication, not intrapersonal." He paused and emitted a slight grin. "Though there are conspiracy theorists who believe the government will one day use NIT-like devices to detect not just what people say to each other, but to themselves. Like reading people's minds. That would be trippy! Hopefully, that's not doable for some time." Tom paused for a moment, then went on, "Still, I recommend that you protect yourself in Zone1. You'll need to cover up your past with certain groups. Believe me, you're a special and distinct young man, Jason, but at times you'll have to pretend otherwise. Ximena FYH will be helpful to you in this regard."

"Zone1? Ximena FYH?"

"Sorry ... no time to explain ... too complicated. You'll meet Ximena soon. Any quick questions before I go?" he asked.

Jason had many questions, of course, but he was too overwhelmed and chose to just leave it at that. Tom stopped pacing and looked closely at Jason for the first time. "Well then, I must be off ... I know you'll make it," he said.

Jason asked, "One last thing before you go ... what's your name again?"

"Tom Stephenson. I'm sure we'll see each other again."

With that, they shook hands, and Tom was out the door.

He seems like a nice person, Jason thought, and I hope many more in Zone1 are like him. But where to now? I can't just hang around in this room.

He decided he would retrace his steps, to make for the stack of books he thought he saw earlier on. Tom had cautioned him to be discreet, so he moved carefully, almost on his toes, and stayed in the darker shadows. Shimmying on carefully, he was soon among the aisles and stacks. It was indeed a library, and he ambled about its aisles, which were extremely lengthy, almost as long as a football field. The shelves were fully packed and reached several feet above his head. It was a queer feeling, being among so many books, reminding him of his trips to the local library at Santa Borough Elementary with Grade 4 teacher Ms. Barrett. Back then, that little library seemed just as big to him, just as endless. Ms. Barrett used to look straight through him and scream, "Jason, put that book back where it belongs!" "But Miss, there are so many books here – will anyone care if one book is out of place?" "Yes, I will... do as you're told!"

He noticed the goosebumps on his exposed arms. Was he nervous, or just cold? He pulled his jacket over his shoulders. Walking and observing further, Jason discovered that the library had dozens of aisles, each labeled at its end:

> ... Zone1 Cluster 4011
> Zone1 Cluster 4012
> Zone1 Cluster 4013
> Zone1 Cluster 4014 ...

He ventured deep into one aisle and pulled a book off the shelf. The cover had a long title he did not recognize, something about an assassination of Jean-Paul Marat, whoever that was. It was old and dusty, with a soft leathery brownish cover and thin pages, and emitted a curious odor.

He scanned a random page and realized it was a play with characters and dialogue. *We want what we want and we don't care how; we want our revolution now*!

Profound, Jason thought, but he wondered why this world would still need a library with hardcopies.

He found a place among the stacks to lay, pulled his hips around sideways, and rested his head using his jacket as a pillow. He felt safe here, surrounded and comforted by books, because he loved reading. At ease among the books, he tried to clear his head to think up a plan, but he kept repeating that strange name to himself: Ximena FYH, Ximena FYH, Ximena FYH. Don't forget the FYH – so you get the right Ximena! Then again, he thought, how many Ximenas could there be? I've never even heard the name and it doesn't sound too cool or popular! I hope this Ximena fellow isn't as nerdy as his name sounds. Since I have nothing else to go with, I'll follow that man Tom's advice and find Ximena as soon as possible.

I need help.

He could not remember ever needing help in any major way. Growing up with his little sister Sarah and Mom, he never asked for much help. It would be too embarrassing. Besides, he never felt he truly needed it. Even from friends at school, he never asked. Sure, he requested assistance with a few minor things, like last night's math homework, spare change for the pop machine, an extra baseball glove, but nothing substantial. From buddies on the soccer team or kids he played with on the block, he never really asked. On the computer, in chat rooms, or even blog clubs, he never got his face dirty enough to ask. Even with his girlfriend Lara, whom he had been dating for a few months, he never showed that kind of vulnerability. Life was pretty good, he thought.

With Ximena that would have to change, and he vowed not to let his pride interfere. Today he had an excuse: this situation here and now, which was unlike anything he had ever encountered! For amid the stacks of a strange library, questions abounded: Why was he here? Where should he go next? Was it safe? Where was his family? He remembered, when he was in Kindergarten, Mom telling him that if he ever needed help all he had to do was ask people who loved him. But who loved him here in Zone1? Not Ximena, who didn't know him. Not Tom, whom he just met. But he was going to need help, and Tom said Ximena would help him.

Ximena FYH, that is.

Though he was hungry, he was sleepier still, so Jason drifted off quickly, leaving this dream-like new world to enter a place of deeper dreams. He napped among the stacks for twenty minutes. When he woke up, he heard the faint sound of people talking. He got up, drew his wrinkled jacket over his slight shoulders, rubbed his eyes, ruffled his hair, and worked his way out of the library toward the voices. Standing concealed at the edge of one aisle, he spied the two guards conversing in front of the office. He listened to them intently.

"Zone1 regulations state that the age of twenty-five is the optimal point for age-decoding," one guard said.

"I'm not arguing with you about that," said the other, who had a much deeper voice. "All I'm saying is that it makes no sense to assume that's the case for every individual. Even the original research indicated that the optimal age variation is plus or minus 5 years, 95% of the time. I think that's one mistake the Zone1 Authority has made."

"Yes, but how do you know which individuals the plus or minus applies to?" said the other. "Oh well, I can tell you one thing for sure, which I hope we can agree on, and that is we can be thankful that *age-decoding* fails only once in a blue moon."

That guard was correct. Age-decoding did not work in a tiny fraction of all cases – about 0.002% – meaning about 220,000 people in Zone1 continued to age biologically, like normal humans. The genetic structure of these humans simply did not respond to age-decoding. They were deemed non-age-decodable. Although their genome was the same as other humans, they did not react the same to the treatment, due to their having one irregular protein. Why it did not, and whether it reacted negatively or in some other way, had never been ascertained. The Zone1 Authority was not overly concerned, however, since practically everyone could be age-decoded and it almost always worked.

Currently, the Zone1 population of about eleven billion people was made up of:

- 38.996 % age-decoded people of biological age 25
- 60.998 % age-decoded people of biological age more than 25

- 0.004 % non-age-decoded youth aged less than 25
- 0.002 % non-age-decodable people of biological age more than 25

All age-decoded people were immune to biological aging. Because immortality was an obvious blessing, age-decoded people were officially known as eubeings, since "eu" was the Greek prefix for "good".

The other guard continued, "But it seems unfair for those it fails, who still grow old, get wrinkles, become frail, and see their world come crashing down when everyone around them–"

"Friend ...we must remind ourselves of the fact that age-decoding succeeds infinitely more than it fails. Let's face it, every system, every method, has failures or exceptions, and age-decoding is no exception. But look at the positive: its flaws are fantastically minor."

"I can't admit that. Think of the actual people, the individuals. How can you say that 220,000 non-eubeings are a minor flaw? That's quite a chunk of humankind."

The guards then turned silent. Jason asked himself, what should I do now? I'm hungry. Where can I get a good square meal?

Suddenly, just to the right of him emerged an apparition – a holographic image like that of many video games he had played. It was fuzzy and fog-like. Before he could react, a soft female voice spoke to him from within the image, "Follow me, so I can begin to help you".

This image, Jason thought, whatever it was, is on my wavelength, because it knows I need help.

Jason was in no position to do anything but trust. His gut feeling was positive, so he obediently followed the holograph, which floated away from the stacks, through another door into a garage-like area. The image moved forward a few more feet, then directly through the open door of a parked driverless car. Jason went in after it.

Presently a large garage door opened and off they went, driven for about ten minutes across New Orleans to a sizable old house located in the Garden District. Like the French Quarter itself, the Garden District was a couple of meters above sea level, so it escaped the severe flooding in Hurricane Katrina in 2005 and even the more catastrophic Hurricane Kate in 2044. The house itself dated back to the 1870s. It was white, with blue-trimmed windows, a two-car garage, and a large, well-kept lot. Two fully bloomed Pink Japanese magnolia trees stood on the front lawn, one positioned at the top of the steps near the porch, blocking part of the living room window, and the other at the far edge of the lawn near the end of the driveway. A garden of limelight hydrangeas lined both sides of the descending natural stone steps.

Waiting for him at the door was a woman, and Jason was immediately struck by her beauty. He lost his breath, and his face took on a full blush. Into Jason's mind popped the word *nubile*, which he had learned from his nerdy buddy Nathan. She gazed at him with her large alluring eyes. She wore a tight, shiny red and black full-body suit that exposed only her fine slender neck and arms and shapely hips. She looked to be a few years older than him. Near her face but mostly on one side clung her hair, which was wavy and dark, almost black. He could not help but notice her perfectly proportioned body. If this was Ximena FYH, and he hoped it was, then she oozed sexiness. The only exception to her perfection was her left hand and wrist, which oddly, were covered by what looked like a large oven mitt.

"Congratulations Jason," she said, smiling softly, "a wise decision you have made to allow me to help you. I'm Ximena FYH. Call me Xi." She paused and looked deep through him. "Now, you're here to ... relax and get away from it all."

He decided to let her take the lead in everything, to let her help, and it relieved him to do so. Besides, he was too riveted by her beauty to manage anything else.

Jason wondered: Was this the future? Or was this heaven?

"Promise me you'll try to be yourself. It's safe at my place. It's the one place I always feel secure," she said with a perplexing smile.

"OK ... Xi," he muttered, though he worried he might never be capable of truly relaxing around someone like her.

She took him by the hand and led him into what she referred to as her bedroom. He did not see a bed. He noted that she was taller than him, even though he was almost six feet tall. The floor was bare, and so were her feet. Embedded in each of the three walls were huge aquariums in which hundreds of fish of assorted sizes, shapes, and colors danced about. The fourth wall contained a complex-looking media system. The room had no windows, desk, dresser, or pictures, and no other outstanding features. He couldn't surmise where the light was coming from, for it seemed to come from everywhere. Jason stood observing the room for a few more seconds, then looked at Ximena.

"Let's lie down," she said.

"Where?"

"On the bed," she said, motioning with her normal hand.

He looked about the room once again, "What bed?"

She flipped a switch on the wall and he immediately felt light pressure at the base of his feet while the rest of his body began to assume a weightless feeling. He slowly shifted above the floor a few inches. Ximena glided toward him. She reached out, held his torso, and steered him into a horizontal position. Although he could not see it, they were resting on an invisible bed located over the geometric centroid of the room. Gravity was reduced to 5% – the level determined optimal for relaxation.

Ximena lay next to him, close enough that he could not help scrutinizing her overwhelming eyes and lips.

If this was going to be his help, he was not about to resist.

"I know what you're thinking," she said.

He could only manage, "Whaaaa?"

"Rest and relax," she said. "I'll take care of everything. Once you're relaxed, we'll be able to do things better."

"Whatever you say," he said, then suddenly got the nerve to ask, "How old are you, Xi?"

"Well, that depends on how you measure it. Chronologically, I'm 211 years old, but biologically, I'm just twenty-five."

"I see," he said. Then he remained quiet and let her do the talking.

For the next fifteen minutes, Ximena described the state of her people, her government, and the age-decoding developments which brought society to this point. From what he could see, she was enjoying the fact that he seemed to be comprehending everything. All the while Jason politely nodded, trying to expunge her alluring beauty from his youthful mind.

At no time did he take heed of her bad wrist and hand, which she kept mostly hidden in the blind spot behind her torso.

She explained how the government lent people immortality through the process of age-decoding, an advanced form of gene therapy in which a carrier molecule called a viral vector delivers desirable genetic material to a human's target cells, infecting those target cells and replacing undesirable genes with the desirable ones. This method was expedited in the 2020s with the successful application of an artificial extra chromosome (the so-called 47th chromosome) in human target cells, which could be used as a "launching pad" for the viral vector.

"But all of this work would not have taken place without the Human Genome Project, decades earlier," Ximena said. "The HGP revealed that the human genome was composed of about 20,000-25,000 genes. The possible combinations and expressions of these genes were tied to the intricacies of human beings, to their essence, to their innate traits and tendencies. It's intriguing to know that the genome, though mappable, is *non-static*. By that I mean that its effects could be modified or even turned on or off by interactions with DNA proteins, hormones, and even the environment."

Jason shifted his position and avoided looking into her eyes. She continued, "Many countries participated in the HGP. It included Australia, Brazil, Canada, China, the United States, France, Germany, Japan, Russia ... I can't remember them all, but it was most of the developed nations. The project brought together tens of thousands of public and private sector experts worldwide from a variety of disciplines. The HGP work was breathtakingly detailed." She kick-started her NIT to drum up more information, which flashed onto the ceiling. "Check out this excerpt from the study, *Generation and Annotation of the DNA Sequences of Human Chromosomes 2 and 4, (Nature, Vol. 434, pp. 724-731, April 7, 2005)."*

Jason read it to himself:

> *Human chromosome 2 is unique to the human lineage in being the product of a head-to-head fusion of two intermediate-sized ancestral chromosomes... Here we present approximately 237 million base pairs of sequence for chromosome 2 ... initial analyses have identified 1,346 protein-coding genes and 1,239 pseudogenes on chromosome 2 ... Extensive analyses confirm the underlying construction of the sequence, and expand our understanding of the structure ...*

"Wow. That's awesome gobbledygook!" he cried.

"And that's only the basic stuff. Though it's all-important. It's about us, our bodies, our essence. The HGP work underpinned age-decoding, a gift no society in the history of mankind has known. And that gift happened *quid pro quo*."

"What do you mean ... quid –?"

Ximena explained, "*Quid pro quo*. This-for-that. You see, Jason, the gift of age-decoding lasted forever, so the government which invented it expected to be highly regarded for a long, long time. After all, the composition of the voting public would not change significantly over time; the deal would be virtually frozen in time. Politically, the Zone1 Authority expected to retain longstanding power. And that's exactly what happened: Zone1 opposition parties folded up their tents long ago and only one party, the Rethinking Party, remained as a weak, almost token competitor. So ... the government gave, and the government received. That's what I mean by *quid pro quo*." Ximena readjusted her position. "Are you still comfortable?"

"Very," replied Jason. "Keep going, Xi."

"It's not an understatement for me to say that the impact of age-decoding was mind-boggling – not only the immediate and obvious impact but also the many unexpected things. In social services: precipitous declines in the need for old-age homes, long-term care facilities, eyeglasses, wheelchairs, golf, bridge, Yahtzee, healthcare, massage, and physiotherapy. In sports: limitless time for people to explore and develop their potential in a variety of disciplines, boundless opportunity to pursue Olympic dreams, to dominate a given sport, to perfect a new method. In commerce: the obliteration of the economic imperative for retirement schemes and pension plans, causing plummeting life insurance premiums. In law: novel approaches to gaining compensation because damages could be monumental with life stretched out so much longer. In medicine: less concern for diseases of old age such as Alzheimer's and Parkinson's and renewed focus on epidemiology and sports medicine. In demographics: the need to control population growth, because life expectancy suddenly changed from less than one hundred years to more than two thousand years."

"That long?" said Jason.

"Yes. So the government had no choice but to decree the right to bear children as a *restricted right* given to a precious few. Hence the start of the *Family Rights Lottery*, which ensured a low replacement rate and steady population, making families with children a cherished right. This contrasted greatly with the situation over two hundred years ago when families with children were commonplace, and high divorce rates tore many of those families apart, in many cases hurting and devaluing the children."

Jason interjected, "I get what you're saying. My parents were an example of that."

"Yes, Jason, unfortunately, they were. I'm aware of that and I'm sorry for you. Now, I want to relate one more effect of age-decoding – a surprising and sad one – which was the increase in suicides, especially among eubeings living in their second century. Spectre Societies, which hosted suicides, emerged as a prominent institution. It was not surprising to see older eubeings committing Spectre Society suicide, but the fact that many clients were not so old, and many were twenty-five, came as a shock. Despite the miracle of maintaining their youthful physiology with little erosion of skin softness or bone structure, and despite retaining their mental capacity with no loss in neuron responsiveness – the seeming magic of immortality within their grasp – many young eubeings simply lost purpose, a condition we call *immortality ennui*. That impacted many eubeings, despite the mass popularity of the Authority's Fundamental Platform."

"Fundamental Platform?" asked Jason.

"Yes," said Xi. "The unwritten agreement that if society gets age-decoded, a central Authority is granted the power to supersede nation-states."

"Sort of like a world government?"

"Exactly, though not for the entire world, and not for all powers. So, ironically, although suicide officially remained illegal, the Authority turned a blind eye to Spectre Societies because they helped eliminate people. Also, the more successful the Spectre Societies, the more generous the government could be in awarding Family Rights Lottery prizes. Last year the Zone1 Authority awarded about 90,000 FR certificates, a direct consequence of the highest Spectre Society suicide rates ever recorded. While 90,000 seems generous, that's less than 1 out of every 100,000 Zone1 citizens winning the lottery. Granted, if a eubeing was patient over their long life they could raise their odds of winning by entering the lottery every year."

She shifted her slender torso on the bed, then continued, "Non-eubeings, too, gradually found their role in this new landscape, and began to organize themselves as a sort of special interest group whose needs were often ignored. What could be worse than being mortal when everyone else wasn't? Although their total members were small, less than a million, the non-eubeings organized effectively to promote their interests."

"What about other Zones on earth?" Jason asked.

"Zone2, the only other Zone, was far too religious, and far too backward from the genetic engineering standpoint, to engage in age-decoding. It never participated in the primary HGP research. Now it contains a variety of dictatorial and cooperative governments in its sub-zones. Overall, Zone2 is inconsistent and geographically fragmented compared to our Zone1. In fact, to this day, Zone2 isn't a cohesive Zone. But it's no pushover. Its borrowed nuclear technology has enabled it to fend off Zone1."

Ximena's description of her world finally wound down. At that point, Jason found the courage to ask her a personal question, "What's it like, being young and beautiful, forever?"

Ximena, flattered by his question, replied, "It's ... interesting. But I don't get out much, and I live with my very old grandfather, so none of that matters."

"How's that?"

"Well, there's more to it than you would think. Being twenty-five years old biologically may seem great, but I'm still getting older, just like you, day by day, experientially. And let me tell you something that might surprise you." She paused and stared off toward one of the aquariums before beginning to speak again. "It bugs me, growing old in a weird way when billions of people before us did so the natural way. It's not all about avoiding physical or mental decline, you know: wrinkles, osteoporosis, arthritis, hearing loss, forgetting. That's the obvious vanity advantage for me, and I wouldn't deny being pleased to no end by that. Who wouldn't? No, there's something else about being a eubeing that bothers me, has been for some time now, though I can't put my finger on it. Let me just say that I find deep satisfaction relating with non-eubeings, whenever I can uncover one. We share an understanding which percolates up in our conversations, which I find difficult to explain."

She turned her head away from Jason momentarily. Then she slowly turned back to face him. Jason noticed her eyes had watered up, which surprised him. She finished, "Hopefully you'll understand one day."

Jason became a bit embarrassed by her emotion but remained intrigued by the details of the world that she had put forward. He got up the nerve to ask her one last question, "What's wrong with your wrist and hand?"

Ximena abruptly raised herself into a sitting position. "Oh, this, yes ... I hurt myself. It's what I call my healing mitt. The doctor says

I'll recover. Now let's go eat. I'll fix you something that reminds you of your mother's cooking."

CHAPTER 5

THE NEW YORK HEADQUARTERS of the Zone1 Authority – comprising three separate structures externally lined with concrete and steel – was designed in the architectural style of Deconstructed Brutalism: a mix of triangular, rectangular, and hexagonal prisms, all concealing, imposing, and menacing. The massive middle building, Block2, served as the grey thorax; the second and third largest buildings, Block1 and Block3, shaped like appendages, emerged from the sides to devour any intruder. This behemoth was impenetrable, engulfing three city blocks. Pesky graffiti on its street-level concrete was removed daily by the authorities. A labyrinth of underground passages integrated with retail venues and subways.

Originally the Authority headquarters was slated to be constructed somewhere in the low Manhattan financial or in the Brooklyn Bay Ridge areas. However, due to the lack of funding for projects to protect these low-elevation areas from rising ocean water level issues – exacerbated by the city's bankruptcy in 2049 – the Authority chose to locate on Broadway Street just North of Grande Street. This decision proved fortunate, as the headquarters dodged the extreme flooding of Hurricane Lester of 2069, the first recorded Category 6 hurricane in the Atlantic basin.

Today the two streets adjacent to Block1 and Block3 were locked down to serve as a temporary outpost for security and communications as well as a makeshift parking lot for the dozens of limousines serving the Authority's Apex200 members and their assistants. The only attendees not requiring limousines were those in the SI Committee and the Core6 itself, who arrived in high-speed flying cars and entered through the rooftop of Block2. President Reubers flew in from downtown New Orleans in less than eighty minutes using his Volocopter Elite, managing to sneak a one-hour nap en route.

They all met in the Ubiquity Chamber, deep inside Block2. Above the head table, near the top of the wall, the vertical infinity symbol of the Authority adorned both ends of a sizeable inscription, which read: *The four avoidable human sufferings are birth, old age, sickness, and death.*

The fifty or so Apex200 members seated in the room knew that, with age-decoding, the government had managed to reduce all four sufferings – with a few caveats over which they endlessly obsessed. All of their meetings stemmed from that obsession.

At the head table sat the Core6 members, leaders of the Authority:

- *Manfred Reubers*, President
- *Dr.[4] Zhuang Zhinghu*, a statistician, and director of the SI Committee; renowned for his leadership on the Committee on Media Control Through Digital Forsaking, which eradicated all unlicensed media
- *Dr.[9] Ahmed Iftikhar*, with doctorates in each of the nine subdisciplines of statistics; his most famous work was his mathematical treatise for predicting chaotic aspects of human behavior
- *Dr.[17] Suzanne Tellier*, an expert in political systems, notably positive feedback loops of dictatorships; each of her seventeen doctorates examined long-lasting dictators, from Stalin in the USSR in the 1900s to Manabe of Zone2 in the 2100s
- *Dr.[6] Randolph Rahilly*, with four doctorates in Psychology, one in Sociology, and four in Psychosociology; specializing in group strategy analytics
- *Dr.[5] Gupta Mantharathna*, a genomics specialist and primary contributor to Dr. Sengmeuller's research on age-

decoding

The meeting utilized NITs for all attendees, including President Reubers. NITs enabled digital communication of all statements to be corralled in a way that was holistically meaningful and efficient. Nobody talked naturally – they needed their NITs to participate, and for the meeting to function. If anyone spoke off-topic, interrupted rudely, repeated previous points, or spoke nonsense, they were electronically de-amplified; and if they committed a transgression twice (a criterion set by Reubers) they were digitally disabled. However, if someone spoke coherently and on topic, their message was accepted, amplified, and used as input for the aggregate messaging triage. Feedback from attendees served as input to this amplification. The system was the referee. The actions and reactions of the people drove the system. A separate input of facial recognition and body language served up yet another swath of data, contributing as much to the final aggregate triage as anything verbal. The output from the system was compiled and displayed real-time, visually, on a schematic device called a *pictoplath*, which provided a platform for rapid, efficient decision making and – always – consensus. An authority meeting could not end without consensus.

And what was the topic of their meeting? Simply, the protection of democratic power.

Reubers, an impeccably patient man, waited for every last person to focus on him before he spoke. Then he began, his gruff yet satisfying voice taking charge, "The Authority had never lost an election, held every thirty years, since the onset of age-decoding. Zone1 voters have enthusiastically re-elected our incumbent government – the Authority – which was responsible for the miracle of age-decoding. I'm glad to report that the Fundamental Platform remains rock solid: popular support exceeds 80%. It's a honeymoon period that's lasted two hundred years: a political streak surpassing records set long ago by Cuba's Fidel Castro. There's never been a political challenge to our party."

He stopped and scanned their faces, seeming to look right through everyone. "However, in the election of 2234, general support shifted modestly to the Rethinking Party, which captured 9% of the popular vote, though it still failed to capture a seat in the Zone1 Assembly. Many did not view this development as urgent. But it was worrisome to me. Although 9% represents a less than potent fraction, it does mean that one out of every ten citizens knows something, feels something, like no other time during the reign of the Authority."

He paused, preparing to ratchet up the drama.

"After that election, I viewed Rethinking as misguided and self-interested. For this reason, our government began more closely monitoring this group, taking the position that it warranted not only surveillance but infiltration. Hence the formation in 2234 of our *ad hoc* Surveillance and Infiltration (SI) Committee. Several of the highest order politicos were assigned to this group, which was given an open-ended budget and a mandate to rectify things before the election of 2254." His voice trailed off for a moment so he could cough and take a sip of water. The pictoplath then displayed a photo of an Asian male with several credentials listed under his name.

Reubers continued, "I will now give the floor to SI Committee Director Dr. Zhuang Zhinghu."

Zhinghu stood up and explained, "As you are aware, in the most recent election in 2224 the Rethinking Party captured 9% of the popular vote. That was a significant improvement for them over the 2194 election." He paused to let that sink in, then stated firmly, "We will not stand for any more erosion. The Fundamental Platform deserves better. We must defend it with all of our resources. As part of that defense, our Core6 group sits before you today, ready to answer your questions on this topic. We are committed to explaining any undertakings of the SI Committee. Who would like to begin?"

The pictoplath displayed the identities of the fifteen people already in the virtual queue. The first question came from Dr. Suzanne Fogarty, a veteran Apex200 analyst, which was highlighted as she spoke, "What do current opinion polls show about Rethinking's popularity, and what might be the governmental impact?"

Dr. Ahmed Iftikhar responded. "It's at levels slightly higher than in 2224. That may translate into actual Assembly seats and more funding. It will also enhance their presence in standing committees, as well as working groups and technical teams. Only *Ad hoc* groups might not be impacted, since they are appointed by the President's Council Office."

Dr. Fred Hishoto, the lead Japanese representative, asked the next question, "What's causing Rethinking's increase in popularity?"

Nobody in Core6 answered. Director Dr. Zhinghu then looked expectantly at Dr. Tellier, who picked up the cue and mused: "We don't know. We speculate it has something to do with the gradual erosion of loyalty to the Fundamental Platform due to ... well, due to the passage of time. It's as if eubeings feel less obliged to support the Authority the more removed they are from its inauguration two centuries ago. But that's speculation, and it's somewhat circular in reasoning. There may be genetic explanations, too, since the composition of those central to Rethinking is not typical and certainly not stable."

At one point the pictoplath disallowed a question by Dr. Sharon Plethwater which had something to do with Spectre Societies because it did not fit with the theme of the meeting. In the lower-left part of the screen, an icon of her name and face popped up, emphasizing her sin. All knew that her icon would reduce in size and eventually disappear if she refrained from further distractions *and* made positive contributions in moving forward. If she were disingenuous enough to ask another superfluous question, her icon would take on the look of a flashing purple nimbus and her NIT would be electronically muzzled for the rest of the meeting.

"Does cryopreservation have anything to do with this threat?" asked Jim Doherty, an up-and-comer in the demographics group.

Dr.Mantharathna answered, "Cryopreservation is a threat because it's a competing technology, and we're monitoring the relationship between Rethinking membership and HF Capital, which is responsible for Anti-Aging Cloning Totipotency (AACT). Of course, it's the dovetailing of cryopreservation with AACT that proves worrisome. That's because it's non-genetic. They are a non-genetic grouping. Age-decoding means nothing to them. So the Fundamental Platform means nothing to them."

The pictoplath expanded and updated its mind map as questions continued. Some answers were amplified in the final schematic; information had to be triaged because it was excessive, whereas the supply of Apex200 time and resources was finitely scarce. The only "known" in all of this was the outcome, consensus, which enslaved the process. Consensus was preordained.

After forty-five minutes, Plethwater's icon finally vanished from the corner of the pictoplath, unlocking her from the clutches of the purple nimbus.

After one hour and seventeen minutes, consensus was reached. They agreed that cryos surveillance and integration should be bumped up to maximum level on the Authority's Artificial Superintellingence FENCODE_11 system, and that the SI Committee be given unlimited resources in this regard.

To lock in the hard-earned consensus, all NITs were temporarily disabled, paralyzing all connecting feeds, except those of Core6.

As was the custom, all attendees except Reubers rose and applauded. They flashed each other broad, enthusiastic smiles.

Images of the vertical infinity symbol proliferated on the pictoplath then sprang off it and floated about the room like untamed cloned apparitions. Reubers sat motionless, sporting a tight grin, as the sycophants revered their ever-watchful leader.

Yet, at some non-superficial level, the group did believe in themselves and the integrity of the Fundamental Platform. So much time and energy devoted together had made them a team, not just humming familiar mantras, but charting the same direction and worshipping the same vertical infinity.

After a raucous minute or so the clapping abated. President Reubers waited for every member to sit down, then stood up and *thought out* the topic for next week's meeting, which, without his uttering a single syllable, materialized on the pictoplath: AACT and the cryos.

CHAPTER 6

WHEN SI COMMITTEE DIRECTOR Dr. Zhuang Zhinghu and statistician Dr. Ahmed Iftikhar got together to discuss things, there was no holding back on the truth. They had to be honest with each other. It was a rare, raw truth, which they each appreciated as a departure from the deceptive, cunning behavior they engaged in daily with most others. Zhinghu was honest with Ahmed because his SI Committee had to be efficient. In his office, a small sign on the inside of the door admonished, "Don't hold back the truth".

If there was any management lesson Zhinghu had gleaned from his previous chairmanship of the Committee on Media Control Through Digital Forsaking, it was that forthrightness was useful in a tight caucus, even if it was counterproductive outside of it. Ahmed, on the other hand, had to be honest because his expertise was data mining, and good data never lied. To explain and predict individual behavior he needed solid data. To transfer this to the SI leadership, he had to be clear and direct. The Authority's primary system, FENCODE_11, depended on authentic data for all its control algorithms.

"OK, Ahmed," said Zhinghu. "You heard Reubers. He's concerned. What do you suggest we do about the cryos and other AACT adopters? I don't have a bloody clue myself. Also, should I call Randolph or Gupta and get them in on this discussion?"

"Call Gupta or Suzanne, but I think we should leave Randolph out of this for now. This isn't classic psychosociology ... although he would make you believe everything is, according to his theory of equifinality." Ahmed stopped, walked to the window, looked out over the steel-framed city of sunlight reflections, then added, "Look, Zhuang, you know as well as I do that chaotic data contaminates unpredictably, especially when it has no digital basis, no history or foundation, and is simply tossed into current reality. It's a classic case of a *spanner in the works*. The AACT folks are the spanner tossed into FENCODE_11, which is beautifully coded works. What I'm trying to say is that we can't throw a spanner into our data mining without damaging the works. Even a few hundred AACTs could do that, Zhuang. If it turns out that way, we'll have a problem."

"OK, OK, then we'll get Suzanne in on this right now." He rang Dr. Suzanne Tellier, which automatically placed on hold her call with the veterinarian, and vaulted her directly into their conversation.

"Hi guys," she said. "What can a high-priced political scientist do for you?"

"Suzanne," said Zhinghu, "we need your opinion regarding the AACT cases. As you know, next week the Authority will be tackling this issue, but we must be prepared and unified before going to Reubers for a meeting. We don't want any fucking nonsense working its way onto the pictoplath like it did last time."

"I see," said Tellier.

"And we also need to protect the integrity of FENCODE_11 data mining, which is threatened," added Ahmed.

"OK. Well, let me ask two questions before I give you my humble opinion."

"Humble my ass, you're the best there is," quipped Zhinghu.

"Thanks, but I still have to ask. First question: What group are these cryos and AACT folks integrating with?"

"With the non-eubeings and others at Rethinking," said Zhinghu. "According to our surveillance, it's a natural fit, and those bastards have been proactive in this regard."

"OK. Second question: How many of these people are there?"

Ahmed replied, "We don't know for sure, but based on preliminary sampling we think there could be hundreds."

"Politically, then, you do have a material challenge. A group of cryos will want to identify and relate, especially emotionally, as soon as possible, with another social group. If they are corralled in an organized fashion and treated fairly along the way, the danger for us is that mutual transference between those two groups creates a sacrosanct bond. Politically speaking, the new mega-group could have potential in the political arena, especially if you factor in the current susceptibility of the Authority to the Rethinking Party."

"You sound fairly confident on this," said Zhinghu, who thought he had followed what she had said.

"I'm very confident," stated Tellier.

Zhunghu asked her, "Should we ring Rahilly for his view?"

"No. Please. I'm getting a little tired of his equifinality theory claptrap. However, his view could prove useful once our surveillance data come together since it should then have a legitimate psychosociological dynamic."

"OK, thanks, Suzanne."

"Anything else?"

"Nope."

"Good, then," she said. "I'll get back to the pooch doctor. My poor little Zippie is sick again. See you both next week."

Zhinghu and Ahmed looked at each other with a measure of accomplishment.

"There you have it," said Zhinghu. "I wonder how Gupta would interpret this. I'll give her a call." He and Gupta were cut from a similar cloth of political optics, constantly validating each other "for the greater good".

Dr. Gupta Mantharathna answered immediately, "Hi Zhuang. How are things?"

"Not bad, thanks. Look, Gupta, we have a scenario developing and I need to pick your brain. Can you come over? Are you in the building?"

"Sure, I'll be right there."

"Good. See you."

One of the great strengths of the Authority was its ability to commandeer absolute dedication from top-level Zone1 scientists. With them on board anything was possible, and the forces which gnawed away at the government's power, which incessantly tried to erode its lifelines of control, could never fully threaten the Authority. It was both heartening and intriguing for those higher up in the Authority to observe the transformation of top scientists – which sometimes took decades, but which was inevitably begotten – from unbiased independents to intellectual mercenaries capable of lavishing themselves with resources to pursue top-ranked research, all the while lapping up political accolades and blinding themselves to any ethical potholes which cropped up. Begotten as such, their intellectual capture was complete. Genomicist Dr. Gupta Mantharathna was a perfect example.

Into the room Gupta marched – a hefty, masculine-looking woman who, ironically, wore perfume that exerted a strong feminine fragrance. "Hi, gentlemen," she huffed. She glanced toward Zhinghu and asked, "What's the development?"

"Thanks for coming in, Gupta," said Zhinghu.

Ahmed started, "It's about the AACT cases, which Reubers mentioned at the end of our meeting. We've got information that hundreds of them may be mingling with Rethinking. Suzanne believes the political angle is threatening, and I'm concerned about the effects of the lack of integrity of this data on FENCODE_11. Now ... do you have any worries about this? From a genomics perspective?"

"Hmm. My gut reaction is that there's little or no danger genetically, assuming we can get our hands on them fairly soon, that is, before they integrate or expand too much. Remember, they aren't infertile. But at least there's no potential genomics danger. Not yet."

"That's it?"

"Yup. Just that one caveat regarding integration. If you take care of it, there should be no problem."

"Good then. Thanks for your input, Gupta," said Zhinghu.

Seeing that Zhinghu was satisfied for the moment and readying to leave, Ahmed left the office. He mulled things over as he walked down to the Third Cup Café to relax and think at four o'clock in the afternoon. It was his favorite place for winding down, serving as his refuge when things got too messy at the Authority. Though he had developed significant adeptness in dealing with Authority politics using his experience and training, he realized he would always be naturally better with numbers, not people. He doubted he could ever become a canny diplomat, even if he lived another two thousand years. No, he was a numbers aficionado.

Ahmed entered the café, ordered himself a ristretto with cream, and settled into his usual seat which gave him a superb view of the sidewalk passersby. People were bustling around either looking for a late snack or heading home early.

He sipped his coffee just enough to test the temperature. His mind wandered to his past. Of his nine doctoral theses, he knew his first was still his best. *Data Mining Synthesis and Antisynthesis* represented a renowned mathematical treatise with tremendous applications in artificial superintelligence. It had earned him a Harvard doctorate in the spring of 2023 at the prodigal age of eighteen. Within two years his thesis was cited hundreds of times in academic publications. To this day, the scientific journal *Nature* had cited it eighty-nine times.

In the year 2024, at the age of nineteen, he joined Celera Incorporated.

He was age-decoded in the year 2053, at the age of forty-eight. But the fact is that he was now 249 years old, chronologically-speaking. He had earned nine doctorates. He often wondered: How many doctorates would satisfy him in the end? And that begged another question: When would it end?

He turned his thoughts away from himself, to the Human Genome Project (HGP), the monumental scientific endeavor which had provided the foundations for his career. The HGP had mapped the human DNA sequence – an exhaustive undertaking which began in 1990, supported primarily by the Department of Energy and the National Institutes of Health of the U.S., as well as the Medical Research Council and the Wellcome Trust of the United Kingdom.

He recalled the original Human Genome Project goals, perusing them silently with his NIT:

- identify all the approximately 20,000-25,000 genes in human DNA
- determine the sequences of the 3 billion chemical base pairs that make up human DNA
- store this information in databases
- improve tools for data analysis
- transfer related technologies to the private sector
- address the ethical, legal, and social issues that may arise from the project

He marveled at how technological advances had enabled the HGP to complete all of these goals by 2003, well ahead of schedule. He knew HGP fostered a deeper understanding of biological systems and set the stage for centuries of future research.

He fondly recalled his initial excitement when Frieda told him she would be spearheading the Authority's ELSI committee for age-decoding, which was modeled after HGP's own ELSI initiative. Her enthusiasm for such work came as a surprise to many who saw her as a driven, pragmatic researcher, and who viewed ELSI as a quagmire that would only serve as a drag on scientific progress. Whenever she talked to him about ELSI proceedings, he appreciated the discussion as a nice break from statistical analyses, a way for him to get a feel for the "softer" issues of genetic engineering.

Frieda devoted almost 10% of the Authority Science Council budget towards ELSI, making it the largest ethical/scientific project in the history of mankind. To her, age-decoding *implored* moral analysis. Post-HGP projects worldwide would bring a new comprehension of life, with applications to medicine, ecology, energy, and the environment. Frieda wanted to ensure that new understandings brought forward by age-decoding had sound moral foundations. Yet she was criticized – primarily behind her back – by many scientists and administrators for diverting too much funding to ELSI, for mandates that were difficult, if not impossible, to resolve.

At a keynote address to the 2038 Seattle Genomics conference, Frieda had explained her stance to the 8,000 scientists: "Probably the greatest danger after unlocking the human genetic code will be in controlling how we avail ourselves of our new knowledge. For this paramount responsibility, we cannot prepare enough."

Ahmed was convinced that Frieda's involvement with ELSI was instrumental – indirectly – in opening his mind and making him a more well-rounded person. He had always been proud of the work Frieda did for ELSI and enjoyed the profound discussions she had with him about that work. ELSI never came close to tackling all the issues, but she still believed in it. He would never forget Frieda's excitement about the challenges. Yet the work she did leading that group of conscientious scientists was all for nothing.

Ahmed eyed more sidewalk passersby and took in a sip of the sweet ristretto. Was it his imagination or did every second woman going by have a cute dog smaller than a purse? He contrasted this with the shepherds in his Iranian past, who used massive Persian Mastiff's dogs to protect their sheep against bears and wolves.

Ahmed shifted his eyes down to his coffee mug and reminisced about issues ELSI was mandated to pursue. These were framed as several questions, some of which could never be answered in the near term because the limitations of age-decoding required long-term data on eubeings, which could take hundreds of years to acquire.

He withdrew from his pocket an old, laminated cue card Frieda had given him, which contained the full set of ELSI questions:

- *Privacy and confidentiality:* Who controls the implementation of age-decoding technology?
- *Individual impact:* How does age-decoding affect individual behavior and society's perceptions of those individuals?
- *Societal Impact:* How does age-decoding affect humanity and the world at large? What are the benefits and potential drawbacks?
- *Unintended Health Consequences:* What are the risks and side-effects of age-decoding? Do scientific and healthcare personnel understand and communicate these to the broader community?
- *Commercialization of products:* Who owns age-decoding technology? Will patenting this technology enable or limit its use for other future technologies?

Of these questions, the very first stood out as most salient, given Ahmed's hindsight into the events of the past two hundred years. He repeated it to himself: *Who controls the implementation of age-decoding technology?*

Frieda, he remembered, feverishly expounded on the ELSI questions, especially the one about implementation control. She had shown incredible foresight in directing a good deal of ELSI resources to this one question, stating with her natural sincerity and solemnness at every meeting, conference, or official occasion that it superseded all other questions. To her, control meant everything, because the "next step" – the logically enticing next step – was to alter the genetic code to influence *human behavior*, possibly to the advantage of those in control. That, Frieda believed, would be the nightmare scenario for humanity.

Ahmed recalled the term Frieda coined to describe this next step. She saw it as the moral antithesis of natural selection, referring to it as *artificial selection*. Natural selection, she argued, was ethically neutral in altering the gene pool and genetic code for any species using generation-by-generation mutations and adaptation. With evolution, traits and reproduction are the drama in the stage of the environment – but no specific individual in the species acts as the director. The director is nature. According to Frieda, the moral antithesis to this entails human "controllers" bypassing the natural fashioning, overriding natural selection, and *selecting codes with a priori human selfishness*. Artificial selection, she warned, could be potentially unscrupulous, subverting not only the majestic forces of nature but the goals of humanity.

When the Zone1 Authority disbanded ELSI and assumed control over all aspects of age-decoding, Frieda must have felt like nobody heard her scream as her fledgling creation – age-decoding – was torn from her arms. He remembered her complaining that after two decades of dedicated ELSI teamwork, it took a few people just a couple of months to wrest it all away.

It was no wonder she took her life because her life's precious work was taken from her. His mental breakdown ensued, including his abandonment of Ximena. Was it all as simple as that?

Ahmed's work for the Authority after his breakdown was a mechanical plodding along for almost two centuries, culminating with his promotion to Core6 over the past thirty years.

He tried in vain to see the upside. But his soul remained sunken. The very fact that he had turned a blind eye toward their *propensity to dissent* manipulations made it impossible for him to claim moral ground. True, he contributed excellent mathematical work; but he was always ethically and emotionally disengaged. His mind, challenged but not over-stimulated, was in moral cruise control. The value of his work was a delusion.

Ahmed scanned more people on the sidewalk. A bearded man on a scooter. Two handsome gay females walking with hands joined. A crowd of old Japanese tourists. All of them would no doubt be impressed by his credentials and work history.

But he felt as inert as a deep black crater in a far-away extinct volcano. He had to face the fact that, as a eubeing, his propensity to dissent had been deactivated. But did that mean he could not try to improve?

To Ahmed, the Frieda years, now long gone, had been so good. Her ideas made sense to him. Her eye to humanity and serving the greater purpose.

He admonished himself: I've got to find a way to break free from the Authority straightjacket, from the amoral immortals. No more mere pondering at cafés. I've got to do something real before it's too late.

CHAPTER 7

AGE-DECODED

SOMETIME IN THE YEAR 2254, Ahmed Iftikhar did something he thought he would never do: he walked straight into a Spectre Society, specifically Chapter 424 in New Orleans. Entering through the light turquoise shadows of the lobby he immediately sensed the spirit of the person whose shoulders he stood upon, Dr. Frieda Sengmeuller, watching him and wondering. He believed he understood her motivation for ending her life, but his own motivation for being here, at this Spectre Society, remained fuzzy.

He was received by a robot that scooted weightlessly toward him and introduced itself as Lolita.

Lolita stood about five and a half feet tall, androgynously composed, yet she still seemed more female than male, and somewhat attractive to him.

How did he know she was a robot? Because she told him so, something all Zone1 robots were required to do when first encountering a person. But he could also tell from the many small signs: her faint lipstick, instead of lying on her skin as with real women, was embedded deep within it; her hair was perfectly set, short and black; her eyes emitted a subtle flow of background energy; and her movement, which seemed too purposeful.

Still, she was alluring. He had to give her that.

"What's your official eubeing name?" asked Lolita.

Wow, Ahmed thought, she said *what's* – a human-like grammatical contraction!

"My name's Ahmed Iftikhar YHHHS"

Without moving, she registered that in her circuitry.

"Is this your first visit, Ahmed?"

"Yes."

"How old are you, biologically?"

"Forty-eight."

"How old are you chronologically?"

"Two hundred and forty-eight."

"Will you pay litecoin, or Visa?"

"Litecoin. How much does it cost?"

"Well, that'll depend on the options you choose. Basic service is L50,000, but it's possible for many expanded services beyond that."

That was interesting, thought Ahmed. "OK, can you tell me about my options?"

Lolita projected the holographic option sheet two feet in front of him at face height.

He scanned it:

Spectre Society MAIN MENU: All figures in thousands of Litecoin

Life review:
oral ... 10
visual ... 100

Will preparation ... 100
Final Messages ... 10 (per message)
Final Fantasy ... 50
Suicide Assistance ... 50

Nothing in the menu surprised Ahmed, except the fact that everything had a price. He had always been under the impression that Spectre Society services were free; that the place was run by volunteers, subsidized by the government. Then again, he had never discussed the experience with anyone who had used the Spectre Society – how could they report back the details?

He wondered what options to go for. Maybe the life review, which would have been uplifting for a man of his success? Maybe not. His being here implied that his life was not much of a success.

He decided to opt for the will preparation because he had plenty of assets and worthwhile ideas about where to direct them. Would Xi be the main beneficiary? After completely failing her as her father, would that provide her some comfort, and him some redemption?

Or should he just give it all to Jesus, to help him with the fatherly responsibilities?

"What does final fantasy mean?" he asked Lolita.

"It means you can live out any fantasy in our state-of-the-art VRC. Any fantasy," she piped up, and he thought he detected a slight grin on her shiny cute face.

"That sounds alluring ... yet I see it's one of the cheapest options."

"Actually, the VRC was quite expensive for us to design and build, but the rest of our services are overpriced, so they subsidize it."

"I see. You're saying that I should opt for the VRC because it's the best value on the menu?"

"Exactly. Now, please," she motioned to a door to her left, "have a seat in the next room where you'll be asked to provide option details. And I want to thank you for courage in choosing suicide at the Spectre Society."

Not knowing whether to say *you're welcome*, Ahmed just stood there as Lolita cruised away so perfectly. He then walked slowly into the room. The room was square and plain, with one simple chair located in the middle of the floor. Designed to minimize distraction, he surmised.

He sat down and glanced again at the option sheet, which hovered again before him. This room was not dissimilar to the last, except the chair was much larger and high-tech.

A few seconds later, a serene, masculine voice began to speak:

The time has come for you to select your options. The universe awaits you. It is open to you, and you're now open to it. Yourself with its earthly ego left behind will embrace the universe, the stars, the superhuman, and all that we do not know. Remove yourself from all earthly distractions, and join the great spectre ...

Ahmed relaxed and considered his choices, while the voice carried on:

... is now just you, a chair, an empty room. You've been called forward, not only from within, but from without, from the universe, and soon you will comprehend the great forces beyond Earth...... dust is made from dust, and so we are thus!

It hardly mattered what the voice was saying. Ahmed had decided. He would purchase the final fantasy, with the suicide assistance. The thought crossed his mind to request the former with an option to decide about the latter, but he correctly figured that the Spectre Society would not allow such dickering.

Presently Lolita re-entered the room and positioned herself off to Ahmed's side, just visible in his periphery. Her slightly femininized left breast gently brushed his right shoulder.

"Have you decided?" she asked.

"I have."

"Good, then please follow me, Ahmed."

It's all so odd, he thought, a robot being so nice and personal. Oh well, that's her job. Ahmed followed her into the next room and decided to put the details out of his mind. What did details matter to him now that his life would be terminated – *relieved* is the better word – in a matter of minutes? Maybe that's the overriding sentiment one feels in ending their life? Relieved? Or was there such a golden rule? Life had taught him to beware of golden rules, the standardization of human experience.

Had his dear Frieda's overriding sentiment been relief, after she took that injection? He could not imagine so. He could never be sure if rational thoughts underpinned her final act. Could she have been rational, knowing the horrible impact on him, on Ximena, on Jesus? She was too good to do that to them.

Did his lovely Frieda simply kill herself for no reason? Or was it some biochemical imbalance? She did suffer bouts of depression, which he admittedly did not help her enough with, dismissing it as her self-pity and mysticism.

Now, approaching his end, he was finding cogency. But such last-minute ruminations did not make him proud to be human. He agonized: If I had helped Frieda, really helped, I could have made a difference. If I had helped with Ximena, really helped, that too could have made a difference.

"What options have you chosen?" asked Lolita, standing close to him and almost whispering.

"I'll have the final fantasy option, with suicide assistance."

"Excellent choices. That's our most popular combination." She pressed a few buttons on her hand-held control. Then she continued, "According to Marcus Aurelius, the great Roman emperor:

He who fears death either fears to lose all sensation or fears new sensations. In reality, you will either feel nothing at all, and therefore nothing evil, or else, if you can feel any new sensations, you will be a new creature, and so will not have ceased to live."

"Well, Lolita, I'm proud to say that I don't fear death. I've just opted for it, and even paid for it." He paused for a few seconds, then said, "But that's a very profound Aurelius quotation. Did you pick that out just for me?"

"To be honest, no. We use that for anyone who selects that combination, which means we've used it eight hundred and seventy-six thousand, two hundred and fifty-five times so far."

Lolita's conversing was impressively human-like. "You've certainly passed my Turing Test," he joked.

She smiled back wryly. Less than one thousand subjects had used that line with her.

Although trained to be patiently accommodating, Lolita was eager to move on with things.

"I need you to take a seat and formulate your final fantasy," she said. "I'll ask you a series of questions. Just give your gut reaction to each, and don't dwell too much before responding. In less than two minutes your final fantasy should be fully formulated; then we'll get the show on the road."

So, it was just some show, killing oneself? Ahmed wondered who programmed that use of language, but then he blinked twice and moved on to the task at hand.

The questions came rapidly.

Is your name Ahmed Iftikhar YHHHS? *Yes*

Will your fantasy be sexual or non-sexual? *Non-sexual.*

Political or Cooperative? *Political.*

Involve fictional or actual people? *Actual.*

Involve superiors or inferiors? *Superiors.*

Entail a monetary issue? *No.*

Entail a moral issue? *Yes.*

Entail abuse of mandate? *Yes.*

Involve a coverup? *Yes.*

Involve blowing the whistle? *Maybe.*

Bzzzzzz. You must answer yes or no. Involve blowing the whistle?

That question hamstrung Ahmed. He rationalized, what good would it do to disclose some grand government coverup to a robot? His propensity to dissent, which had been disengaged so long ago, was welling up inside and trying to bust out, but like all eubeings, he could only conceptualize dissent, not easily emote it or act upon it. As much as he tried, even with nothing to lose moments before ending his life, he could not muster up the nerve to blow the whistle on the Authority. *If I can't do the right thing here, in a simulated fantasy, could I ever do the right thing in real life? How pathetic.*

It all demoralized Ahmed, magnified by a realization that he had been an integral part of the corrupt Authority for most of his life.

Bzzzzzz. You must answer yes or no. Involve blowing the whistle?

"Forget it!" Ahmed shouted. He bolted up from his chair and cowered in the corner of the room. "Forget it! I'm backing out!"

By his sudden change, Lolita appeared almost resigned, certainly not shocked.

"Cancelling is still your prerogative at this stage," she said calmly. "But there'll be a small service charge for the preliminaries. About 3% of our clients do exactly as you have just done. I should point out that if you had completed the final fantasy, we would never have let you cancel the suicide assistance. Letting clients do that sort of thing would render this place an amusement park, not an authentic Spectre Society."

Ahmed hardly took in what she said, for he was congratulating himself for his sudden reversal.

He requested that she usher him out immediately. She grasped him by his left arm – firmer than necessary, he thought – and escorted him down three hallways and through two rooms, finally releasing him a few meters from the front door.

"Well, Lolita, thanks for your help."

"You're welcome, Ahmed. And may I wish you all the best in the future?"

"You're too kind. Thank you."

With that, Ahmed strolled out of the building with a spring in his step. His brush with death brought a surge within, an unequivocal resolve to do just one thing: to become the good person that Frieda and Ximena once loved.

CHAPTER 8

AGE-DECODED

THE HAND-WRITTEN MESSAGE came unexpectedly to Ahmed Iftikhar.

Ahmed: Meet me at the downtown Hilton.
Two o'clock in the front lobby. This is vital.
Regards,
Tavon Brooks, Apex200

Ahmed was curious. Why would an Apex200 member want to meet him now, at a hotel? He did not know Tavon Brooks. He checked Tavon's employee records and found he was a statistical aficionado; he was also the recipient of the African American Heritage Award, based on his journey from a poor district in Detroit to the top of his class at MIT. He truly wondered why this young man was so eager to meet him. Hence Ahmed's cautious disposition when he shook hands with Tavon in the lobby.

Tavon opened, "May I suggest we go to the hotel bar for a drink?"

"Sure."

They walked slowly across the expanse of a gorgeous lobby, which was adorned with six scintillating Rosdorf Park chandeliers, as well as four large works of Cecily Brown abstract art, including *Puce Moment,* whose sexual anatomical components taunted and laughed at both of them. Upon reaching the other end of the lobby, a hotel clerk ushered them over to two large, green, comfortable lounge chairs. A waitress with a friendly smile approached to take orders. The place was almost empty.

"Greetings, gentlemen."

"What'll you have?" Tavon asked Ahmed.

"Scotch. No ice. Lime on the side."

"That sounds good; bring us two of those please," said Tavon. The waitress nodded and hurried off.

Ahmed examined Tavon for a moment. He had a normal build, with a wide, warm face. His eyes, without discernible color, exuded a wideness, an awareness, an acute connectivity. His long mahogany-brown hair was set partially in dreadlocks which swirled their way magnificently about his forehead and almost to his shoulders.

Tavon turned to Ahmed. "Look, you're a busy man, so I'm not going to waste your time—"

"I've got lots of time," Ahmed interrupted with a slight smile. "I've got all the time in the world. Time is almost limitless these days, remember? Don't rush on my account."

"That's not the case for me, as I'm not a eubeing yet. Two more years to wait."

"Yes, I figured you were younger than twenty-five. You've certainly made great strides at the Authority, being so young."

"Well, Thanks ... Look, as you know, I'm part of the data mining team helping the SI Committee. The other day I picked up your visit to the Spectre Society. At first, I thought it was a false positive mistake, but FENCODE_11 validated it, triangulated it with two other data sources."

Ahmed's expression did not change, but inside he began to worry.

Tavon went on, "I haven't yet disclosed this to anyone, but you probably know that, according to SI protocol, I'm obliged to pass it on to someone at or above your level." He stopped to give Ahmed a chance to react. "That would mean someone in Core6."

Ahmed tried to read Tavon's expressions, to make use of his extensive psychological training. The situation was serious, so a valid assessment could be vital. He noted how Tavon appeared strong, resolute, certainly not confused. Was Tavon waiting for him to say something? Ahmed decided it would be wiser to say nothing, to bide his time until he got a better read on things.

Tavon continued, "Though I'm obliged to disclose your visit, I'm here to tell you that I won't."

"Uhum," said Ahmed, barely audible.

"I won't because I think something like that is too personal to be reported to other bureaucrats ... what's your opinion?"

Ahmed was relieved. He sensed Tavon opening up. The young man was, of course, his subordinate, but he seemed to be inviting Ahmed to converse with him on a personal level, not as his work superior.

Tavon found himself thinking about the power of coincidence, how it could play a part in shaping things. What a coincidence that he alone in the Authority was privy to the FENCODE_11 tracking of Ahmed's visit to the Spectre Society? As fascinating as it was unfathomable, Tavon knew this coincidence, more than anything else, had brought them together this evening.

Ahmed risked a bit more, "I agree with you ... about some things being too personal. Not everything is reportable in a systematic way. Sometimes a real heartfelt discussion is better."

The drinks arrived and they both helped themselves.

Tavon then reaffirmed to Ahmed, "FENCODE_11 is aware, but nobody in Core6 knows – except you, of course."

Ahmed reminded himself that his position in Core6 still gave him the upper hand in this conversation. Or did it? He again scrutinized his young subordinate. Nothing truly suspicious registered. But he would need to dig deeper to decipher Tavon's motives. Why were they here, face-to-face? He decided to probe but to do so indirectly.

He asked, "Don't you want to know why I visited the Spectre Society, since I obviously wasn't there to kill myself?"

Tavon knew otherwise. FENCODE_11 had transmitted the Spectre Society conversation between Ahmed and the robot Lolita, which he had analyzed. But he feigned ignorance for the sake of saving Ahmed's face.

"That's why I wanted to see you, Ahmed. I was worried, frankly, that you might be depressed or ..."

Ahmed looked straight at him, "No need to worry. I was merely there in my bizarre way to pay respects to that great scientist and amazing lady – Dr. Frieda Sengmeuller. She ended her life by killing herself and I finally mustered up the courage to check out a suicide parlor, not as a curiosity ... but more as a tribute. I admit it was a strange thing to do, and most people wouldn't understand my need to do it, but I had to finally get it out of my system. I wanted to experience the *feel* of suicide, to know what a person goes through when they are about to say goodbye to the treasure of life... to themselves ... I wanted to share Frieda's experience without going through with it. It was cathartic, in a way, and I really should've done it a long time ago. That robot Lolita was kick-ass." He paused for a quick chuckle, then added. "I'm not sure you know how well I knew Frieda."

Tavon knew all about their relationship, but asked anyway, "How well?"

Ahmed took a sip of his drink. "At first she was my co-worker ... but then that turned into a romantic relationship. She eventually became my soulmate, the love of my life. Sometimes, though only in private, she called me *Crunchy*, a reference to me being a number-cruncher. I was never a believer in corny soulmate stuff, but Frieda changed that. We moved in together, and soon after had a child."

"*Crunchy* ... that's cute," Tavon said. He then asked, "Is your child alive?"

"Yes. Our daughter Ximena lives in New Orleans. But she and I are estranged. I'm ashamed to admit that I abandoned her right after Frieda killed herself. I must have had some sort of a nervous breakdown, and blamed Frieda for everything. But leaving my daughter was my doing."

Tavon was surprised by Ahmed's openness. "I'm sorry to hear that," he said.

"I'm sorry too, believe me."

Unsure of whether to ask anything else about this matter, Tavon shifted his glance to the far end of the bar. It disturbed him, how he could know so much about another person, without even knowing that person. This is what it must be like to secretly read someone's diary, he thought.

After the delay became uncomfortably long, Tavon returned his gaze to Ahmed. "Look, I respect you immensely as a professional. But I was concerned because I couldn't justify reporting a Spectre Society incident like that involving my superior. I figured you must be struggling with a personal matter. I've struggled too, you should know. I'm sensing we share some things in that regard. We both have big roles in the Authority, are highly regarded, but we're not perfect human beings, nobody is. Does that make sense?"

"Of course, and I agree. Especially the part about not being perfect."

They were genuinely loosening up. It was noteworthy that, although they were both statistical gurus, they were not conversing about mathematics, which was furthest from their minds.

"That drink went down well," exclaimed Ahmed, "another?"

"Sure."

Tavon was surprised yet assuaged by Ahmed's subtle potshots at SI culture and protocol. Though they were not treasonous criticisms, they opened the door just enough to intrigue Tavon who, in a few cases, adjoined with tiny remarks of his own.

The waitress delivered their second round of drinks.

As their mutual respect rose, so did the risk level of their discussion. Tavon knew he was prone: he had to trust that the concerns Ahmed expressed to Lolita in the Spectre Society – about government corruption; about blowing the whistle – were valid. He needed to eliminate all doubt here and now.

The second round of drinks began to take effect. Tavon related the story of how his mother won the Family Rights Lottery twenty-four years ago and, though she was poor, had exercised that right instead of selling it to another person. Hence his current age of twenty-three, both chronologically and biologically, meaning he was not yet a eubeing.

"Good for her, good for you," said Ahmed. "Almost all poor people who win end up cashing out their Family Rights."

"You'd have to know my mom," said Tavon. "She doesn't take no for an answer."

Tavon then gathered his nerve. It was time for him to take a chance, as he might not again have this opportunity. He took a deliberately slow sip of his drink, pushed a few dreadlocks off his forehead, then plunged in.

"Look, the reason I wanted to meet you was to let you know that I'm probably going to leave the Authority altogether. I've had enough. Please keep this between you and me, Ahmed, just as I've done regarding your visit to the Spectre Society."

That statement was the crowbar that tore everything wide open.

Ahmed gathered himself and rejoined with a subtle nod, a tiny gesture that fortified their trust.

He then shocked Tavon with his response, "I'm thinking of doing the same."

Each man gathered themselves and quaffed a good portion of their scotch.

"Let me explain," said Ahmed, who was about to make a huge move away from his long-held safety in the Authority to the riskiest position he had ever held. He decided to justify his reasons to Tavon, and in doing so he divulged the Authority's deactivation of the propensity to dissent. Never had Ahmed discussed this with anyone outside of Core6. Over the next few minutes, he outlined how Frieda and Gupta had together discovered the genetic basis of the *propensity to addictive behavior*, then the propensity to dissent, well before Frieda unlocked the solution to age-decoding. He described how easy it was to deactivate the propensity to dissent while people were age-decoded.

Tavon listened to these revelations with astonishment. "That's incredible," he said. "How many people know about this?

"Just Core6."

Tavon replied, "If you don't mind me saying, that's not just incredible, it's despicable. I never imagined our leaders had used science like that. Though I must say, I was suspicious that something untoward had transpired during age-decoding because – as a fellow statistician, allow me to indulge you – all political data after the Fundamental Platform seemed diametrically skewed. The skewing was trenchant, statistically unnatural."

Ahmed took a gulp of his drink. After what he had just disclosed to Tavon, there was no turning back now. He knew he had to change, and over the last few minutes, he proved he was changing.

A clever thought came to him, which he then shared with Tavon, "They erroneously thought that since they made people immortal, their power should be immortal too."

Tavon let out a brief, gasping chuckle. "It's funny, critics of statistics say it's often used to tell lies, but that isn't necessarily the case. I specialize in using statistics to *detect* lies. What befuddles me is that although my analysis showed something untoward, I couldn't have inferred the exact evil nature of this. I'm stunned." He drew in a large breath, "This inspires me to not only leave but to work against these people." He paused, reasoning that this statement would further test Ahmed.

Ahmed said, "I've already crossed the Rubicon by telling you about the propensity to dissent. We're in this together now."

For Ahmed and Tavon, the dangers of conspiring to work against the Authority were profoundly clear. It was also clear neither could live with themselves if they did nothing.

For Tavon, their conversation today rewarded his patience in trying to uncover a strong ally without incriminating himself. For Ahmed, it brought real possibilities for redemption, a need which had recently taken hold of him. Perhaps one day he would be able to bear his haggard image in self-reflection.

Tavon spoke next, "I just can't believe what they did. Now that I'm aware, it makes so much sense. It's a complete breach of trust of the people by the Authority, a wicked act. A government should serve its people, not deceive them. You can probably figure, Ahmed, that as an African American I'm very aware of my ancestral past, and the history of black slavery in the United States. The horrors of humans subjugating other humans. This stuff is in my veins. After what I've learned today, I feel the actions of this Authority are just another form of slavery ... in this case the slavery of *all* people, regardless of skin color."

"I can't disagree. But don't beat yourself up about not figuring it all out with your statistical deciphering! It's been set for two centuries, and nobody's figured it out. Though, to be honest, I'm surprised people haven't been more suspicious."

Half-jokingly Tavon said, "Maybe propensity to dissent subsumes the *propensity for suspicion*. Could they be part of the same trait?"

"Actually, that's not so far-fetched. Who the hell knows? I'd wager the people who did this to billions of people don't even have a clue."

The two men remained at the Hilton bar until almost two o'clock in the morning. When they finally left and were standing outside on the sidewalk, Tavon brought up one last thing.

"Look, Ahmed, I think you should know that I knew all of that about your daughter."

"Yeah, I figured that. I'm guessing you may know more about her than I do."

"Sorry, it's my job—"

Ahmed gently touched Tavon on the shoulder. "Hey. You don't need to apologize. We must respect each other. We're on the same team now."

"Based on our talk today, I have a suggestion to make about your daughter. Why don't you try reuniting with her? She's working with Rethinking, so we're really on her side now, and if she learns that it could be huge. After what I've learned today, it makes sense for you to try reuniting with her. Would you allow me to set that up?"

Tavon paused, waiting for a response.

At the mention of his daughter, Ahmed's emotions spiked. He felt compelled to ask, "I was aware Xi had done some work with Rethinking. She's still involved with them?"

"Yes, in a big way. I had to analyze that as part of my job. Believe me, you'll be proud of her when you get the details."

"Isn't it way too late, for getting back together? I've thought about it many times, even met with her grandfather Jesus about it, but he told me she had shut me out and would never go for it. This has haunted me for so long, how to persuade her to forgive me. After two centuries I don't think she —"

"I don't think redemption sets time limits. Do you?"

"OK, well said ... but how do you think she'd react? What do you believe, as an external observer?"

"At some point, you'll have to ask her for forgiveness, even if she asks questions you can't answer. I'm guessing she'd be more open to it now. There's only one way to find out."

Ahmed conveyed a measured nod, "OK, you have my permission. It's been a remarkable evening, Tavon."

With that, they shook hands firmly, then headed into the New Orleans night in opposite directions.

Ahmed walked southeast along Bienville Avenue, gingerly stepping on every fourth sidewalk crack. Jazz music became louder as he approached a corner bar called, *We're all Imperfect*. A male voice bellowed out in baritone:

Oh when the day of judgment comes,
Oh when the day of judgment comes,
Oh I want to be in that number,
When the saints go marching in.

A giddy, childlike wave shot through Ahmed. So much was changing so fast, he thought, after years of nothing. Years and years of absolutely nothing.

Tavon headed northwest along Bienville Avenue. He knew things would change remarkably after tonight. As a start, instead of surveilling Ximena and Jason, he wanted to meet them in person, better understand the AACT issue, and offer to help Ximena with the Rethinking Party. There could be no turning back.

CHAPTER 9

JASON RESTED SLOUCHED on the couch, with his neck at an awkward angle, and his head reclined, peering almost straight up. Ximena had told him to make himself at home, but not to fiddle with any gadgets he did not comprehend. That seemed reasonable to him.

Ximena, sitting in a nearby chair, noted the young man's solid jawlines, brown, thick, wavy hair, deep and sentimental eyes, and strong, symmetrical nose. His skin, though fair, held a hint of darker color, especially in his arms. He was above average height, but lean.

Jason was thinking about his mother and sister. He vaguely recollected the accident. Something loud; silence and dampness. His sister screaming. A fire truck, a police officer, Mom groaning on a stretcher. Yet as hard as he tried, he could not get beyond these recollections to picture the accident *per se*. How did it happen? He would someday broach that topic with Xi.

His mind moved on to his coming out of the cryopreservation. Who put me in that state? Was this common, or am I a special case? Am I the same person now as I was before, or was I somehow messed up? *I feel the same as ever*, he thought. I don't feel messed up, but who knows? Can I be a reliable judge of myself?

I want to watch TV – but where is it? This room seems entirely non-electronic, like an enclosed garden porch or sunroom. I can't imagine a house without a TV. I'll try surfing the net to see what's out there, see if I recognize any sites or games or clogs. But how? I don't have an NIT. He went to the kitchen, activated the e-paper, and scanned the headlines: *Reubers Enshrines Indigenous Peoples Treaty; Xeta-3 Trials Successful Against Tay-Sachs Disease; Zone1 Authority Questions Zone2 Nuclear Intentions; Pitbulls and Poodles Making a Comeback.*

Jason began reading the lead article about Indigenous Peoples but soon his thoughts shifted back to his family. His mother he had always sympathized with, because of what had happened between her and his father. He knew she had tried her best to raise him and Sarah on her own. From the time he was ten years old she did so without any help from Dad or any other man. Sarah, eight years younger than him, had a maturity that was an immense help to Mom in that regard. "You'll be a great mom someday," he recalled his mother saying to her. Indeed, his mother praised Sarah and him excessively, to the point where they were often embarrassed or ashamed by it. Perhaps they felt they didn't deserve it, guilt-ridden by what had happened with their father. In his heart Jason always held the urge to reach out to his mother, to say he was sorry, to hug her – but he never did.

Ximena came in from the backyard. "How's it going?"

He turned as she entered, looking beautiful, although he detected a slight imbalance in her smile. Interestingly, her sexual effect on him had waned each day as he got to know her, though it still existed at a modest level.

"I'm OK, Xi," he answered.

Ximena said, "I just saw my father, Jesus Sengmeuller. I'd like you to meet him, but that'll have to wait a little while longer. Anyhow, he says he wants to meet you. He's not really my father ... he's my grandfather. I won't discuss my real parents; that's a sad story. No, Jesus is my surrogate father. He filled in when nobody else was there, back in the time when most children were reared by one or two loving parents. I had no real parents after the age of ten – except Jesus. He was age-decoded over two hundred years ago when he was seventy-four years old. What makes him so interesting is that, while he isn't getting any older, biologically, he also isn't getting any younger, so he's locked into ripe old age, prone to the typical aches and ailments of old people. But he's managed to hang in there and survive for almost two centuries. That's quite a feat, don't you think? According to my doctor, the chances are one in three that someone of Jesus's biological age would survive that long. I'm lucky he has

MARK P RYALL

... he's the sweetest man ... always a wise twinkle in his eyes ... and a wacko way of looking at things. You've got to meet him. Did I mention that he's as sharp as a tack, the smartest person I've ever known?"

She went on to explain to Jason how age-decoding was applied to everyone in Zone1 who was twenty-five or older. Typically, people had it done on their twenty-fifth birthday, as part of a ceremony. The procedure was painless and fast, as easy as a medical checkup. Anyone older than twenty-five simply locked into whatever age they were at, and never grew a day older after that. Thus, the government managed to "freeze" that portion of the demographic bell curve exceeding the age of twenty-five (except for the few non-eubeings). Eventually, over the next few decades, the curve gradually reshaped itself and clustered a little closer to the age of twenty-five. This happened for two reasons. First, when younger people reached twenty-five they were age-decoded. Second, people who were age-decoded at a biological age over twenty-five, especially those beyond middle age, died at a much higher rate, as evidenced by the effects of the Covid superbug in 2099, as well as the increased participation rates of older eubeings in the Spectre Society. The Zone1 demographics eventually converged to: almost nobody younger than twenty-five (just a few byproducts of the Family Rights Lottery); many people exactly twenty-five; and even more people older than twenty-five, though few who were very old. Overlaying this were a few non-eubeings who aged normally.

"Jesus is unfortunate to be so old," she added. "Yet he's never gone near a Spectre Society. I love him so much, I'd kill him if he tried! He is, to me, everything good in one person. About twenty years ago it was rumored the Authority was about to announce a breakthrough in reverse-aging, but nothing happened. Rumors persist that they are now close. Jesus, trapped in his frail state, would be a perfect candidate for reverse-aging."

Jason asked, "Why is his name, Jesus?"

"Oh, that's easy, he changed his name to Jesus when he converted to Buddhism, which was soon after he was age-decoded. His real name is Igor, but everyone calls him Jesus."

"But Jesus is a Christian name, not Buddhist, right? Why would he choose the name Jesus when becoming a Buddhist?"

"He explained that to me once. When he turned Buddhist, he still wanted to respect and retain part of his Christian heritage, so what better way than to adopt the name of the most prominent Christian of all time, Christ himself?"

"I see," said Jason, still bewildered. He wanted to ask Ximena about her parents but was not sure it would be appropriate to do so. Instead, he asked her if she had any information on his own past, his family, his accident.

"I thought you'd never get to that," said Ximena. "That's covered already. We're meeting with a person named Tavon Brooks tomorrow. He'll have all of that information. Let's wait until then to discuss this."

"OK, Xi."

"Good. Now it's been a long day. Why don't we watch some TV?" She activated her NIT. "Here: I'll feed in the taste parameters for you. Action?" she asked. "Yes," he replied. "Fiction?" "Yes." "Popular?" "Yes." "Violent?" "No." "Comedy?" "Yes."

"Well, she said, "that narrows it to the following twenty-six shows – pick one." Jason scanned the list which hovered about one foot in front of him at eye level. He pointed to a show called *Harrowing Harrows.* The lights in the room dimmed down, and an awesome three-dimensional holographic show filled the room.

Ximena pretended to watch, but she was more entertained watching Jason watch. She could see he must have been a big TV fan in his day.

At some point, with the young man so engrossed with the show, Ximena began to rub the surface of her healing mitt with her good hand, as if her wrist was itchy underneath. She did not remove the mitt, but rubbed it, aggressively, as if by compulsion. Jason did not notice, except on one occasion when he turned quickly to her to ask a question.

The next morning, as they ate breakfast, Jason casually said to Ximena, "I asked you a question in my dream last night." He helped himself to another spoonful of cereal, a sip of juice, then continued, "I asked you why people sleep, and whether we could find a way to avoid sleep. And you replied the following:

No they haven't. Dr. So-and-So and his small research team at Such-and-Such University were fascinated with this question in the mid-2100s... but when he died in a traffic accident, his scientific leadership in this area was lost, and funding dried up because there was no practical benefit to answering that question. Dried up like a newly washed patio on a hot sunny day. Think of it: eliminating sleep and adding extra wake time to each day – it's not worth it when age-decoding adds hundreds of years to the average life ... and imagine if reverse-aging was discovered!"

He had been mimicking her voice as he spoke, which amused Ximena. But she was more impressed by the validity of his dream because it was close to reality. She praised him, "Well done! Age-decoding indeed snuffed out the need for sleep avoidance research, as it snuffed out so many other things – often unexpectedly."

After she spoke, Jason took on a worried expression. This did not surprise Ximena. Although she was doing her best to help him – that was her assignment – she had been warned it would be difficult for him emotionally and to watch for this. She cheered him up by reminding him that a man named Tavon Brooks was coming to visit him later that morning.

Thirty minutes later Tavon did arrive at the house, carefully camouflaging his visit using methods he learned in Apex200. Yet he knew he was rolling the dice. He vowed as he walked up the steps to be as sympathetic as possible with the young man before devising any strategy. Last year's Apex200 personality profile had shown that he needed to shore up his relationship skills; he enrolled in a course, *Reaching Out*, which taught him to listen to people instead of pretending to listen; it also taught him to pay close attention to the many signals of body language. Tavon needed to understand Jason well, to get to know him, and to glean what he could about him from Ximena.

He rang the doorbell. As he waited, he used his NIT to call up one of his favorite sayings, by John D. Barrow, who long ago taught mathematical science at the University of Cambridge:

> *When there is an infinite time to wait then anything that can happen, eventually will happen. Worse (or better) than that, it will happen infinitely often.*

Tavon was depending on Barrow's statement to guide his actions, focusing on the bracketed "or better" aspect, determined as he was to expedite the demise of the Authority. As a member of Apex200, he knew he was risking his career – his life? Even this one visit brought elevated risk. But he knew it was the right course of action. *Anything that can happen, eventually will happen.*

Ximena opened the door with a cautious smile. She spoke to him naturally, of course, "Hi Tavon – come on in."

"Thank you, Ximena," he said, reminding himself to not use his NIT.

"How are you?" she said.

He did not answer but offered a slight smile.

Ximena said, "Let's go to the garden room so you can meet Jason right away."

"Good."

She led him down the hallway, through the kitchen, and into the garden room, where Jason was just beginning to read Suzanne Jifton's hot-selling dystopian fiction *Preternatural DY4*, which Ximena had recommended. Jason disengaged himself from the novel and stood up to greet the guest.

"Hi, Jason. I'm Tavon Brooks, Tavon Brooks NHH to be exact." He extended his hand.

"Nice to meet you, sir," he said, and they shook hands.

They both sat down while Ximena went to retrieve refreshments.

Tavon said to Jason, "I know you've been through a lot in the past few days, but believe me when I say you're lucky to be looked after by Ximena."

Jason nodded lightly, as Ximena brought in sweet-tasting drinks on ice.

Tavon continued, "I have details about your family, but first I want you to promise to keep this information between the three of us for now. Will you promise that?"

"Yes."

"OK. The good news is your little sister is alive ... but I'm sorry to say that your mother's not." Tavon waited a few seconds, then went on, "They attempted to save all three of you, but your mother's condition and age did not warrant the risk. They were able to make her aware that you and Sarah would live on, and she passed away soon after that. I'm sorry to tell you this, Jason. I'm terribly sorry."

Jason tried in vain to control his breathing. Strangely, he could not picture his mother's face. But his love for her engulfed him.

Ximena covered Jason's hand with hers and spoke, "Jason. I know how much you loved her and how important she was in your life. We're so sorry."

Her kind words did not help. His ache was as real as the day his father left. Jason got up from the couch, avoided looking at anyone, and walked into the backyard, deep into the expansive garden. He observed his favorite flower. He was unsure of its exact type – it looked like an orange rose, only with larger leaves, unique in the sea of wonderful flowers. Before his wide eyes that singular beautiful orange life tended back and forth in the playful breeze. Sunlight darted through its wavering gaps. He reached out and delicately touched it with the fingertips of his left hand. *Then it appeared – a perfect image of his mother's face.* It sallied toward him from the garden green. Flush with that sacred reminder, he longed for her. His jaw and neck tensed insurgently, as he restrained something which refused to be held back, something he was not accustomed to. When it came, it was a sobbing cry, genuine and tearful.

After another ten minutes of garden solitude, Jason decided to go back to the house. Tavon and Ximena welcomed him back and they all sat down to start clarifying things for him.

Tavon began, "I don't expect you to understand all of the detailed science, but I'll give you the brief version. Would you like to hear that?"

Jason nodded.

Tavon went on, "OK. What happened to you after the accident is the miraculous result of the two new technologies: Anti-Aging Cloning Totipotency and cryopreservation. The first, known as AACT, is a method which, in contrast to age-decoding, does not directly alter the aging process; rather, it uses genetic cloning methods to re-manifest specific parts of the human body – such as vital organs – if ever they deteriorate; dovetailed with advances in medical diagnostics, it's a powerful "indirect" solution for aging and was used to regenerate several of your injured body parts. The second, cryopreservation, is easier to explain but no less remarkable: it "freezes" people. Unfortunately, the two corporations which held rights to these technologies became embroiled in legal proceedings for almost two hundred years. The Zone1 Authority, obsessed as it was with the Human Genome Project and age-decoding, didn't trust AACT and cryopreservation, so it got involved in disqualifying AACT. The deadlock was finally resolved when HF Capital, the largest financial services corporation in the world, stepped in. It was the only private firm with the financial might to support this without government intervention. So that's the condensed version of the story, Jason. Now here you are, and your sister too, and a few others like you – AACT cryopreserved and completely legal."

Jason sat bewildered. "Wow, that means I'm a heavy-duty consequence of science!" he cried. "How about my sister Sarah? Do you know where she is?"

"I don't know, but I'm working on that. I believe she's alive, at least that's what my contacts at HF Capital are telling me."

"Can I see her? Will you arrange that?"

"Please be patient. I promise I'll do what I can as soon as I can. You'll see her as soon as it's safe to do so."

The conversation then drifted elsewhere, as Jason related stories of his family life, sports, school, and girlfriend Lara, being careful not to mention his mother or father for fear of losing control of his emotions. Ximena and Tavon listened assiduously, asking here and there for further details. They enjoyed listening to the young man, who intellectually and spiritually seemed more like a mature adult than a nineteen-year-old boy.

After a bit more chatting, Jason asked to be excused to take a nap. He went to his room and lay down on the bed. Adjusting the pillow, he asked himself, why me? Why my sister? What did we miss as the world went on and we were stuck in that frozen state? Were there physical or mental side-effects of doing that?

Back in the kitchen, Tavon was preparing to leave. He said to Ximena, "He's a fine soul, that boy." Then he joked, "I wonder if cryopreservation made him such a good person, or if he was just born that way?"

"Shut up, you're terrible," said Ximena, smiling. "Don't even think such a thing! I can't see how being frozen could improve a person's personality."

Tavon grinned back at her. They were at the front door now.

"Ximena, may I call you Xi?"

"Yes."

"Xi, I have to be frank, this contact worries me. Please, remind Jason and Jesus of the importance of confidentiality and avoidance of any etalk."

"I will. And thanks for what you're doing. I do appreciate it."

"No problem. I'm glad to help Jason, and you."

Tavon departed, headed back to New York.

Later that day Ximena fixed Jason a meal of spaghetti, salad, bread rolls, and Coke.

The young man got up the nerve to ask her, "What's happening with sex these days? Do people still have it, or has that been removed from your society as well?"

Ximena was surprised and amused by his question. She explained to Jason that sexual urges were as strong as ever, but age-decoding brought infertility. It turned out that three of the four fertility genes overlapped with the age-decoding genes, so infertility was an automatic side effect of age-decoding. Only if you won the lottery would they bring you back into the fertility arena – assuming you did not mind undoing your age-decoding for some time.

"Weren't people against losing their fertility?" asked Jason.

"Some, yes, but surprisingly few. The vast majority didn't care, given the allure of the fountain of eternal youth! You're young, so maybe that seems odd to you. But most people, most voters, are not young. Immortality was potent, unsurpassed in the realm of human offerings. While anti-aging remedies had been predicted as far back as the 1900s, the day the discovery was announced was like none other. They say the celebrations lasted for weeks! You can't imagine the stunned delirium and unprecedented jubilance. Jesus tells me they sang William Penn's "Death cannot kill what never dies" in the bars, parks, offices, and homes. After the parties wound down, the Authority discovered that most people – no matter what income level, ethnicity, sex, etc. – were perfectly willing to sacrifice fertility for age-decoding. The tradeoff was minor; the benefit so remarkable. People also recognized the other societal benefits, such as rendering birth control pills obsolete and ensuring population control. But that wasn't why they cooperated with the fertility tradeoff. No, they signed for one simple reason: *they loved the thought of living forever!*"

Jason asked, "Didn't people miss the chance to have a family, you know, like two parents, some kids, living under one roof?"

"People could still win the right to have a family, or purchase that right from some other winner. The age-decoding procedure was reversible, and so was fertility. But remember Jason, and this is the key, most people already had children. What happened here was that people gained immortality and gave up *most other peoples'* rights to have children: the rights of younger people, the rights of people who might not be old enough to vote, the rights of people too young to appreciate the worth of having children and raising a family, and the rights of the future unborn. The government's Fundamental Platform was popular because it was an intergenerational tradeoff. Over time, it all settled into utmost respect for the Authority, sustaining itself without no political challenge." Ximena paused, then grinned, "Mind you, sex has sure changed since your time."

"I wouldn't even know about that," Jason replied with a sheepish smile. "My girlfriend and I were *straightedge* about everything: no drugs, no booze, no skipping classes, and no sex. It sounds lousy, but it was pretty cool being that way … different."

Ximena smiled with what he said, "Straightedge, eh? – we could use more of that today."

CHAPTER 10

AGE-DECODED

LATER THAT DAY, SATISFIED that Jason would be safe for now, Ximena descended to the downstairs washroom, closed the door, set the lights to their dimmest level, and carefully pulled the healing mitt from her left limb, all the while watching herself in the mirror. Misgivings swarmed her mind like a disturbed hornets' nest. Her mother left her by killing herself. Her father left her by dispossessing her. Could there be another child in this world so utterly tossed aside? What did she do to deserve this?

She unwrapped the medicated gauze, then paused whimsically in admiration of it: the base of her wrist and most of her hand except her thumb, reduced over the years to a grotesque amalgam of dangling flesh, exposed bones, and disjointed arteries, vein, and nerves.

Her breathing hurried as she flexed her jaws, licked her tongue wide across her upper then lower lips, and watched herself begin. First, she gnawed at the flesh which hung from the limb, disheveled and fresh; then she chewed off tiny bits, not ferociously, but diligently, savoring each episode as an orgasmic defense against those she despised. Especially her father. At the thought of him, she swallowed all that was in her mouth.

She gnawed and gnawed for a few more minutes, fervidly, victoriously.

All of the pain was pleasurable.

As was her custom, when she ceased she held her arm up close to the mirror, at shoulder height, rotating it slightly to the perfect angle to project through the background faint, blue light the optimal image of the dangling parts of the appendage and blood drops dripping down, deep down, into the sink, while at the same time she spied the backdrop of her reflected face which comforted her, liberated her, in a way she would never comprehend or be able to explain to anyone.

Now done, she reapplied fresh gauze with the tender care of a nurse, then pulled the healing mitt back into place.

This grotesque routine somehow lent Ximena more meaning, more courage, more self, more everything. Quite aware of the abnormality of the act, she did it for the salvation it lent her.

Even Jesus, who had once caught her in the act, dared not question her about it, let alone try to decipher it. He rightly figured it was her *rire sous cape,* her way of laughing in her sleeve against it all.

CHAPTER 11

IN THE YEAR 2061 WHEN Ximena turned eighteen, she gained new rights, including freedom-of-information rights to view the Coroner's Report and the Authority Police Report of her mother's death.

She sat with Jesus in their living room as they poured over the reports. The Coroner's Report was conclusive: suicide induced by the drug secobarbital; the autopsy uncovered a puncture wound on Frieda's right lower arm. The evidence pointed to direct injection of *secobarbital* as the "cause of death," although the coroner did not conclusively state the "manner of death", i.e., whether Frieda injected herself. However, according to the Authority Police Report, an injection needle was found on the floor, containing her fingerprints; it was also noted that Frieda had access to this drug through her workplace: scientists used secobarbital to euthanize animals such as rabbits, sheep, and monkeys. Finally, testimony from interviews with Ahmed showed that Frieda had suffered from past bouts of depression and that she was particularly upset about the ELSI situation and overwhelmed by the implementation of age-decoding.

None of these details surprised Ximena or Jesus; they knew all of this from direct communication with Authority Police after Frieda's death, as well as the extensive news coverage.

However, there were two items they did not know about, both contained in the Police Report. First, a mention that freshly spilled coffee was detected on the floor near her dead body. Second, the fact that Frieda sent a brief message to the Authority Police moments before killing herself, probably figuring they would respond promptly because she was a high-priority scientist. Her message, shown in the report, was:

This is Dr. Frieda Sengmeuller. I am about to end my life, for reasons too complex to describe. Please send someone urgently to tend to my body so my daughter does not return home to see me dead.

There were no witnesses to her suicide. According to Authority Police, Ximena was the last person to see Frieda. Interviews with her indicated that she spent some time reading with her mother that morning, then left to go to the apartment park before Frieda's unfortunate end.

Over the last eight years, as she grew to become a young lady, Ximena had always questioned whether her mother killed herself. She was never willing to accept it, and for that reason held out hope for some clue in the evidence. To her, Jesus and most others were too absolute in their conclusions.

After they had both read through the reports, Jesus stated, "I'm not learning anything new here. And I hate doing this. She was my only daughter, and it saddens me to replay and rethink all of this."

Ximena touched Jesus gently on his forearm and said, "I hate it too. It's the last thing I want to do. The only new things I learned from these documents were her final message to the police and that bit about spilled coffee. The Authority Police report does not explain why coffee was spilled on the floor near the time of death. My understanding is that the effect of secobarbital is not instantaneous: it requires one minute to dismantle a person's central nervous system. So why, if she took the drug, would she suddenly spill her coffee? Or why would she even be drinking coffee if she knew she was about to die?"

Jesus speculated, "Maybe she spilled her coffee a few minutes before she took the drug. Anyhow, I doubt they can pinpoint the exact timing of the spill relative to her death."

Tears clouded Ximena's eyes as he said this, and she said wistfully to him, "Yeh, I guess. But it just doesn't sit right with me. This whole thing has never sat right, and never will."

Jesus gave Ximena a full, heartfelt hug, then slowly headed off to the study.

Ximena's tears subsided, but not her sadness. Would she ever know the truth? She walked over to the fireplace mantle and took hold of an old photo, bringing it close to her face. It showed her as a seven-year-old, standing on a docked sailboat with her mother and father, arms around each other, readying to head out on Lake Pontchartrain. A wonderful memory.

CHAPTER 12

IN THE FALL OF THE Year 2150, Ahmed made an earnest attempt to reach out to Ximena. Over the past ninety-six years, he had conversed with Jesus about ten times, enquiring about her, and gleaning what he could from what Jesus had to say. In the early years, Ahmed provided financial support for Ximena's education as she earned her Master of Science degree from Tulane University with a specialty in Behavioral Health Psychology. After that, he sent monthly support payments to Jesus to ensure the two of them could afford to stay in their house in New Orleans.

But that was it. Effectively he was still her estranged father, and he yearned to somehow change that, or to at least approach being a real father to Ximena. Jesus had made it clear to Ahmed that his daughter never asked about him and refused to talk about him, so Ahmed knew that if he tried to reach out to her his chances for redemption were slim.

He often wondered what it would be like to get back together with Ximena, not necessarily living in the same house, but participating in her life, as a true father might: talking and sharing; giving her the love that he knew he could. But as years and decades passed the shame of his leaving entrenched itself and wore away his hopes. If something other than shame was holding him back, he could not figure out what it was. Perhaps if she reached out to him? But why should he expect that?

On this typically hot and humid New Orleans day, Ahmed was visiting Jesus in person to broach the topic of a possible face-to-face meeting with his daughter. He felt that physically visiting the house would help him reacclimatize to the environment and get a feel for what he was attempting. Jesus assured him that Ximena would not be there.

As Ahmed's car parked itself in front of their house, his thoughts turned surprisingly not to Ximena, but himself. I'm so happy and successful at work, he thought, and I've moved on from Frieda's horrible passing, even had some decent relationships with other women. That's all well and good. But what I did to Ximena, or didn't do for her, was never right. Unlike the death of Frieda, which is slowly fading in my life's rear-view mirror, my estrangement with Ximena is weighing on me more and more.

He knocked on the door and Jesus answered. The old man looked exactly as he remembered, though Ahmed resisted saying, "You haven't changed a bit," because it made no sense to say that to a eubeing.

Both men were uncomfortable, as they had not talked face-to-face for almost one century. They worked their way down the hall, through the kitchen, and out the back door to the shaded area on the back porch, where an external fan kept the air circulating nicely. At the center of their table was a pitcher of ice water and two tall glasses.

"Thanks for seeing me, Jesus."

"You're welcome. I'm doing this for Ximena."

"I get that. I'm trying to do the same."

"Boy, it's humid. This reminds me of my work in the Brazilian rainforests. Go ahead, help yourself to some ice water."

Ahmed took a sizable gulp, then said, "I noticed the picture of Ximena in the hallway, of her winning the Science Fair. Funny, I remember that like it was yesterday. Grade 3. She made Frieda and me so proud."

Jesus's serious countenance shifted to a slight grin. "She is a smart one, just like her parents."

"And her grandfather."

"That too."

"I remember when she won that prize Frieda cooked her an extra special meal, blueberry pancakes with whipped cream – for dinner!"

"Well, I can't say she indulges in that anymore." Jesus said, "Look, Ahmed, I've got to ask you straight up, why wait ninety-five years to do this?"

Ahmed replied, "What's ninety-five years for a eubeing? It's just a blip in time these days."

Jesus raised his voice, "I can't believe you would say that! Ninety-five years is still ninety-five years, and that's a long time to make your daughter suffer!"

Ahmed retorted, "OK, OK. Please don't yell. What happened to the Buddhist way of practicing patience?"

"Real Buddhists don't shame each other for expressing emotions. You're mistaken in your view that Buddhists avoid anger. Thanissara, a Buddhist nun, wrote long ago, *Anger is a healthy response to injustice ... is clarifying.* You have an idealistic, mystical image of Buddhism, not real Buddhism."

Ahmed backed off and told himself not to escalate things. This conversation was meant to be constructive.

Silence dug in between them and both men took in some more water.

Jesus peered out across the yard at the sage green leaves of willows, which shifted modestly in the tender breeze. He then explained to Ahmed, "Look, it's not that Ximena believes she doesn't have a father. She knows you exist. To her, it's much worse. How did she express it to me once? ... Oh yes, she said her father didn't want her as his only daughter. His only daughter. It's as simple as that."

Ahmed chose not to respond. How could he defend himself?

Jesus continued, "You may not know this, but she's ever reluctant to believe in Frieda's suicide. I'm not sure if she believes it didn't happen, or if she can't believe it did happen, which are two different things. This has spilled over into her struggles. She remains nervous about going out with men; a recent relationship went sour when she discovered the man was a statistician; another went sour when she discovered the man hadn't seen his mother in five years. She is also prone to self-harm, physically."

"Physically? What do you mean?"

"Nothing, it's under control. But I do worry about her."

Jesus wasn't sure if Ahmed knew one more thing about Ximena, which he promptly revealed, "And did you know she's working for the Rethinking Party, has been for almost thirty years? Something just doesn't sit right with her about the Authority. Just like something never sat right with her about Frieda's death. She seems to conflate the two."

"I wasn't aware of that," Ahmed said, genuinely surprised.

"To be perfectly frank, I think she's with Rethinking because you're with the Authority."

That disheartened Ahmed. Could really this be true?

Jesus advised, "Look, Ahmed, I can't sit here and casually tell you what to do about her, how you might reconnect with her. But I will say that I fear you coming here to see her personally. I can tell you she won't agree to that."

"OK, I get it. How about etalk? Do you think I should try just talking with her?"

"Even that is not a promising idea. Some years ago, yes, you could have tried that. Before they invented NITs and before she joined Rethinking. But now it would be risky for you, wouldn't it? Nobody really knows if they track conversations with these new NITs. Perhaps you know, working so high up in the Authority? What I'm trying to say is that NIT etalk with her could signal your conversing with a direct adversary. What would your employer think?"

Ahmed knew his point was valid. FENCODE_11 would undoubtedly raise red flags. He asked, "Well, could I hand-write a letter to her and leave it with you? I'd be willing to write it here and now."

Jesus did not address his question. Instead, he proffered, "Ultimately, I believe you can't change the relationship with your daughter until you change your relationship with yourself. When you've done that, she'll be ready."

That hit Ahmed hard. But he carefully took in what Jesus was implying and realized there was no point in continuing this vein of the conversation.

"And how are you doing?" Ahmed asked.

"I'm fine. Staying out of trouble, working on a new book."

"Interesting. Tell me about it."

They talked on for about fifteen minutes, then Ahmed politely suggested he not overstay, thanked Jesus, and departed.

While driving away, Ahmed selected Classical Favorites on random play, and his car, perhaps sensing his mood, chose *Premiere Gymnopedie* by Erik Satie. That's uncanny, he told himself, because he felt just like Satie might have ... that his life just wasn't as good as it should be.

CHAPTER 13

THE SI COMMITTEE ALWAYS met in the depths of Block2 of the New York Authority headquarters. They met for real, not virtually, because after they finished their work President Reubers wanted his prestigious group to experience two days of everything the city had to offer. They treasured the historic venues: the Guggenheim Museum, the Statue of Liberty, the September 11 Memorial, Central Park, Times Square, jazz music at the Village Vanguard, deli food at Katz's, and soul food at Sylvia's. They also explored the modern venues: the Alphabet Robot Colosseum, the Columbia University Quantum Computing Centre, the World Diversity Complex, the New York State Nuclear Fusion Facility, and the new satellite location of the U.K.-based Earlham Institute Biotech Collaborative.

At the head table for the SI meeting sat the Core6: Manfred Reubers, (President), Zhuang Zhinghu (SI Committee Director), Ahmed Iftikhar (statistician), Gupta Mantharathna (genomics specialist), Randolph Rahilly (psychosociologist), and Suzanne Tellier (political scientist). The room was packed with the forty members of the SI team. Not a single member was absent.

President Reubers sat slightly off to the side from the other Core6, so he could retain an unobstructed view of both the head table and the crowd. His large rectangular face, tight grey sideburns, completely bald scalp, and deep eye sockets contributed to his authoritative presence. He sat comfortably in a chair designed to counteract chronic back pain and followed the proceedings by moving his eyes rather than shifting his head. He was known to be a patient person, though capable of decisive action and even losing his temper when called for.

Zhinghu insisted on launching SI Committee meetings with what he called *grassroots analysis*: a presentation of work in progress by a researcher in Apex200. The idea was to give them feedback, steer them along, troubleshoot, and, most importantly, lend them the chance to impress co-workers and top brass.

The presenter today was Tavon Brooks, the rising star who had been hand-picked for today by Zhinghu and Reubers.

Tavon stepped forward. His dreadlocks were pulled back behind into a tight ponytail for this occasion. His reputation was climbing rapidly in the ranks of the Authority, as he was already deemed by Zhinghu and Reubers as one of the top five minds in Apex200. Moving deliberately and efficiently, he did his best to mask his nervousness.

Ahmed was the only person in the room who knew Tavon's inner motives. And vice-versa.

Tavon presented fresh data on Spectre Society usage. "As you can see from the graph, eubeing usage rate continues to climb steadily; we haven't even reached the point of inflection. Last month's rate, expressed on an annual basis, was 1 per 9980. That's a breakthrough. Never has it been below 1 per 10,000".

"To what do we attribute this increase?" asked Ahmed.

"We're unsure. *Post facto* hyper-regression analyses of both the oral and visual life reviews indicate positive themes, predominantly; psychological indicator regression reveals non-depressed personalities. Frankly, it's a bit of a paradox: the people killing themselves are normal, psychologically, if not supernormal."

"Have you done group cluster analysis?" asked Rahilly.

"Yes. There's nothing definite there," Tavon answered.

Zhinghu looked around the room. He asked if there were any more questions. Everyone was silent. Even the pictoplath lay still.

"OK," he said, "Let's schedule an updated analysis in a few weeks. Magnificent work, Dr. Brooks. Thanks very much."

Polite, steady applause followed, and Tavon took his seat near the front.

President Reubers then rose and walked to the front, adjacent to the head table. His back was giving him more trouble than usual today, but he mustered up the energy, as this would be his last chance to speak live to this group for some time. He knew the research: nothing technological had ever been invented that was superior to an old-fashioned face-to-face pep talk from the leader, something at which he was good. He attributed his speaking success to his speech writing. But others attributed it to his appearance, body language, and gestures, which lent him unwavering confidence.

It was time for Reubers to speak about the threat posed by AACT and the cryos. Since SI Committee members were at two levels of knowledge – those in Core6 knew much more – he had to tread carefully by talking only generally. "Thank you, everyone, for being here. We're at perfect attendance. I'm ever impressed with the dedication of this group."

The pictoplath highlighted the Authority motto in tangerine orange: *The four avoidable physical sufferings are birth, old age, sickness, and death.*

Reubers went on, "Today's meeting concerns a group of non-eubeings who were very recently resurrected by HF Capital. These humans were locked in cryopreservation for about two hundred years. That's after being subject to AACT. As you are aware, both of these technologies are unproven. HF Capital was originally interested in these methods because it gave them a potential low-risk, realistic method of testing the two techniques simultaneously. With the backing of the U.S. government and the cooperation of several large drug companies, they hastily implemented their study. Our Authority did not promote this experiment. We at the Authority are not in any way responsible for the recent de-cryopreservation and recognition of these individuals, nor the re-emergence of AACT."

Reubers carried on for twenty minutes, describing the threat of bad science and imploring everyone to follow his instructions carefully regarding this case. He argued that this new group of cryos might be even more dissenting than non-eubeings, since they were historic relics, with no experience in current society and no appreciation for what the Authority had done. They were a consequence of profit science, selected for use by a capitalist corporation. He admitted he was worried about the threat posed by AACT humans and believed the Authority should begin to control that threat.

Everyone absorbed what Reubers said. They were not surprised – the word had been getting around for a few months now – but Reubers dispelled all rumors by crystallizing this threat.

With that, Zhinghu stood up and announced several housekeeping items. Everyone then recited the confidentiality pledge and the meeting adjourned.

As people filed out, the head table remained seated and watched.

Now was the opportunity for Reubers to move on to the second level of understanding: Core6. This tight group, responsible for his lengthy stay in power, was always a more fundamental worry to him – because of the secrets they held.

Zhinghu led them into the much smaller conference room. As they settled into their seats, he matter-of-factly scrutinized each of them. His forehead bore chagrined wrinkles. "We need more information on the AACT threat."

Ahmed responded, "The latest information coming from FENCODE_11 shows that AACT was applied to all cryos around the same time by HF Capital Incorporated. About 10,000 of them. That's a damned lot more than our original estimate. For HF Capital, there was a minimal risk, because most clients were injured, or in extremely poor health, and their families were, well, bloody desperate. Cryopreservation complicated things but had to be used by HF Capital because of *ad nauseam* legal issues. The bottom line is that AACT combined with cryopreservation had a scant likelihood of scientific success, and we were prudent to ignore it at the time as a political threat. But now, about two centuries later, it seems their methods were based on solid science ... surprisingly solid."

Zhinghu piped up, "It appears we have competition all of a sudden". He then turned to Dr. Tellier and asked, "Suzanne, is the threat as political as it is scientific?"

Tellier stared at Zhinghu. "Yes, I'd say, very political. If AACT catches on, it could jeopardize age-decoding for a few reasons, from what I can surmise. First, because totipotency directly tackles diseases such as cancer, i.e., health conditions independent of age, it would prevent most causes of death if made widely available. Further, in acute cases of severe injury such as car accidents, AACT can save a person, whereas age-decoding cannot. That's what I'd call the competitive threat to age-decoding."

"Agreed," said Mantharathna.

Rahilly had not spoken, though he was considering launching into one of his equifinality diatribes; but even he could not see an application of his perspectives to this messy situation.

"Anything else, Suzanne?" asked Zhinghu.

"Yes, I'd say, something much more serious, politically," said Tellier. "If AACT ever caught on, our Fundamental Platform would be jeopardized. Remember, AACT humans are naturally fertile, so their relative numbers will grow markedly over the coming decades compared to eubeings, who are infertile. Without the need for age-decoding, without peoples' trust and the unwritten social contract which has supported our government for so long, we could lose access to peoples' genetic code. And let's not forget that if humans use AACT, the Authority can't realize the glorious side-effect of the deactivated propensity to dissent."

Side-effect of the deactivated propensity to dissent.

Everyone was stunned when she said it. It stung Ahmed to even think about it. For decades nobody had dared use the term *propensity to dissent*. Tellier had violated Core6 protocol.

Reubers relieved the pressure with a grin and mischievous wave of his arms, joking, "I couldn't have said it better."

CHAPTER 14

IT WAS ANOTHER HOT afternoon in New Orleans with the strong sunlight interrupted occasionally by small cumulus clouds. The cicadas buzzed in unison every few seconds to protest the heat.

Ximena sat on her back porch on tenterhooks, stretched on the rack of patience. She stared out across the expansive backyard, which contained several English-styled gardens, a pond, a cabana, a Gazebo, and six different hedges, including one continuous tall hedge along its perimeter. A shy breeze played softly with the thin branches and tiny leaves of the willow trees.

She had not heard a word from Tavon for about two weeks. He had instructed her not to try calling; to wait for him to make contact. She worried on behalf of Jason, who was eager to see his little sister Sarah.

Ximena knew she was an ideal person to look after Jason. The young man needed to hide out and settle down, and Ximena had spent her life at this house, seldom leaving the property. Her discomfort was borderline agoraphobic: a fear of external people and places. Her drive for security would help Jason stay safe.

She wondered, had something terrible happened to Tavon? Had he been uncovered at the Authority? Was he in danger? The techniques of the SI were well known. She admonished herself to be positive, even if she felt anxious. So she arranged a surprise for Jason, a special visitor for lunch. "Someone you just have to meet ... and now is a perfect time," she told him. When he heard this, Jason tried to make her reveal the guest's identity, but she did not relent.

For Jason, the last few days had been most unsatisfying. Though Ximena was an excellent host and gave him lots of tasty food, conversation, and freedom to read and relax, he missed connecting with younger people: classmates, friends on the block, his girlfriend, even his sister. When he asked Ximena if there were any young people in her neighborhood, she just shook her head. He passed the time reading, finding solace in a new science fiction novel called

Age-Decoded II. This work reminded him of his current situation, trapped and frustrated as a scientific object of experimentation, a person important to everyone but himself. Except the "person" in that novel was an AS robot.

Later that morning Jason noticed Ximena guiding an old man from the driveway around the side of the house toward the backyard; she was holding him by one arm and shoulder as he struggled to balance on the stone pathway. Jason figured the visitor had to be Ximena's surrogate father, Jesus, so he went through the back door to greet him.

"A mean path makes a meaningful journey," were the old man's first words upon reaching the edge of the porch in the backyard.

Ximena added, "Jason ... I'd like you to meet my dear grandfather, Jesus Sengmeuller."

Jason immediately noted the starkly defined crow's feet at the corners of the old man's eyes. He extended his hand politely. Jesus, rather than shaking it, placed one of his hands below Jason's and one on top, gently squeezing in between. "Take me to a nice porch perch, young man."

This man connects, Jason thought.

After they were seated, Jesus said to Jason, "Son, I'd like to welcome you back. You and I come from the same era, except you are younger, with more potential. I am merely a bit wiser."

A bit wiser – what an understatement, Ximena said to herself. That was the essence of her grandfather: humility. "It's absolutely beautiful out here if you don't mind the heat," she said before heading in to get refreshments.

"Beautiful like you" Jesus called behind her. "Don't you think my daughter is beautiful?" he asked Jason.

Embarrassed by the question, Jason nodded shyly.

Jesus negotiated his chair closer to the table and, looking down at the ashen beige Appalachian patio stones, said, "Jason, I don't mean beautiful in the literal, physical sense. I mean it in the sense of pure beauty, the beauty of being, of human essence. Xi has what we Buddhists refer to as *smriti*, or mindfulness, that is, an awareness of the essence of each and everything, in and of itself. That, to me, is a beautiful quality for a human being." A wide smile lit up Jesus's face, accenting to the crow's feet near his eyes. He added, "Whenever I'm with Xi, her *smriti* renders me more in tune with things, making me stronger. Xi renders everyone around her more in tune and stronger."

Ximena returned with the drinks, "We've got coffee or juice." She placed two containers on the patio table. She poured coffee for her grandfather, juice for Jason and herself, then sat down.

She decided to share some of Jesus's life stories with Jason. "My grandfather was an outstanding intellect, completed his master's degree in Biology from Stanford University, *summa cum laude*. That means the top of his class, Jason. He specialized in species identification and biodiversity. After he graduated, he enrolled in a PhD program at the same university, to research plant and insect species in Ecuador (the lowlands and the forests). But he became distracted by a project in the Choc Ó forest regions of Columbia, where he applied many new methods of specimen collection, providing the groundwork for his book, *Biodiversity Unplugged*. That book was acclaimed by scholars and widely read by citizens!"

Ximena took a sip of her drink, then went on, "Jesus never finished his doctoral studies because he was too involved in the study of life unfolding around him. Twice he tried to extract himself from the ecosystems to return to North America and finish his academics, but each time he was drawn back to South America. Did I mention he was also involved with a group of scientists who resisted the formation of Zone1? I don't know much about that, and I doubt he'll tell you much. But I do know that their efforts failed. When the Authority was set up, Jesus was age-decoded, and soon after that he disassociated himself from the group and converted to Buddhism. Is that a nice little biography of you, Dad? Did I do you justice?"

Jesus grinned, "You're much too gracious, dear Xi. Let me bring things down to reality for Jason." He then focused all his energy on the young man, talking softly, slowly, commanding Jason's attention. "Son, age-decoding was a disaster for me, because I lost my interest in politics, my zest for critical action. I wondered many times over whether a man my age, an old man, should have chosen to be age-decoded in the first place. I can see the allure for a twenty-five-year-old or even a fifty-five-year-old. But for me, was it worth it? Yet, like everyone else, I succumbed to the temptation. Immortality is a universal attraction for humans."

He then changed the subject, pivoting to his role with Ximena. "Interestingly, I effectively won the Family Rights Lottery the very next year, but not through the Lottery itself. What I mean is that my son-in-law suddenly offered me the role of raising his child. Hardly anyone gets to raise a child in Zone1!"

Jason's eyes popped wide open. "Do you mean raising Xi?" he asked.

"Yes. My son Ahmed was desperate for help in fathering her, and so he offered me the role of surrogate father." Jason noticed Jesus's eyes twinkling. "The way I see it, my son knew himself, knew he needed help. It must have been tough for him to ask me to do that, but he wanted what was best for Xi."

"But why was he incapable?" Jason asked.

"Because his wife had just killed herself. His wife was Dr. Frieda Sengmeuller."

That name jolted Jason's memory. Tom Stephenson, the man he met earlier on, had told him about Dr. Sengmeuller, the famous UCLA scientist who invented age-decoding. Wow, that amazing woman was Xi's mother?

He turned to Ximena, "That's so sick! You didn't tell me your mother was that famous scientist. That's unbelievable!"

Ximena blushed, "I wanted to let Jesus tell you."

Jesus went on, "Jason. Allow me to tell the story of Siddhartha, more commonly known as Buddha, which might intrigue you. Prince Siddhartha as a young man ventured out from the insurance of his luxurious palace, yearning to discover what the world was really like. The King, who was very protective of his son, instructed the guards to hide all sick and suffering people from the tender eyes of Siddhartha during the journey. That was impossible, of course, and the scene unfolded as follows:

> *"Driver," said Siddhartha, "what is wrong with that man?"*
>
> *"He is old, my lord."*
>
> *"And what is 'old'?" asked the prince.*
>
> *"'Old' is when you have lived many years."*
>
> *"And will I too become 'old'?"*
>
> *"Yes, my lord. To grow old is our common fate."*
>
> *"If all must face old age," said the prince, "then how can we take joy in youth?"*

That one decision to find out," continued Jesus, "led eventually to Siddhartha's *satori*, or enlightenment. He at once understood *interbeing* – the interconnectedness of life – a fundamental principle of Buddhism."

Jesus took a sip of his coffee, then explained, "You see, Jason, before I was age-decoded, I studied diverse organisms in ecosystems and uncovered numerous new species and interrelationships of ecosystems. I saw first-hand how insects and plants relied on each other in ways that most people couldn't even imagine. Thus, enlightened by *interbeing,* I was already a Buddhist at heart. But after age-decoding, I became limited, trapped, sheltered from mortality. Siddhartha was wise enough to never return to the palace. In contrast, the palace and its powers seduced me to return. I was not alone: everyone naturally sought that shelter. I can't think of one person who didn't desire it. There was even talk of reverse-aging."

Though Jason was not religious, he appreciated the importance of what Jesus was saying. He said to the old man, "That story about Siddhartha is intriguing. I'll try my best to remember it. I am curious, however – do you still do plant and insect research?"

Jesus was pleased by the young man's interest. For a moment he smiled and stared across the backyard and beyond willows to the adjacent properties. He held back his response, then responded, "No, Jason, I seem to have lost my zeal for challenging science, challenging authority, challenging anything. There's no other way to describe it. Something about age-decoding tamed me. Buddhism, however, has helped me cope."

"Would you go back if you could?"

"You can't. Once you're age-decoded, you're not allowed to reverse it. Unless, of course, you win the Family Rights Lottery and need to regain your fertility to conceive a child. But a more important aspect of all of this is not what happened to me as an individual, but what happened to humans as a species. While age-decoding is alluring for individuals, it impedes the natural selection of our species. I spent my best years uncovering the wonders of nature's way: the Giant Amazon Water Lily, bamboo, figs, epiphytes, parasites, the Harpy Eagle, and the complex colonies of Leafcutters. Each of these amazing species is the consequence of thousands or millions of years of natural selection. So, you see,

Jason, when Zone1 implemented age-decoding, that single genetic engineering act obliterated natural selection for our species."

Jason sat puzzled. He had heard of natural selection in high school biology class but knew little about it except that Charles Darwin was famous for discovering it.

Jesus sensed the young man's confusion, "Look, I don't expect you to comprehend all of this. Let me explain a bit more if you're interested."

"Please, go ahead. I'd welcome the challenge!"

Smiling over the fact that this young man was a veritable sponge, Jesus went on. "Natural selection is the life-explaining process ... the grand jewel of biology. Darwin's 1859 publication, *On the Origin of Species by Means of Natural Selection, or the Preservation of Favoured Races in the Struggle for Life,* which goes by the popular shorter name, *Origin of Species,* was the first full description of the process and remains a profound turning point in human understanding of life. In this work, Darwin explains that life species descended from other species and that life transforms itself using random individual genetic mutations. These mutations are passed onto future generations if they are proven to be advantageous to the survival and reproduction of the individual in the environment in which it lived. That made sense, Darwin explained, since if the probability that any individual lived longer and procreated was increased by a particular genetic mutation, that mutation was more likely to be "passed on" through reproduction, or "selected to" the future gene pool of the species. That's how future generations adopt mutated genes and their traits."

Jesus paused to take a sip of his coffee, then continued, "Look, Jason, what I'm saying is that life is selected by nature. That process is *natural selection*. According to Darwin, genetic mutations, though rare, have been the driving force of evolution for all life on earth. One intriguing notion put forward by Darwin was that aging itself was a trait. It should not, at first glance, be naturally selected, since it offered no competitive advantage to individuals of a species. Oddly, Darwin could not explain the existence of aging. That one trait – aging – seemed to defy the fundamentals of his theory. He recognized this contradiction and suggested that a limited life span somehow helped the species as a whole, even if it did not benefit individuals within the species."

Jason commented, "That's pretty complicated, but I think I get what you're saying."

Jesus added, "There's an old scientist, much older than I, named Theodore C Goldsmith, who explored this topic intensely in the 21st century. Though he was an electrical engineer by training, he wrote a book in 2003 called *The Evolution of Aging*, which he shared publicly on the internet to foster collaboration. He was age-decoded at the biological age of ninety and is still alive, as cogent as ever, but incapable of communication – except by twitching his right pinkie finger. They say he's working on another book even in this state. I'm telling you this because Goldsmith appreciated interconnectedness so well; he lived interbeing like a real Buddhist. Think of it, Jason, through one tiny part of his anatomy this old man still manages to stay interconnected."

The curious story made Jason chuckle.

Jesus paused and gathered his thoughts. He was pleased to see Jason still listening intently. "Darwin's *Origin of Species* was published," he explained, "well before the discovery of DNA, but Darwin knew that genes were an important building block in the blueprint of human life, that they coded information and passed forward ancient and emerging traits. Of course, many were not prepared to accept his explanation. Darwin knew that religious Creationists, who attributed the intricate designs of all life to the hand of God, would view his theory as sacrilegious. That's why, in the second edition of *Origin of Species*, he tried to quell Creationist criticism by inserting three new words, *by the Creator*, in the following:

> *There is grandeur in this view of life, with its several powers, having been originally breathed by the Creator into a few forms or into one; and that, whilst this planet has gone circling on according to the fixed law of gravity, from so simple a beginning endless forms most beautiful and most wonderful have been, and are being evolved."*

Clearly, Jesus had just utilized his NIT, but Jason still marveled at the old man's ability to use his mind to find these passages so quickly. Jesus went on, "Those three words – *by the Creator* – did little to quell their criticism because by that time things had gotten personal and battle lines were fully drawn."

The conversation between Jesus and Jason continued until dinnertime. Jason sat intoxicated by Jesus's description of how the Anglican Bishop of Oxford Samuel Wilberforce viscously attacked Darwin's ideas at an 1860 British Association meeting; how many of Darwin's friends and associates deserted him; how, over the ensuing decades, fossil evidence burgeoned and opposition to the theory gradually weakened, with wider acceptance of terms like mutation, variation, and survival of the fittest. Notwithstanding this, Jesus stressed that the Church never totally relented on the theological front regarding the Book of Genesis.

Jason had learned much from Jesus that afternoon. He figured Jesus was the wisest person he had met so far in Zone1.

CHAPTER 15

IN THE YEAR 2166, MORE than a century after her capture, Frieda was recuperating in her apartment after an intense ten hours working with Authority scientists. Sitting in her American Shaker traditional rocking chair next to the only window, she scanned the too familiar view of the adjacent apartment buildings and distant street-level shops. She had only a vague idea of the building that contained her. Whenever she pressed her eyes against the left side of her window, she could detect elements of its flat-faced cement structure, rectangular steel outcrops, and rows of small windows which were at such a sharp angle to the line of her eye that she could not perceive what was behind them, could only receive their daylight reflections.

In fact, Frieda was held in the bowels of Block3 in the Deconstructed Brutalism headquarters of the Authority in New York. Gupta informed her that her window was graphene-lined unbreakable and that the rest of her hyper-confined space was just as secure. At the start of her captivity, Frieda had tried screaming and pounding several times a day. Gupta took pleasure in watching these bouts on the remote monitor for several weeks before informing Frieda she was wasting her lungs and her hands.

On this day Frieda let her mind meander and stew. As long as I'm alive, which is solely at their discretion, I'll find a way to work against them. Of course, I must always feign that I'm helping them. But how would they know how long it should take me to invent reverse-aging? I can create "extra" time for myself to use against them.

Luckily, I control the development of my pNIT technology. This device is orders of magnitude tinier than the NIT, at the pico-level rather than the nano-level, hence its nifty name, pNIT. They naively believe it's an innocuous adjunct to reverse-aging technology, but it's much more than that. I've been able to craft and improve it with the help of some excellent scientists over the decades. Made it more adaptive and more nimble, two properties that I knew needed to be enhanced. I might soon be able to utilize it for my clandestine purposes. And when will that time come? That I don't know. I still need help in terms of timing and circumstance, to break the logjam of my total confinement. For decades and decades, I've been contained in this apartment working with Authority scientists, but always virtually, with no direct contact with humans except Gupta herself. No idea of how the world has evolved, no inkling of how my family is doing out there. Just this solitary confinement and the singular mandate to develop reverse-aging.

They couldn't do it without me, obviously, or why else would they keep me in this line of research, supplying me with a line of top-shelf scientists? Brilliant of them to label me as Chief Genomicist (CG) to oversee the work with their cadre of scientists. All communications I have with those scientists, other than Gupta, are muffle-altered to feign me off as the nonhuman CG, an artificial superintelligence entity. I'm rendered a mere AS abstraction, a deception which I find just as demeaning as my solitary confinement.

As to my working with these scientists, Gupta made it clear from the start that she would have me executed if I even hinted at my true identity with any of them.

I can't envision how Gupta became so rotten to the core. When I first met her, back in 2044, I took her under my wing and mentored her. I shared my knowledge and she gained confidence. She seemed a decent person back then; a hard worker, perhaps a bit self-centered, but nothing out of the ordinary. We did excellent work together, sometimes in conjunction with others, decoding the genetic basis of many psychological traits, most notably the *propensity to addictive behavior*. That single discovery unleashed enormous publications and citations, and, more saliently, applications for improving human lives. It brought us the recognition that most scientists could only dream of. The propensity to dissent was another decoding line we discovered, though the applications for this trait were more of a slippery political slope, so we published those findings in modest, more general tones, and chose not to pursue any applications. All the work Gupta and I did – we co-authored about one hundred publications – represented superb scientific collaboration.

Then yesterday, Gupta hit me with it: The Authority had genetically debilitated the propensity to dissent in anybody who was age-decoded! I was speechless. She bragged on about it, framing it as a clever scientific application that would keep society stable and content. But I believe she told me that to hurt me, knowing I was always nervous about its applications. Why else would she divulge that horrid information?

Never did I envisage that Gupta could be anything but a positive force. Yes, I may have overlooked a few faint early signs: I recall now that when I broached the "softer science" topics related to the ELSI Committee she was generally unwilling to engage or inquire further. I also noticed how aggressively she mingled with scientific leaders and Authority administrators at parties and conferences, such as those from the National Institutes for Health. But these were unremarkable instances, and certainly did not augur her extreme turn for the worse.

Is she a bad person in a bad system? Or a good person in a bad system?

Now she's just helping them suck my brain dry, and I've no choice but to prostitute my scientific mind to survive.

Or so they think. I'm turning the tables on Gupta and the wretched folks she answers to. They should know better than to try containing me.

No doubt they want me alive only to serve their purpose of researching reverse-aging technology, which they seem obsessed with as their Holy Grail. This to me seems misguided, however, because reverse-aging would serve to enhance all the shortcomings of age-decoding. First, it would eliminate what is left of the old and the young segments of the population, rendering all humans whatever age they chose, which would likely be about twenty-five years old, as research proved that this is the average "sweet spot" most humans would select, given the choice. Who would want to be much older? Who would want to be much younger? Physiologically and psychologically, that's the sweet spot. Thus reverse-aging would exaggerate an already distorted population distribution, which would mean fewer and fewer old people as they slowly died off or killed themselves. A hyper-distorted distribution, perhaps even no distribution, would result. One doesn't require an ELSI Committee to see how wretchedly unnatural this scenario would be. Secondly, reverse-aging would bring evolution to a standstill, even more so than age-decoding, since deaths and births would be rendered nonexistent and the gene pool would never be revitalized. The many other drawbacks of reverse-aging I can only hypothesize since I would need to know what unfolded in the real world.

One added fear I have, knowing what Gupta told me about the deactivation of the propensity to dissent, is that one never knows what other genetic tampering the Authority might attempt while implementing reverse-aging. It's a slippery scientific slope.

Now I'm fashioning something which excites me and gives me great hope, but it's going to take much more time to carefully sculpt into the intricate piece of art it must become. I'm sculpting this pNIT surreptitiously, adding critical components they will never suspect. If they found out, they'd no doubt eliminate me once and for all. In this pNIT work I'm coordinating with many scientists, but only in such a way that, under my command, they are unaware of the grander mission of my masterpiece. Gupta's threat to kill me if I reveal my identity does not deter me.

But what of my family, what is unbeknownst to them? My existence, I assume.

AGE-DECODED

I fondly remember those times Ahmed and I spent with Jesus and Xi. After two hundred years the memories are stronger, not weaker. Like the night we played scrabble together, Jesus and Xi teamed up to beat Ahmed and me in a game that came down to the one word, *quixotic*, which they laid down on the last turn by attaching *quixoti* to the ending letter of our word *chic*, and doing it all on a triple word tile, scoring an amazing 117 points! How we all laughed to the point of crying. I remember the great hikes we did whenever we traveled, such as Laurel Canyon (Los Angeles), the Fraser Valley (near Vancouver), the Eiger Trail (Grindelwald), and of course right at home, the many walks around New Orleans. These outings were great for exercising but were also an opportunity to share, chat and laugh together, which we did – old and young alike. I also remember the countless hours we spent glued to Netflix, binge-watching series such as The Mad Scientists and Robotic Romances, ravenously consuming pretzels (Jesus's favorite), Fruit Roll-Ups (Xi's favorite), Ritz Crackers with cheddar cheese (Ahmed's favorite), blueberry yogurt (my favorite), or popcorn (everybody's favorite!).

Can society afford to eradicate such cross-generational treasures? Xi. Jesus. Ahmed – what has even become of them? My disappearance must haunt their poor souls. In what manner did I perish, were they made to believe? Was my murder faked? Or did the Authority concoct something more sinister – should I call it evil? – such as staging my suicide? That would enable them to blame me and to increase the already unfathomable burden on my family! I so wish to know what my family *thinks* happened. I also wish they knew what *really* happened. I'm alive!

I yearn to hug your blessed souls, Xi, Jesus, and Ahmed. I love you all more than ever.

CHAPTER 16

THE MORNING AFTER JESUS'S visit, Jason was asked by Ximena to read a short story called *The Ants*. She said it was written by Jesus in 2054, one year after he was age-decoded, the same year he converted to Buddhism.

Ximena explained to Jason, "Before being age-decoded Jesus only wrote non-fiction: books, articles, lectures, conference presentations. But afterward, he took up different interests. I was young at the time, so I can't tell you much firsthand, but that's what Jesus told me. He believes this short story represents a mysterious personal revelation. He calls it his "unresolved revelation," though I find that to be an oxymoron, and I told him so."

Anyway, give it a read and let me know what you think."

"Interesting," said Jason, who got comfortable on the couch and plunged right in:

Mezhar Brolnik noticed the insect – an ant – in his periphery, late at night, while lazily reading a short story from Billardos' latest collection, Passages of the Noon. The large black ant was camouflaged somewhat by the dark brown dresser upon which it climbed, slowly, almost straight upward. It was early Spring when the house tended to creak in untoward ways, and animals outside were just awakening to launch another warm season. It was a time of imbalance and change. If the ant was disquieting, it was likely owing to Mezhar's grey, inward disposition after many months of harsh winter and dark mornings and evenings; but now sunlight hours were beginning to widen across the days, and Mezhar believed his discomfort would wane as surely as the snow melted. To him, the ant was simply part of nature's transition to Spring. Who could deny that? Any house in the city had ants in the Spring. The ant he saw was thus: a tiny sign of the natural, seasonal transition. How could he consider this tiny insect a threat?

The next morning Mezhar brushed his teeth and stared at his unkempt figure in the mirror. He remembered dreaming about ants. He could not recall any details but was certain of a dream. The deep thoughts of the night spurred him to spend some time searching the Net regarding ants. He worked only part-time now and had no family to bother with. He had a lot of free time.

He quickly learned that ants live in large colonies. One colony may have hundreds of thousands or even millions of members. Although the colony will probably exist outside a house, some ants may enter a house to look for food or water. He also discovered that ants may colonize within the walls or other structures of a house. No sane person living alone would fancy that!

He read of two types of ants: the males, who live solely for the function of mating; and the Queen, who lays eggs and tends to the nest. A colony may have one or more Queens, depending on the species. He then read about the third type of ant, about whom much was written: the workers. All workers are females. Some workers, those with larger heads, specialized in transporting food – carrying it and/or eating it then later vomiting it up, to share with other colony members. Other workers, with smaller heads, cared for the scores of young ants back at the nest. A third type, known as the scouts, conducted surveillance for sources of food. Finally, workers who aggressively protected the colony from any threat were known as soldiers.

By lunchtime, Mezhar concluded that the ant he had spied yesterday must have been a worker – likely a scout on a surveillance mission, scanning his house as a potential food and water source or, perhaps, as a location for a future colony.

He knew that one worker was a negligible aspect of an organized multitude of ants. But was that scout he saw negligible? The question churned in his mind.

While preparing his lunch, Mezhar noticed three more ants on the kitchen floor. What a blessing it must be to do what they do! Knowing that their energy is naturally spent in total purpose; adventuresome undertakings, far-reaching journeys to secure vegetable morsels, cat food crumbs, or even dead pieces of skin or toenails. The variety of nutrition would secure the health of the colony. What a noble contribution those workers were making to the colony and the Queen!

Mezhar could have stepped on all three ants and quashed their tiny lives, but he restrained himself. He was above that.

AGE-DECODED

It occurred to him that if he cleaned the house impeccably, he might influence the early surveillance workers and pre-empt the onslaught of a multitude of ants. With the spying and bugging process underway, it might not be too late to do something proactive. Yet, instead of cleaning, he hastened to learn about ants, then act reasonably. Stepping on three ants in the kitchen would be a futile move, and he was proud of his decision not to do so. Unrefined maneuvers would be ineffective against a complex of ants. He was not a child and would not act like one. Yet if he dawdled and philosophized, that would also be futile. He knew that Lasius Niger, the common black garden ant, was well-known for cutting out nests under stones or against walls and for even invading the nests of other ant species, are feared by people because they could take control of their houses. If they control your house, they control you.

To Mezhar, living alone seemed a disadvantage, since he was the only defender. Yet as he pondered this further, he figured that living alone might lend him advantages: unbridled means to defend, to take bold personal measures, to act swiftly, to preclude being held back by committee and the need for consensus.

Mezhar Brolnik's edge, he thought, would be his singular ingenuity.

That evening he scoured the Net for more material regarding ants. Spring implied life and birth and growth, and Mezhar's first tactic was to learn more about ant birth and ant larvae. An ant's life span is only a few months, though the Queen of Lasius Niger can live for up to 15 years. He discovered that larvae hatch from eggs and look like tiny hairy maggots. They have no legs but can hook together and can accomplish small movements such as tilting their head in the direction of food. More importantly, the larvae phase is the period when ants grow over several weeks – so they have to eat liberally. Larvae voraciously suck up food juices and regurgitated food offered to them by worker ants. With some species, such as Lasius Niger, the larvae spin themselves a cocoon within which it will transform from larvae to adults. To spin a cocoon, the larvae must be pressed against a solid object, such as a wall, or at least buried well in the soil where it can be dug up later by the workers. If feeding goes well, an adult ant will likely arise from this cocoon. Ironically, a newly born black ant emerges from the cocoon looking as white as freshly fallen snow. But within hours its exoskeleton hardens and turns black.

Upon gleaning this information, Mezhar knew it would be futile to try to destroy larvae or cocoons. There were likely millions of them nearby, perhaps even within his house! How could he, even if he wished, find these infinitesimal larvae? It discouraged him that his new knowledge did not yield immediate strategies for defending his home and his life.

Mezhar went to bed ... was soon contained in a cocoon, regressing into larvae form. Subconscious of the situation, he could only wiggle and bobble to try to escape the cocoon which was his own making. Avoiding regression to a pre-larvae state would be futile unless external help could be found which would enter the ingress of his trap. Wiggling and bobbling intensified Mezhar's endangerment because it only served to re-spin the cocoon and tighten the ingress. He called to worker ants to help, but his voice was not developed enough to produce sound and was degenerating; he could spy the Queen through the thin cocoon wrap; yes, though ants can tunnel several feet down when crafting their colony, and finding the Queen is like finding a needle in a haystack – there she was! Yet he had no means of getting her attention; besides, he knew she was too important to be troubled by his trivial recession to pre-larvae form. He went back to calling worker ants to help, but his voice was ineffectual, and they bypassed the diminishing ingress of his cocoon to serve the thousands of other larvae...

In the morning Mezhar recalled his dream vividly.

Before breakfast, he went to the hardware store and bought nine ant traps which he planted cunningly about the house: five on the main floor where the kitchen was, and four upstairs. According to the package, the active ingredient in the ant trap was borax, with an added food attractant. Worker ants visiting these traps will transport poison back to their colonies, share it, and kill the colony. It was interesting to Mezhar that one chemical could solve so much. After more web research he discovered that ants use many chemical mechanisms. To differentiate nest mates versus ants from other colonies, two worker ants meeting will "sniff" one another for trademark chemicals, using their antennae. If chemistry indicates different colonies, the ants will either fight or run away from each other. The black ant also uses acid to attack. Worker ants will react to danger by releasing alarm pheromones, signaling soldier ants from the same colony to move toward the location of this chemical and attack what doesn't belong there. Although ants can be savage in their chemical attacks, they can also be gentle and caring. For instance, some ants tend carefully to aphids and shield them from parasites and predators – so they can eventually extract from the aphids the delectable honeydew chemical.

Mezhar was counting on one chemical, borax, to fool these very intricate chemical creatures. Was he expecting too much?

He anticipated an increase in the number of ants once they detected the new sources of food contained in the traps. Ants, he learned, communicate with fellow colony members by releasing pheromones (chemicals with many different smells) and leaving scented trails for others to follow. These chemical trails contain information about the quantity, quality, and distance of food. Strong enough to withstand most washing or heavy rain, the chemical trails are laid down in such a manner as to minimize overlapping with trails of other colonies. Given his knowledge of these trails, Mezhar correctly figured that worker activity should escalate around his traps and along pathways leading from his traps to the colony sources. He also made the correct decision to avoid killing any of the worker ants that would be marching so boldly across his floors now that the traps were laid, because killing them would prevent them from transporting borax to their colonies and their Queen(s).

Mezhar ate a late breakfast and was disheartened – for he saw no ants.

The rest of the day he spent at the downtown office. A semi-retired accountant who had built up a reputation as very safe and methodical during thirty-three years with four companies, Mezhar had the luxury of working whenever he wanted as an independent contractor. When he returned home, the sun was still exerting a slight influence above the horizon, but the main floor of his house was grey and begging for light.

He switched on the kitchen lights he saw, for the first time, many ants. A couple of dozen were scattered about on the kitchen floor, and more were on the counters. His reflex was to strike. But he restrained himself and remained rational. His strategy must be upheld.

Watching TV later that night he perceived an ant scaling up his leg. Though he did not see it, he assumed it was an ant and subconsciously flicked it away.

The next morning, after a restless sleep with no dreams, Mezhar discovered a large dead ant near the baseboard crevice in his bedroom. He picked it up and descended the stairs to the kitchen. Using a magnifying glass, he scrutinized it for parts he had read about. The trunk, with six legs attached; sharp claws at the end of each leg, enabling the ant to climb. The head, with two attached antennae – sensitive organs of smell, touch, taste, and hearing; jointed, so that they can be extended forward and retracted back; also from the head arose two pinchers, used to dig, carry food, and defend; and the large mandibles (jaws), which bite and tear food into smaller, edible pieces. And, at the rear, the metasoma (poison sack); just like wasps, some ants used stingers for defense. Mezhar turned the ant every which way and revisited its body parts. What a marvel was this ant! He decided to drop the specimen into the kitchen garbage can, but at the last moment, he changed his mind and hurled it into the backyard as far as he could.

After deciding not to go to work, Mezhar went about town accomplishing several errands. Although he was a solitary figure who craved his independence, he always made a point of greeting the shopkeepers he had done business with over the years. He thought of broaching the subject of ants with Mr. Fraser, the butcher, but decided against it. Miss Clepworth, the coffee shop owner, asked him, "How ya keeping, Mezzie?" and he merely said, "Good, thanks." No mention of the ants.

Returning home before dinner, Mezhar walked wearily to the family room. He turned on the TV weather channel, stretched out on the couch, covered himself with a wool blanket. He posited that there had been a significant increase in ant traffic in his house since the traps were laid. This pleased him. After tracking the weather for a few minutes, he dozed off ... he conjectured: most of the hundreds of thousands of ants, especially the young adults of the colony located just to the West of his house, were currently within the depths of the colony nest, minding the Queen; when they got a little older, they would certainly reassign themselves to tasks nearer the surface of the ground and, eventually, leave the security of the nest to venture out: first into the gardens, then into his house; if he attacked, their chemical defenses would be substantial; but what worried him most was their nonchemical defense, which might be more potent, for ants can also defend by overwhelming opponents with sheer numbers; to a small invertebrate or small mammal, the sight of hundreds or thousands of ants swarming towards them is intimidating – would it not also intimidate a gentle old man like himself? ... the dream again draped him in that cocoon ... he called to worker ants to help, but his voice had degenerated completely now; he could still see the unattainable Queen through the thin wall of his cocoon, he had receded to early-larvae form; he tried to arouse a shout from deep within his midsection, but sound was impossible now and the workers passed him in droves to serve the thousands of other growing larvae; the imperceptible ingress of his cocoon was a portal to nowhere; he was lost ...

The sound of his own snoring extracted Mezhar from his sleep. He opened his eyes expecting the sight of the weather channel, but the TV was off. The house was dark, except for the faint street light which entered the room through two windows. Mezhar could hear an unfamiliar noise emanating from the kitchen. He knew an ant could create sound by scraping together its roughened body parts. But such noise was only detectable by a person whose ear was within an inch of the ant. Or by a person one room away, if thousands of ants were scraping.

Jason placed the document on the coffee table and tried to comprehend the story. He did not know why, but it bothered him.

Questions poured across his mind. Why would Jesus write this? What did it mean? Was the character Mezhar supposed to be Jesus himself? If so, why was the character so paranoid of ants when Jesus was an ant expert who loved studying them?

Jason's analysis labored. He wanted to talk to Ximena about the story.

"Xi, where are you?" he called.

Ximena came into the room. "What's up?"

"I don't think I understand this ant story. I mean, I have some hunches, but they could be far-fetched."

"Don't worry, the meaning may be unattainable. I told you that Jesus himself was perplexed by what he wrote. Sometimes you just have to let it happen and soak it up for what it's worth."

"What's that supposed to mean? I was taught in Grade 10 that stories have meaning; that stories and poetry and other types of art are supposed to say something ... they called it a theme. Don't you think Jesus had some theme he was trying to express?"

"Yes, probably," replied Ximena.

"What do you mean?" asked Jason.

"Probably, but maybe not in the rational sense. Sometimes themes can't be figured out, can't be rationalized. Perhaps it was pure intuition that drove him to write this story about the ants. Some art is like that, don't you think? I believe some art is created to make both the artist and the recipient wonder and question, instead of boldly projecting a clear, rational theme. Examples in visual art might be abstract artists like Yayoi Kusama and Helen Frankenthaler."

Ximena knew it was silly for her to cite artists whose works Jason didn't know, so she added, "Maybe I can give you an example from sports. Have you ever seen an athlete make a move which you've never seen before, which defies explanation because it couldn't have been taught, yet magically happens?"

"Yes. I watched old clips of the basketball star Michael Jordan, who played for the Chicago Bulls. He was amazing! He made some crazy sick moves, like his switch-hands layup!"

"Good, then you know exactly what I mean."

"But I'm still wondering about that short story. Maybe Jesus had a clear message and we just don't see it."

Ximena gently giggled, "That's possible too."

CHAPTER 17

AGING RESEARCH BEGAN long before the HGP. For example, in 1935 Clive McKay from Cornell University claimed to have slowed aging in laboratory rats by reducing their caloric intake while maintaining their consumption of nutrients needed for good health. The animals lived healthier and longer. The effect of calorie reduction on humans (while carefully maintaining essential nutrient intake) was investigated much later at Louisiana State University, in 2006, supported by the National Institute on Aging. Metabolism slowed and insulin levels rose – pointing to increased longevity. Similar research was conducted at the University of Florida Institute on Aging. Based on these findings, a small but devoted contingent of human calorie restriction adherents emerged, like a new religion, ready to evangelize others to its cause of longevity.

Much early aging research was linked to genetics and Darwin's Theory of Evolution. In his 1952 classic, *An Unsolved Problem of Biology,* Peter Medawar proposed that aging was caused by minor mutations slowly weeded out by natural selection but replaced by other minor mutations. He argued that natural selection wanes with age and that genes beneficial early in life (which help with survival and reproduction) are naturally selected over genes beneficial in old age. His thinking dovetailed nicely with Darwin's original evolutionary theory. But why had humans not evolved to grow older and to reproduce at older ages, as might be predicted? Was aging itself a hereditary trait? Or was it better viewed as a condition – a disease?

In the 1960s Dr. Leonard Hayflick of the University of California discovered that a cell had a pre-programmed limit for the total number of times it could replicate itself or divide, which became known as the *Hayflick Limit.* He speculated that aging was associated with such a limit for normal cells. In 1999, Michael Rose from the University of California at Irvine showed that this limit could be extended in fruit flies. Rose used selective breeding of older fruit flies to enable the natural selection of flies capable of breeding at older ages, creating generations of longer-living fruit flies. He proposed that the life span of humans could be lengthened through similar manipulation.

In 2003, the HGP completed its final mapping of the human genome. However, that mapping was not without controversy, due to a competing nonprofit (but business-backed) group known as The Institute for Genomic Research (TIGR), headed by U.S. researcher Craig Venter, who once worked for NIH. His group joined forces with Celera Incorporated and used different techniques than the HGP in competing for the same goal. Both groups claimed to have completed the final mapping of the human genome as early as the year 2000, but they were politically forced to cooperate and publish simultaneously: HGP in *Nature* and Venter's group in *Science*. This pressure to finish and cooperate was so strong that gaps accrued in some of the data, most notably that of TIGR. HGP accused TIGR of piggybacking on HGP's work to correct their mistakes. Still, the mapping of the human genome was completed, with huge significance to genetics and aging research.

With that, aging research became inextricably linked (some would say inextricably) to genetics. For example, in 2005, research led by Andrew Dillin at the Salk Institute for Biological Studies, California, uncovered one gene in roundworm cells as the key to extending its life by shifting the metabolism to the enhancement of cell maintenance. "Until recently," his team suggested, "the mechanisms that control the aging process were thought to be immensely complex and nearly impossible to dissect at the molecular level."

Amidst such developments, some began asking bolder questions such as, should genes be patented? Author Michael Crichton argued in 2007 that patenting genes was tantamount to patenting "snow, eagles, or gravity." Private corporations had no right to do so, as genes are naturally occurring phenomena, not human inventions. Crichton believed gene patent infringement concerns stifled information exchange, research, and medical testing. In a related article, "Staking Claims in the Biotechnology Klondike," John Sulston of the World Health Organization Human Genetics Commission also argued that genome sequences should be part of the public domain, not privatized or patented. A life form as it occurs naturally, he argued, cannot be "patentable" because there is no inventive step of human intervention.

Aging research marched on, with huge private sector involvement. Calico LLC, a subsidiary of Alphabet Inc, was created in 2013 to research aging and age-related disease. Google founder Larry Page was elusive about its specific goals and research, but their budget rivaled the combined aging research spending of the two most involved government agencies in the world: the U.S. National Institutes for Health, and the Natural Science Foundation of China.

Various other anti-aging companies arose in the early 21st century, such as Unity Biotechnology, Life Biosciences, Juvenescence, Insilico Medicine, Quest Diagnostics (a subsidiary of Celera Corp), Genentech, and AgeX Therapeutics. These companies made useful discoveries about the aging process and associated aging-related disease, but their progress was painstakingly slow, such that their share values generally declined through the 2020s as the initial enthusiasm about solving aging was dampened by the complex reality of the undertaking. The lack of collaboration among competing commercial interests also limited progress.

In the year 2012, the scientific community started making widespread use of the extraordinary Clustered Regulatory Interspaced Short Palindromic Repeats (CRISPR) gene editing technology. Genes of living things could now be engineered. Scientists targeted human diseases and disorders such as HIV, cystic fibrosis, Alzheimer's, heart disease, and cancer. They also targeted non-human sources of disease such as malaria in mosquitoes, Lyme disease in mice and ticks, and swine flu in pigs. Examples of corporations involved were Beam Therapeutics, Novartis, Editas, Intella, Biogen, Cellectis, bluebird bio, Vertex Pharmaceuticals, and CRISPR Therapeutics. Notwithstanding concerns that CRISPR gene-editing could cause unintended damage or mutations to DNA bases, research advanced rapidly as these methods became precise.

In 2020, Jennifer Doudna of UC Berkeley and her European collaborator Emmanuelle Charpentier of the Max Planck Institute for Infection Biology won the Nobel Prize in Chemistry for their pioneering work on CRISPR-Cas9. This was a breakthrough in genetic engineering efficiency. A plethora of public and privately funded scientists refined and improved this technology, making significant strides in repairing genetic "mistakes" while minimizing unintended consequences. In the years 2020 through 2030 breakthroughs in the use of *guide RNA*, greatly enhanced the timing and sequencing of CRISPR-Cas9 applications. This progress was buttressed by the use of *protein nanobodies* to enable CRISPR-Cas9 to effectively turn genes on and off, further minimizing untoward side-effects.

By 2033, a new CRISPR-SHARP mechanism came into play which, combined with advancements in Artificial Intelligence and Qubit Quantum Computing, proved useful for aggregating and analyzing data in anti-aging work. The two dozen or so primary genes involved in human aging were isolated, though with fuzziness regarding the specific role of proteins of the aging-related genes – a collective known as the *aging proteome*. Proteomics research exploring the role of proteins rather than genes *per se* intensified. One gene in this proteome, SIRT6 (known as far back as 2020 to play a key role in organizing proteins and enzymes for DNA repair) was linked to longer lifespans in mice, mole rats, and beavers. The protein structure specific to this gene, also known as SIRT6, and the amino acids that comprised it, were eventually resolved in many other animal species, including humans. This research clarified the complex role of proteins in the aging process.

In 2044, the theoretical foundation for a genetically-based method to arrest the aging process in all animals was uncovered by Dr. Frieda Sengmeuller in conjunction with associates from the UCLA Memory and Aging Research Centre and the Peking University Institute for Aging Genetics, all funded by the U.S. National Institute on Aging and the Natural Science Foundation of China.

At the press conference announcing her team's anti-aging breakthrough, Dr. Sengmeuller stated that more comprehensive animal trials had already begun, to substantiate their hypothesis. She coined the term "age-decoding" for her discovery, a reference to the decoding of genetic structures and processes required to make it work. Five years later, her group began human trials.

Nine years later, in 2053, Dr. Sengmeuller proudly announced her team's assessment that age-decoding could be safely and effectively applied to humans. That same year she was awarded the Nobel Prize in Medicine.

In the face of the massive potential financial impact of the discovery of age-decoding, the U.S. government attempted to wrest control of the technology. But even it was not capable of underwriting the necessary legal and economic support: the U.S. $500 trillion government debt and $200 trillion central bank quantitative easing load were massive financial straitjackets, making it too weak to control the technology as one nation. Hence the impetus to form the first "Zone1 Authority", created to administer financial support for age-decoding across the world's most highly developed economies. The U.S. initially led the way, but China rendered equally strong financial clout because of its slightly larger economy and decent fiscal situation. Not by coincidence, most Zone1 countries had been key partners in the HGP.

With compensation came control, and the Zone1 Authority morphed rapidly into a loose, quasi-government organization with responsibilities spanning all contributing nations. The United Nations challenged the formation of the Zone1 Authority to control age-decoding. The challenge was based on the Convention on Biological Diversity, which had been ratified at the Rio Earth Summit in 1992 by 188 countries, including all countries attempting to form Zone1. That agreement called for "the equitable sharing of the benefits arising out of utilization of genetic resources".

This challenge was rebuked by the U.S. and China, with help from India, Germany, France, Canada, and the United Kingdom. These "Big 7" members of Zone1 were entitled to inner circle Authority power. They pointed to U.N. Convention's own "*Article 2. Use of Terms*", which defined "Genetic resources" as *genetic material of actual or potential value*; and "Genetic material" as *material of plant, animal, microbial or other origin containing functional units of heredity*. Age-decoding, they argued, was a process, not a material, so there was no obligation for any single country to share it. They also claimed, ironically, that the Convention provided a mechanism for the creation of an Authority, such as Zone1, by permitting the formation of Regional Economic Integration Organizations, "*constituted by sovereign States of a given region, to which its member States have transferred competence in respect of matters governed by this Convention and which has been duly authorized, in accordance with its internal procedures, to sign, ratify, accept, approve or accede to it.*" The final argument of the Big 7 was that the Convention was signed in good faith by its countries in 1992 and could therefore be rescinded in good faith at any time – a right which the U.N. could not deny them. Ultimately, then, because of its very own regulations, the U.N. challenge to the formation of the Zone1 Authority failed.

A further challenge to the Zone1 Authority was mounted by 125 out of the 150 member countries of the World Trade Organization (WTO), an organization with considerable influence in the domain of biotechnology products. These nations maintained that restricting age-decoding applications to Zone1 would be contrary to WTO free trade principles. However, the WTO's Trade-Related Aspects of Intellectual Property Rights II (TRIPS II, negotiated in 2029) mitigated against the right of WTO countries to access intellectual processes. TRIPS II set minimum standards for most forms of intellectual property regulation within member countries, primarily as a protection for owners of property from international piracy. The WTO was hard-pressed to challenge the right of the Zone1 Authority to apply age-decoding exclusively to its member populations, given that the Authority was the originator of that intellectual process. With all eighteen key participating countries of HGP counted among the twenty-four countries attempting to form Zone1, TRIPS II served as a solid defense against WTO challenges, which dragged on for years, but ultimately fizzled out.

Thus, by the year 2055, the Zone1 Authority was installed, and the unwritten Fundamental Platform took hold in the minds and souls of age-decoded eubeings. Nation-states under the Authority still held decentralized powers, but key governing decisions for most of the world's developed nations lie in the hands of the Zone1 Authority. The remaining nations and regions that never recognized the jurisdiction of Authority collectively comprised the less organized, less sophisticated region known as Zone2, where age-decoding never happened.

CHAPTER 18

VERY LATE AT NIGHT, well past his normal bedtime, Ahmed found himself reading an essay he had not read for over 200 years: C.S. Lewis's *The Abolition of Man.* Frieda had once told him that if he ever read anything when he was in a spiritual mood, that should be it. It was a good sign that he remembered this now, he thought, because he had mostly shut out anything about her from the moment he joined the Authority. He had to, for there was no other way to reconcile her ethics with his corrupt, well-compensated career. Her goodness was wasted on him. Now, however, he was eager to bring her goodness back, to embrace everything he could about her.

He wondered: How could I have lasted so long at the Authority, inside that rotten structure, given what I knew, what I did? How could I have shunned her love, shut out her goodness, letting it die with her suicide?

Now, in the dark of his study under the power of one light, he activated his NIT again and poured through more Lewis, relishing Frieda's genuine soul at his side:

In order to fully understand what Man's power over Nature and therefore over other men, really means, we must picture the race extended in time from the date of its emergence to that of its extinction...

If any one age really attains, by eugenics and scientific education, the power to make its descendants what it pleases, all men who live after it are patients of that power. They are weaker, not stronger...

Ahmed deliberated: what a contrast was the foreboding of Lewis with the bold confidence of Teilhard de Chardin – trumpeted inside the Authority – of the powers of human reflection which rendered humans above all other life forms; humans riding the *axe et flèche de l'Evolution, i.e.,* Evolution's Arrow; the totality of human thought beneficially coalescing upwards, imminently, to a final point of unification. Due to their innate optimism, Chardin's conceptualizations were advocated by the Authority. That included the concept of the *noosphere* (distinct from the physical *biosphere*): an intangible, psychic layer of human thought that gradually progressed through history from Point Alpha, the beginning, to Point Omega, the final aggregate of shared consciousness. We in the Authority were swept away by Chardin, Ahmed mused. Lewis's ideas never stood a chance.

But were we not the victims of philosophical propaganda? Now, beholding Lewis's powerful sobering words, Ahmed experienced more than a twinge of humble anchoring. Inside the Authority, Ahmed thought, the feeling of humility was foreign.

He asked himself, had Frieda embraced the ideas of Teilhard de Chardin? That he doubted. Even if she had, she would have preferred Lewis. How ironic, he thought: two wildly popular Christian writers with largely incompatible ideas.

He poured through more Lewis:

> *... there is therefore no question of a power vested in the race as a whole steadily growing as long as the race survives.... within this master generation (itself an infinitesimal minority of the species) the power will be exercised by a minority smaller still ... the rule of a few hundreds of men over billions and billions ...*

I was clearly and unabashedly in that privileged group, Ahmed admitted. Plodding along for two centuries, amid all the secrecy. I was that minority, affecting the billions and billions in ways they could never imagine. How is it that we overlooked the wise words of this philosopher? Did Lewis's message just fizzle out in our world? Or did we choose to ignore it?

My time working in that privileged minority flew by, more like fleeted, he thought. And all for what? Nothing to me now, or even less than nothing. Amazing that I've only now woken up.

His thoughts freshly circulating, he giddily read another line from Lewis:

Human nature will be the last part of Nature to surrender to Man.

With that awesome quotation, Ahmed forced his eyes away from the holographic text. But his eyes shifted back to savor it one last time. Had the full surrender transpired or was it merely transpiring, such that there was time, though perhaps very little? He had to believe there was time. He read one last passage:

... critics may ask 'Why should you suppose they will be such bad men?' But I am not supposing them to be bad men. They are, rather, not men (in the old sense) at all. They are, if you like, men who have sacrificed their own share in traditional humanity in order to devote themselves to the task of deciding what "Humanity" shall henceforth mean. 'Good' and 'bad', applied to them, are words without content; for it is from them that the content of these words is henceforth to be derived.

"Haunting!" Ahmed shouted to himself.

Lewis's words – could they have been written over three hundred years ago? – spoke to him in a humane way that made him quiver with emotion, something not normal for him.

Ahmed knew now what he must do. It was simple: find a way to become good once again. Redemption was his only path. The meaning of those words would help bring him to the goodness of Frieda, into her loving arms, to where he should have been all along.

He mused that he was lucky to be a eubeing because it afforded him the time to redeem himself after two wasted centuries.

Both regret and optimism overcame Ahmed Iftikhar at this late hour. Regret for so much pitiful waste; optimism for his unlimited future.

CHAPTER 19

BECAUSE OF HIS POSITION in Apex200 Tavon was aware of the goings-on of the cryos and HF Capital under the auspices of Rethinking. He secretly arranged to escort Jason's ten-year-old sister Sarah to Ximena's location so she could be with her brother. It had been three weeks since their cryopreservation ended, and the siblings were anxious to see each other. The use of NITs would have enabled close and convenient contact between them, but they did not yet have these devices.

Without communication, Jason knew his little sister would be worried. He was concerned for her, a concern he found odd because he and Sarah had never been that close, separated as they were by nine years, with completely different interests and friends. Besides, he thought, brothers were not supposed to show concern.

When Tavon brought Sarah in, Jason sprinted forward and gave her the biggest hug of her life. A tingly sense of growing up filled Jason.

With no supporting father and the death of his mother, Jason recognized that Sarah was his only family. She looked older somehow, but still held that cute innocence of a ten-year-old girl.

Ximena and Tavon left Sarah and Jason alone for a while. Sarah, immensely excited, told Jason about her stay with other cryos, who she felt were very nice people to stay with, and how, despite this, she had asked them to connect her to him as soon as possible. She also wondered aloud why Jason had not also been put in with the cryos.

She asked Jason, "Why do you think you were set apart in the first place?"

"I have no idea – I just know that I ended up with Xi, who has been very good to me." He paused, then asked, "Who looked after you with the cryos?

"We were looked after by several people in the Rethinking party," she said, "which is an underground party, although I'm not sure what that means because they certainly don't live under the ground. Also, nobody has explained eubeings and non-eubeings to me very well – can you do that?"

Jason deflected that question, and asked, "Do you know about Mom?" He hoped she already knew their mother had died, that he would not be the first to tell her.

Surprise enveloped Sarah's face, indicating she did not know. She waited while Jason figured out what to say next.

He decided to be direct. "Mom passed away long ago."

Sarah twisted away quickly and cowered near the window. She rested her head on the ledge and looked across the emerald and shamrock green flora of the vast backyard.

Jason knew how close she was to Mom. Should he go over and hug her again? What should he do?

Just then Ximena and Tavon entered the room, and Sarah burst out, "What's going on here? What's happened?" She was sobbing and shaking.

Ximena, who sensed what was going on, said to Sarah, "Please don't try to deal with everything right now. We can make sense of all of this ... gradually. I'd like you to stay here with me and your brother for some time. So much has happened."

Sarah, looking down, responded with a slight nod. She suddenly looked up again and asked, "What about my mother ... how can you be sure she's not alive?"

Ximena answered, "What Jason told you is correct. I'm very sorry, Sarah. I know you were extremely close to your mom and loved her dearly... can I take you out to the garden for a short walk?"

She offered her right hand to Sarah and led her out back to where the Ixora, Junipers, Bougainvillea, Jasmine, and Orchids would, in their light and mystical way, soften Sarah's heavy thoughts amid the fragrant breeze. To Ximena, the presence of God was ever-present in this beautiful backyard, and Sarah needed that.

Tavon and Jason remained in the front room.

Tavon said, "Unfortunately, cryos like you and Sarah have not been made aware of much. Though you are together now, which is good, you have been isolated – perhaps insulated is the better word. The Authority wants it that way and, ironically, Rethinking sometimes does too."

He then used the opportunity to tell Jason that Ximena's real father Ahmed was coming to visit tomorrow. He asked Jason to stay quiet about it because Ximena was extremely nervous about the meeting. Jason promised Tavon that he would, then suggested to Tavon that Jesus should be present to support Ximena during the meeting. Impressed by Jason's foresight, Tavon assured him that Jesus would be there with her.

Tavon beamed when Jason said that. "You remind me of me when I was young. Except maybe you're smarter."

Blushing noticeably, Jason said, "I doubt that, but thanks for the compliment."

CHAPTER 20

APPROACHING NOON THE next day, Jason, Ximena, and Sarah ate brunch together. Jason loved the English muffins, onto which he spread Gelnoni, something that reminded him of margarine. Sarah preferred the scrambled eggs and bacon. Jason asked his sister to tell him more about the cryos group, but she was more interested in talking about their family.

"Do you remember anything about Dad?" she asked him.

"I remember a few things. Dad spent a lot of time reading science fiction to me in the family room. Never children's books, always grown-up books. Always old books, too, books that he grew up with. He read to me Jules Verne's long adventure called *The Mysterious Island* and Margaret Atwood's creepy *The Handmaid's Tale*. He read me numerous short stories, too. One story I recall, by Ursula K. Le Guin – *The Ones Who Walk Away From Omelas* – spooked me so much I asked Dad to read it several times. I also asked Dad to make me a rocket, as the father did for his son in Ray Bradbury's short story *The Rocket*; Dad read that story to me one night when a supermoon was rising rose from the horizon, and he said he'd try his best to build that rocket. But it wasn't all science fiction that Dad introduced to me. He also read me long passages from the *New American Standard Bible*, which I found a bit boring, though some parts in the Old Testament such as David and Goliath, the Tower of Babel, and the story of Job, were memorable. Probably the funniest stuff he read was the ancient short story written by Mark Twain, *The Celebrated Jumping Frog from Calaveras County*. I should read you that one, Sarah. You'd find it hilarious!"

As she listened to Jason relate all of this to his sister, Ximena admitted to herself that she was becoming more and more impressed with him.

Jason continued, "But what I remember most about my Dad was his coming home late, sometimes after dinner, parking in the driveway, and sometimes Mom and him shouting at each other out there while I secretly watched through the front window. Though I was young and lacked all the facts, I felt sorry for Dad. I figured he was hungry and wanted to come in for dinner, and Mom was keeping him on the driveway, just standing near the front steps yelling at him. Why not feed him like she did us? I especially recall the time Mom told him to leave for good. Dad picked me up in his arms and said to me directly for the first time that he loved me. He promised that Mom would do a fine job looking after me. He said he had to leave so Mom could do her best without him messing things up. You were asleep at the time, Sarah, so Dad asked me to say goodbye to you. He then put me down, patted me on the head, glanced oddly at Mom, then simply walked out the front door. I can still hear his footsteps on the hardwood floor. But I didn't imagine he'd leave forever. I remember it all."

"Did you tell me he left?" asked Sarah.

"No. I didn't ... because you were too young. Mom didn't tell you either. I guess we both sort of denied it ourselves and tried to keep it from you. Only time ... yes, lots of time .... made us come to believe it and reveal it to you. For a while, we just gave you the story that he was away on a long trip."

"You should've told me right away."

"We were protecting you."

"Could I talk?"

"Yes, but barely."

"Could I say, *Daddy*?

"Yes," said Jason. He then shifted the subject. "Xi's mother is the famous scientist, the one who unraveled the mystery of age-decoding and won the Nobel prize – Dr. Frieda Sengmeuller."

"Wow!" Sarah cried, turning to Ximena, "That's cool. I would love to meet her. What about your father, Xi? Is he also famous?"

"I don't know him very well. I know he works for the Authority, but I've never spoken to him since my mother's death."

Sarah looked at her. "Really? Did she die? That's sad."

"I'll explain it all to you later," said Ximena. "Luckily, someone else stepped in to be my father. A dear old man. His name is Jesus, who couldn't have been a more incredible father to me. I'll let Jason tell you all about him while I prepare for his arrival. He should be here soon."

"Jesus?" exclaimed Sarah. "I thought Jesus died eons ago. Aren't we two hundred years into the future?"

Jason and Ximena glanced at each other and laughed.

Ximena explained, "Not Jesus Christ, Sarah. I'm talking about Jesus Sengmeuller, the man who became my surrogate father!"

Ximena busied herself in the kitchen while Jason and his sister finished their lunch and talked some more, mostly about the current society, which Sarah was very curious about. Jason did his best to explain eubeings, non-eubeings, age-decoding, the Zone 1 Authority, and the Rethinking Party. The cryos had explained little of this to her. They paused to ask Ximena how long she had been working with the Rethinking Party. She explained that her involvement started when she found out that her real father was working with the Authority.

Jesus arrived just after one o'clock, about an hour before the planned visit of two other guests.

Jason brought Sarah directly over to the old man, who raised his head slightly from his crouch, revealing crow's feet at the edges of his twinkly eyes, which bestowed instant magic upon her. Sarah smiled and shook his hand, distracted by its deep wrinkles and strange veins. Jesus then reached into his pocket, turned slowly to Jason, and placed a copy of *Biodiversity Unplugged* into his left hand. "Take this, son, and learn from it. Teach your little sister well. Of it, I'm very proud. I composed it in my prime, well before I was age-decoded."

Ximena said to Jason, "That's the classic I told you about. It's more valuable than any PhD could ever be."

Jason held it tenderly using both hands. The book was old, very thick, with a dark blue leathery cover. He opened it and flipped through its thin pages of fine, small print. He was eager to begin reading it now but knew that would be rude.

"Thank you so much, Jesus," he said.

Sensing the young man's eagerness, Jesus replied, "Take your time reading it, son, and share it with your sister. Don't speed read ... peruse it slowly, immerse yourself in it, allow it to sink in... and, of course, feel free to ask questions along the way. Doing so will put you on a path to comprehending interbeing, which, as I have said to you before, represents the interconnectedness of life – the essence of life. Life ... it finds a way through interconnections." Jesus's eyes shone as he continued, "What I'm trying to say is that there are no isolated independent parts of nature separate from all others. You'll learn of the connections between the incredible number of species of fauna and flora of the westernmost uplands of the Amazon; the sublime biotas of the rainforests of the Atlantic Brazilian coast; the wild coffee and the African violets of the Usambara forest of Tanzania; the unique plant species of the Himalayas in northern India, Nepal, Bhutan, and western China, and how these are rapidly disappearing due to human development; the variety and origin of reptiles, lemurs, and amphibians endemic to that great island, Madagascar, and their relationship to the enormously complex biota of mainland Africa; and the extinction of the eight-foot-tall kangaroo in Australia due to climate change and hunting. You'll also learn how competitors share limited space; how insects support plants, and vice-versa; how organisms emigrate to new habitats; how species thrive, change, or die; and how entire ecosystems maintain or shift their dynamic balance, sometimes spiraling out of control. With all of this, Jason, you'll discover that humans have an impact – often, but not always, in a negative way. The book is my effort to unravel interdependency, to endorse complexity, to seek simplicity, and to acknowledge natural beauty. Nature is one; nature is interbeing. Humans as part of nature should know and respect this. I trust that you will."

All Jason and Sarah could do was nod appreciatively. How could they respond to that dissertation?

Sarah then asked Ximena, "What is it like to not grow old?"

"But I am growing old, dear. Sure, I'm age-decoded, so my body doesn't age, and I always look young. But in my mind and my heart, I still feel like I'm growing older."

"But he's a lot older," said Sarah, pointing to Jesus, realizing right after she said it that she might have insulted him.

Jesus smiled modestly, "Yes I'm old, but not growing any older, which is amazing. But it's also a trap when you're as old as I am. An unnatural trap. I'm just stalled, a step away from death. My body and mind, ever weary, never rest. They just hold on, having long ago accomplished everything worth accomplishing." He paused to reflect, then went on, "As for the younger age-decoded individuals, you might be surprised to hear that all is not so rosy for them either, though it would take me much more time to explain that to you. Perhaps we'll find some other time. Ultimately my view is that people like you, who haven't been age-decoded, the very rare few, have it best!"

Sarah and Jason were surprised by what Jesus had said. How could growing old be better than staying young? It made no sense, but they still respected his view.

Jesus carried on, "Never overestimate; always underestimate. Applied to oneself, that's known as humility. Charles Darwin, for one, was a very humble person. He said of himself late in his life:

> *with such moderate abilities as I possess, it is truly surprising that I should have influenced to a considerable extent the belief of scientific men on some important points?*

Do you see how humble he was, this man of such greatness? I should add that, twelve years after publishing his famous book *Origin of Species*, after he had convinced so many naturalists, scientists, and others of the merits of evolution and natural selection, Darwin imposed a general humbleness on all humans with the publication of another book, *Descent of Man*. This work placed special emphasis on the human species in the realm of natural selection and treated humans as subject to the same natural laws as all other living things. He argued that humans were just another animal, leveled or grounded, connected with all forms of life, but not above the laws to which all life is subject."

Jesus contemplated for a moment, then asked them, "Do you see the humility in all of this?" Using his NIT to pull up one of his favorite quotations, he said, "Only a great and humble person like Darwin would write:

> *I remember when in Good Success Bay, in Tierra del Fuego, thinking ... that I could not employ my life better than in adding a little to Natural Science. This I have done to the best of my abilities, and critics may say what they like, but they cannot destroy this conviction."*

Jason marveled again at Jesus's memory and glanced over at Sarah to see if she too appreciated what the old man could recount.

Jesus remarked, "Don't think I have all those quotations memorized. Remember, I have an NIT and you don't."

"Oh yes, almost forgot!" Jason replied as Sarah let out a giggle.

He knew what his sister looked like when uninterested and he could see with relief that she did not carry that look. She, like he, knew that Jesus was teaching them much more than they could learn at school. And even though it was not simple material, Jesus somehow made it understandable.

Ximena then said, "My mother tragically killed herself around the time age-decoding was brought in. Some believe she lost her mind, but Jesus thinks she lost her soul ... something to do with her work with a group exploring the ethical, legal, and social issues of age-decoding. That group, called ELSI, examined how age-decoding might impact the human life cycle and the progression of the human species. However, we'll never know for sure what ELSI looked at since it was terminated by the Authority. Thus, Frieda's leadership of ELSI was discredited and any research from that group was never released. The destruction of Frieda's efforts ... we can only assume it drove her to take her soul."

"You see," Jesus added, "Xi's mother was special, but even she, with her superior intellect, ELSI knowledge, and many followers within the scientific community, did not stand a chance against the powerful lure of age-decoding, wrapped up in the newly minted Zone1 Authority. Some say Frieda was politically naïve, focused too much on science and not enough on the use of that science. But I think it was the opposite: she focused too much on the use of science and not enough on science. However you look at it, I believe agelessness, which humans have been dreaming of ever since they could dream, and writing about ever since they could write, was far too alluring for a wise woman like her and a few key associates to contain with cautions and caveats. No matter what Frieda did, the dam was going to burst, and my daughter could only do like all others: get out of the way and let it flow. And that she did. My dear daughter found her way of getting out of the way."

Sarah and Jason, though saddened by his explanation, understood.

Jesus handed Sarah a folded piece of paper and said, "She wrote this the day they announced the Nobel".

Sarah opened the piece of paper. She cried, "It's a poem! Should I read it?"

"Sure. Why don't you read it out loud to us?" asked Ximena, who knew the poem well and looked forward to hearing it again and seeing how the youngsters reacted to it.

Sarah read:

The Brilliance of Hue

The fall, late in its arrival,
strives to hold on to an age long since
removed.
Four months from summer's beginning
autumn has yet to show color;
lost in the withered greenery of a season past its time.
Is this a sign of youth?
Or of summer trying to place itself
in a misbegotten way?
One must wonder whether these green leaves,
lost in early reverie,
will ever reveal their brilliant hue
by growing old.
(F. Sengmeuller).

"That's beautiful," said Sarah. "She must have been a very talented person, to do great science and then write beautiful poetry."

"Not all scientists show an artistic side. She clearly had some Leonardo da Vinci in her," said Jesus.

"Who's Leonardo?" asked Sarah.

Jason piped up, "He's the famous painter who drew the Mona Lisa."

Jesus used his NIT to project an image of that painting, which Sarah instantly recognized.

"He wasn't just an artist?" she asked.

"No," said Jesus, "He was as much a scientist as an artist."

With that, Ximena asked Sarah and Jason if they could move outside and explore the creek area for a couple of hours. She explained that two other guests were coming to the house, and Jesus and she needed privacy for that meeting. Though Jason had already been told by Tavon about Ximena's real father coming to visit, he pretended he was unaware and agreed to go exploring with his sister.

Ximena was fighting to quell her nerves. Tavon Brooks and her father were on their way.

CHAPTER 21

TAVON BROOKS AND AHMED Iftikhar arrived at Ximena's house well into the afternoon. They planned to sit down with Ximena and Jesus, have Tavon speak first, hope for some positive response from Ximena, then let her and Ahmed converse with each other, probably on their own.

Jesus was hesitant about the meeting, and only agreed to allow it because Tavon informed him that Ahmed was shifting his priorities against the Authority, and he figured that might open the door with Ximena. Jesus had informed Ximena about the plan, and he could not believe she agreed to it.

Ximena and Jesus stood at the doorway ready for their guests. They were spared the direct sunlight they would have encountered if they had stood there a couple of hours earlier. The angle of the sun's rays had shifted and shadows lengthened such that the front steps were checkered with multiple umbrae from garden plants and flowers. The air was humid and warm, though hints of summer's final stretch abounded: the waning hue of the leaves of the poplars, the tranquility of fewer insects, and the hummingbirds abandoning their nests and headed to Mexico with their young.

Tavon approached first along the walkway, and as he came into focus for Ximena she said to herself that he looked as striking as ever. The man trailing behind him had broad shoulders and a Middle Eastern complexion. She knew he must be her father, and she avoided eye contact.

The two guests followed Ximena and Jesus into the foyer.

Ahmed felt surprisingly good; his nerves were under control. He tried his best to appear relaxed using body language techniques he learned through courses at the Authority. Moving slowly and confidently was the key.

Everyone introduced themselves but not before Tavon reminded them all to speak naturally and to avoid using their NITs. They proceeded to the dining room and sat down at the large mahogany

Hugues Chevalier table. Jesus and Ximena positioned themselves on one side, directly across from Ahmed and Tavon. Ximena noted Tavon's eyes, exuding the capacity for sharp logic. His deep black skin and fancy dreadlocks simply added to his persona. She still had not looked at her father.

Tavon began by asking, "Where are those youngsters, Jason and Sarah?"

Jesus replied, "They're out exploring the creek, which runs adjacent to the west side of the backyard. Lots of flora and fauna there to mingle with."

"Well hopefully I can say hi to them later on," Tavon replied. He then kicked things off, "Today is an important day for both Ximena and Ahmed. Their connection is most fundamental: Dr. Frieda Sengmeuller, who was Ximena's mother and Ahmed's wife. For Ximena, it is amazing that Ahmed has come here today to finally bridge a gap and reconnect with you, his daughter."

As his words began to sink in, Ximena's heart accelerated. Inside her welled the urge to lunge across the table at this man – to grab him by the throat with her good arm and strike him with her bad one.

Tavon detected Ximena's building emotion, but he pressed on, "In recent confidential meetings, Ahmed expressed to me the deepness of his conviction to finally do what Frieda would have wanted him to do, rather than avoiding things for so long. As you all know, Ahmed recently shifted his allegiance and is now working against the Authority. That's a blessing for us all. You should know that by meeting here today, Ahmed is not only changing his life, he's risking it."

Ahmed then spoke for the first time, turning to look at Ximena, who was looking down towards her lap. "Please, Ximena, forgive me for leaving you. Jesus, you did what a good man should, and for that I'm indebted. Forgive me, both of you, for wasting all of these years and –." Suddenly his jaw froze. He was whelmed with a visioned of her as a child, an innocent young child left alone. He pulled himself together to continue, "Believe me when I say I'm ready to move forward as your father, Xi, to try to make amends. You deserve –". His jaw locked up again and he looked longingly up to the ceiling.

Jesus spoke, "Ahmed is here today to take a positive step towards redemption with you, Xi."

For the first time in two hundred years, Ximena looked directly at her father. Their eyes locked for a few seconds, but it felt like an hour to him as she peered right through him. In a trice, she jumped up and the full weight of her bad arm swung across the table, just glancing off his cheekbone and hitting the chandelier hard.

Her healing mitt dislodged and fell onto the table.

The lights wobbled and jangled above. Shadows of yellow dodged across the walls.

Everyone's eyes were not drawn to the healing mitt – but to her exposed hand, a gruesome red and purple mass wielded at eye level.

Ximena cried out, "You asshole! ... how dare you show your face!"

She darted out of the room and out the porch door.

Ahmed broke the silence first, "I'm so sorry everyone. I should have figured." He walked over to the back window and peered longingly into the backyard, but she had already disappeared into the gardens. His face bore the scars of emotional self-cutting.

Turning to look at Jesus, he said, "Time, even when you have tons of it, is too important to waste, and I've wasted it both in my work and in my personal life. People may never understand why I left. Even I don't completely understand. I must have had a nervous breakdown after your daughter's suicide, just walked away from any reminders of her. Ximena was, of course, the biggest reminder. Please, please, I don't expect anyone to forgive me here and now, but maybe you can understand just a bit. I abandoned her, and I'll try for as long as it takes to make up for that."

Ahmed stared desirously out the window again, to the far reaches of the yard. Under his breath, he whispered, "Please ... please ... let me back in, Xi." He then stated more loudly, "Witnessing her innocence and beauty today makes me certain I'm doing the right thing. She ... has her mother's eyes, have I ever told her that? Seeing her today was like having her mother's soul return."

Tavon then turned to Jesus, "Though the task will be arduous and risky, I'm also proud to be putting my mind to the right cause: to exposing the corruption involved in age-decoding and revealing the truth to those who have for so long vested their goodwill with the Authority. The Fundamental Platform, I hope, will be shown for what it is. Of course, we can't do any of this if we're not genuine ... that's why Ahmed finally tried to reconnect with Xi today."

Jesus requested that they provide him with more details, "Corruption is a serious word," he said sternly.

Ahmed promptly filled him in, describing how the Authority deactivated peoples' propensity to dissent, rendering them less capable of political challenge. The ease with which he told Jesus this belied the longstanding top-secret nature of the subject: nobody outside Core6, not even anyone in Apex200, was aware.

"Less capable of political challenge? Are you serious?" asked Jesus.

Ahmed nodded his head, then said, "All age-decoded humans have been set, without them knowing, to a very minimal level of potential dissent, that is, to high compliance with rules of authority. Rendered sycophants. In many societies and political systems, this can happen, using means such as dictatorship, propaganda, materialism, magic, and religion. But in this case, it happened through genetic engineering."

Jesus contemplated for a few seconds, then observed, "That helps explain the durability of the Fundamental Platform, why no political challenge has ever been mounted." A second, more personal thought came to him, which he did not share: he saw his life split into two diametrically opposite periods: the first great and productive; the second encumbered, listless. It all horrified and disgusted him.

Jesus gathered himself for a few seconds, then asked, "If everyone who was age-decoded lost their propensity to dissent, why is Ximena working for the Rethinking Party? Do either of you know how that could be?"

Tavon answered, "The deactivation of the propensity to dissent was not genetically efficacious in about one out of every two hundred subjects. Ximena may be in that small fraction of exceptions, which still amounted to about fifty million people across Zone1. But Ximena's behavior might also be explained by the fact that a propensity of a trait represents a tendency, not anything absolute. So eubeings could potentially dissent if pushed hard enough by their feelings and thoughts. What I'm saying is that for someone like Ximena, strong internal forces could override a deactivated propensity to dissent."

The conversation between the three of them extended for about half an hour. Ahmed spoke, mostly, while Tavon and Jesus soaked up what they could. He told them he was certain he had made the right decision in trying to meet with Ximena today, and that her intense anger towards him was not a surprise. He also confided that he believed the events of today would help him rebuild his relationship with her.

As Jesus listened, his respect for Ahmed grew. He too was pleased by today's developments. He now understood the latter part of his life – his inertness, his lack of resolve. Things also crystallized for him on a grander, non-personal scale. He now understood the secret, antiseptic manner by which the Authority rode the laurels of genetic engineering.

As their conversation neared its end, Jesus surmised for everyone, "I have learned much with our meeting. Now I see why, after age-decoding, I was out of tune, critically. I had excess *dukkha*, or suffering, the First Noble Truth of Buddhism, and not enough *marga*, or liberation, the Fourth Noble Truth. I lost what Buddhists call *mindfulness*."

Though Ahmed and Tavon found Jesus's pontifications amusing, they nodded respectfully in unison.

When Ahmed and Tavon got up to leave, Jesus thanked them both for their bravery and honesty. Turning to Ahmed, he added, "Don't worry too much about Xi. As she calms down, I believe she'll put much thought into your efforts today."

Tavon thanked everyone for their time and reminded them to safeguard everything about the meeting.

Meanwhile, pacing solo in her favorite backyard garden, Ximena imagined herself giving Ahmed a long-awaited, exalted hug. He was, at last, her redeemed father. She pictured him taking her good hand in his and tenderly saying, "I love you." Blissfulness consumed her in this hypothetical state.

On the drive home, Tavon assured Ahmed that he took every precaution to ensure their meeting with Ximena and Jesus was beyond Authority scrutiny. Nevertheless, Ahmed remained edgy about the whole thing. "I'm used to snooping, not being snooped on. I don't like the feeling coming from the other direction."

"Nobody likes being snooped on," replied Tavon.

Ahmed nodded, then said, "One more thing, speaking of snooping. Before you drop me off, I'm going to give you the deactivation code for FENCODE_11. That's the code needed to debilitate its surveillance in a specific setting. You or I may need to avail ourselves of this code in the near future. We must, however, be extremely cautious in our approach."

"OK, then, what's the code?"

"For heaven's sake, I can't just give it to you. I'll tell you how to derive it, OK?"

Tavon waited, amused.

"I base it on my lucky number: thirteen. I don't know if you're aware, but Chromosome 13 of the human genome spans contains about 113 million base pairs in one strand of the DNA. The double-helix strands of DNA are each composed of millions of nucleotides of four possible types: adenine (A), cytosine (C), guanine (G), and thymine (T). Base pairs are two nucleotides that bond across the double helix. They bond in a complementary manner, such that a C on one strand always bonds with a G on the other strand, and an A always bonds with a T."

"OK," said Tavon, bemused, "Where is this headed?"

Ahmed explained, "I took the luxury of reverse-rounding that to 113,113,113. I then figured out the number of composition permutations possible for chromosome13, making use of the four possible base pairings." He stopped to notice Tavon grinning even more, then added, "Combinatorics mathematics puts the total possible genetic codings for this single chromosome at $4^{113113113}$. The result, which has more than six million digits, is of course impossible to remember. But I don't want a code I can remember. Why should I commit to surface memory something so important? I'll never forget how to arrive at the number since the way of determining it is so wacky."

"It's wacky, alright. It's not as large as the famous Graham's number ... but I do like it!" cried Tavon.

It was evident to them both that their partnership had enormous potential. As Ahmed stepped from the vehicle, he said, "Thanks for setting up today's reunion, Tavon. It was the right thing to do."

"You're welcome, my friend. I do believe she'll come around."

CHAPTER 22

FRIEDA YEARNED TO HEAR anything about her loved ones Xi, Ahmed, and Jesus. But whenever she asked Gupta for information about them, she was stonewalled.

That was Gupta, she mused, phlegmatic as ever.

After a few years, Frieda gave up asking, though her wondering never ceased.

Once, after almost one century of captivity, Gupta was delivering some supplies to Frieda's apartment and made the unusual move of sitting down at her kitchen table. Frieda took that as an invitation to chat, and they did, reminiscing about working together as young genomicists well before the discovery of age-decoding. The conversation lasted about half an hour. For the first time in her captivation, Gupta spoke to her as a person, not as a captive. Frieda was careful not to broach the topic of her own family, but they did talk about things such as whether age-decoding worked in the long term (yes it did, perfectly) and whether global warming became the disaster most expected (not quite, as nuclear fusion technology obviated the need for carbon-based energy by 2075). She felt a fresh little connection forming between her and Gupta, and was about to offer her a refreshment when suddenly Gupta stood up and announced that their discussion was just a ruse, a test to see if Frieda still enjoyed feeling like a human. Gupta promised it would be the last genuine conversation between them. She kept her word.

This evening, as with most, Frieda asked herself, what has become of my dear Xi? When I was taken away, she was just ten years old, a lovely soul, the daughter I had always dreamed of. She had already exhibited scientific curiosity and talent. She was naturally awestruck by new knowledge, though I tried not to overwhelm her, and I didn't want her taking things too seriously since she was just a child. Xi never stopped asking me questions about my work, about the human genome, the aging proteome, age-decoding, and ELSI. Indeed, she showed special interest in the ELSI project, sensing even at her early age that it was vital to "counterbalance" the unfettered application of age-decoding. Has my dear Xi become a genomicist, like me? Or has she pursued some other passion?

My eyes are now tearing up. But what is the point of my crying? Nobody will see my tears, except perhaps Gupta, who will ignore me, or, worse yet, revel in my sadness.

Whenever I reflect upon Xi, I have this strange recurring thought that she's suffering more than she should. I don't mean suffering in missing me, but in some other, abnormal way. I don't know why I think so. It disheartens me, and I wish I could reach out and help her as a mother should. I can only hope that Ahmed is looking after her.

Frieda's eyes were still watery as she answered the door to let in Gupta, who brought dinner: chicken parmesan, with beet and spinach salad, and a glass of soda water.

Gupta walked straight to the kitchen table to deposit it.

"Here you go, Frieda. What the fuck are we crying about now?"

With that, Gupta departed without another word.

Her nastiness did not overly affect Frieda, as she had grown to expect it. Still, she missed the days when she could count on someone to console her. Ahmed was always the best at that. She wondered, what has become of him? I know he chose to be *age-decoded*, so he must still be alive, middle-aged, and healthy. He's likely met another woman, probably settled down long ago with someone to help him raise Xi. Xi's new mother. Bless her soul and her love for them. Does Ahmed work at a University? For the government? For a private company? Has he started his own business, or returned to school to earn another PhD? With him living so long I can only wager that someone with a mind like him would earn multiple doctorates. Ahmed wasn't just a one-dimensional statistical whiz. He had interests in many areas, including literature and poetry. What I would give to know how his life is going! Does he think often of me? Does he hate or resent me for what I did? Does he blame himself? He had nothing to do with it! Those who did this to me did this to him.

And what about Jesus? What has become of Dad? Is he alive? I doubt it. He'd never have succumbed to the allure of age-decoding. He's too much a purist and a critic. I can only guess he lived for ten or twenty more years after they took me, then died a natural death. I cherish and miss Jesus, though I'll never see him again. I was blessed to have him as my father, and always proud of his rebellious but thoughtful nature. Such an intelligent, interesting man he was! What insurrections was he churning in his final years? I'm sure he was stirring some pots. Of anyone I know, Jesus is the one I think most likely to suspect my death was not a suicide.

Frieda decided to cease her ruminations, so she pulled up a short story she had just written a few days ago, a work she hoped someday would be read by many others.

Why not read it to herself? She could appreciate its message here and now.

She curled up on the couch, took a sip of her soda water, and began reading *Russell the Real Scientist*:

> *Russell Wezword is a person I'll never forget. Smart and wide-eyed, forever argumentative, he'd draw you into any debate then throw you back out again two hours later and never let you forget he'd beaten you with his logical whip.*

> *He was a Real Scientist. A damned good one, according to what people said. In the area of Physics his PhD thesis had caused chaos in the National Institute of Technocracy (NIT) because Real Scientists had found his results too amazing to be true – despite his rock-solid experimental procedures and statistics. It all had something to do with refuting the theory of the 11th dimension. Anyone who tried explaining it to me was, of course, wasting their time, so I won't even begin trying to explain it to you.*

In the year 2079, eleven floors down in the NIT lab area, Russell and I first met. He was finishing his thesis work at the time and I was just starting mine. In those days practically anyone who got through high school went on to do a PhD. Adjacent to the Physics wing, in the Nutritional Soft Science Lab, I worked trying to recruit subjects for a study having to do with Vitamin D as a possible cure for the common cold. Ten years ago it had been proven Vitamin C didn't work. So my thesis advisor, Dr. Morrison, was counting on Vitamin D to take his place in history.

I wasn't so big on the Vitamin D idea. Or nutrition in general. I had wanted to study sociology, but only one University in North America still offered this course and it was rumored to be severely underfunded.

So off I went one day, obediently, to recruit subjects who would catch a cold then binge on Vitamin D for the sake of Soft Science and especially Dr. Morrison.

That's how I met Russell Wezword.

"Want to be in a nutrition study?" I asked him in the hallway.

"I don't subscribe to the efficacy of vitamin therapy," was his immediate reply. The guy sounded like a computer.

I reasoned with him. "We'll pay $1000 for each two-hour session, plus you'll get three square meals a day for an entire week."

"To the money, I'm indifferent because it's insubstantial. But the meals are enticing, I must admit." He paused and looked directly at me for the first time. "So the latter factor is enough to persuade me."

"Great," I said and got his name and number. "I'll call you soon."

He ended up being a pain in the neck as a subject. We supplied terrific meals; he complained about high-density free radical additives. We supplied all the Kleenex he could ever need; he pointed out that Kleenex had recently been linked to nose cancer. We supplied reams of video entertainment; he demanded reading materials.

And it soon became apparent that he knew much more than I did about nutrition.

"I'll never understand you nutritionists," he said to me one day in the lab as I monitored his heart rate and blood pressure. "You're more like psychologists because although you play with people's diets you are really tampering with their minds until it becomes possible to hypnotize billions of people into believing Vitamin C can cure their cold." He coughed. "Then it takes half a century for one of you to discover you were all wrong about Vitamin C. So what happens next? Vitamin D, the next letter in the alphabet soup of megavitamin therapy research, becomes the most likely hero. How Soft Scientific!

I should explain that currently, students studied either Soft Sciences or Real Sciences. All University programs were either one or the other and it was no secret that most of the good minds and money went to the Real Sciences.

I struggled to re-attach an electrode that had fallen off his chest. "Well," I said, "Most of us –"

"And don't think I'm not aware of the connections between the NIT Nutritional Soft Science Lab and the vitamin industry. If I wasn't a starving graduate student I wouldn't be here right now earning tainted LIVECO dollars."

LIVECO was the world monopoly supplier of Vitamins A through W.

"Mind you," he added, "it's impossible for a Soft Scientist like you to completely understand this in the purely sequential, logical, unbiased manner we Real Scientists do. I just try to disseminate whatever I can to Soft Scientists and hope they take in as much as possible, and approach a partial understanding almost by osmosis.

I was Soft and Russell was Real, but, believe it or not, we became good friends. Often we went drinking after long days in the lab and I let him impress me with his wondrous knowledge base and amazing reasoning abilities. His lectures would be in full swing before the first gulp of beer hit our stomachs. And I lost many bets with Russell over the next couple of years – mostly over trivial things like who invented the self-cleaning garage or what year the ozone layer completely disappeared. I once bet him over the origin of the word knowledge. I thought it was Latin but he didn't waste any time proving that it was Greek. That bet cost me $500. I was *sure I'd get him back good when he offered to take the Black Sox in the opener of the 2020 World Series. The Expos were favored, so I put more than the usual on them. They lost 7-0. "As I say," he told me afterward, "Real Scientists know the factors best so you're destined to lose in the end, bud."*

Russell tended to call me "bud" when collecting a win. I didn't mind it, but I wasn't crazy about it.

Life didn't change much for either of us over the next few years. Russell continued to win all wagers and we both got our PhDs. My thesis wasn't nearly the hit his was, though, for in the meantime several Soft Scientists from all over the world had independently found that Vitamin E, not D, was the cure for the common cold. Dr. Morrison missed fame by one letter.

"The Real Science notions of today," Russell expounded one night at the Grad Club Pub, "will become the true laws of tomorrow." He paused, sipped his beer, then went on "Tomorrow, the environment will be perfectly protected because today Real Scientists are rapidly amalgamating all information concerning its preservation. Technology will respond appropriately because Real Science will respond, and Real Science will respond because we have faith in it."

"True," I nodded.

"And within 30 or 40 years all nonatheists will become atheists. God or Allah or Gautama or Graham will be rendered redundant because the rigorous domains of nonchaotic Real Science will have satisfied all humans – Soft or Real – in both the spiritual and rational sense. It's happening already. Did you know that over half our current population is atheist? Back in the 1960s, it was only 1%. In the 1990's it was 20%. Today it's over 60% and rising!"

"Hmmm," I said.

"And no more will countries be required to spend up to one-third of their GDPs on space defense systems because the sheer intricacies of the new offense-oriented developments will prove indefensible, making all defense programs either obsolete or imponderably expensive." He stopped and took

one long guzzle, then said, "Man and woman will become supreme Real controllers."

"All this within 30 or 40 years?" I asked.

"Plus or minus ten."

"That soon?"

"Certainly. Technocracy, the wave of the present, will be the ocean of the near future," he said, poetically. "By then our knowledge base – now doubling every three years, will have increased a thousand times. By then rationalism will reign supreme, and ideas such as God and the afterlife will be extinct."

"Extinct? The afterlife too?" I asked. His last comment had disturbed me a bit because—though I was not certain about the idea of God – I had always thought there was life after death in one way or another. It seemed natural and hopeful.

"Of course the afterlife too!" he cried.

"Wanna bet on it?" I asked, reflexively.

"What?"

"I'll bet you there's an afterlife of some sort," I said.

"OK. Let's wager the usual amount," he said, then added, "As usual, I'm betting for the principle of it, bud, not the money."

As we shook hands I noticed the sweat beads which had built up over each of Russell's eyebrows because he had done so much energetic talking. And continue to talk he did that night.

All the while I found myself smiling more and more on the inside as it gradually dawned on me that I may have made a bet that I couldn't lose! Here's why: if after we died, there was no afterlife, then neither Russell or I would exist so I wouldn't be able to pay Russell his winnings. On the other hand, I couldn't possibly be required to pay Russell before we died because we had to die first to discover if there was an afterlife.

So I might win, but I couldn't lose!

I was only a Soft Scientist, but to me, the logic of it all seemed very nice.

If Russell ever saw this logic, he never admitted it. I didn't expect him to. What was entertaining, however, was his up-front cockiness as he showed me Real article after Real article proving the nonexistence of the afterlife. For instance, he spent an entire afternoon with me at McWalldin's Bar and Grill reading out loud to me a study by Dr. Rushenwhale et al. which proved within 99.7% certainty that when you died neither your mind nor your soul lived on. They had used electromagnetic Green-particle waves to get their results. According to Russell, any research based on Green-particle was big these days.

"We'll only know for sure after we die," was my simple response. Then I'd change the topic if I could.

The details of the rest of our lives on earth I shall spare except a few. Russell died at the age of 76, suddenly, a victim of the deadly Ho Chi Minh flu, just two weeks after having been named Honorary Chair of the Real Science Society. I died three years later, idiotically, in a drinking accident – crashed head-on into a parked police car after being waved over for a breathalyzer test.

Yet I died with something to prove.

Yes, I met Russell up there.

Yes, he was embarrassed to see me.

"Here's your money," he said the moment I arrived.

"Thanks," I said.

"No problem," he said, floating in front of me with a funny look on his face. "Up here you'll find that money doesn't do much good anyway."

"Oh?"

"It's practically useless," he said, grinning now. "Which makes your winnings worthless, which means –"

"Principle," I interrupted.

"What?" he asked.

"Principle," I repeated. "That's why you said you bet – for the principle, not the money."

My friend hovered there for a bit and did not say a thing.

Finally, I spoke, "Well, I'd better get going. I've got an appointment to go to."

"Sociology Club?" he asked.

"I'm not sure. I've just been told it's with someone important. We'll talk soon ... eh bud?

"Yeah ... soon," was all Russell the Real Scientist said before coasting away in a daze and I knew he meant it.

Reading this story made Frieda feel good about the work she had done on the ELSI project. It vindicated her, validated her, and, most importantly, gave her some good company.

CHAPTER 23

AGE-DECODED

FRIEDA HAD NOTIFIED Gupta months ago that reverse-aging technology was "good to go" whenever the Authority needed it. For Gupta, this was a tremendous boost, because she had told Reubers that the risk of containing Frieda was worth the potentially huge reward, and this unfolding of events was proving her right. They were about to hit the jackpot, and Gupta would soon bask in the accolades from Reuber and, more saliently, from the Nobel Committee.

Today Gupta was taking the first step in setting forth the machinations for bringing reverse-aging to the people in Zone1. The entire Core6 realized the importance of a reverse-aging rollout before the next election, which was to take place in three months. Since elections took place just once every thirty years, why not lock in the political advantage now?

And who in the Authority did Reubers and Gupta choose to collaborate with Frieda on the implementation?

They selected Ahmed Iftikhar himself.

Gupta had two compelling reasons for using Ahmed. First, she knew that Ahmed was a numerical crackerjack, so he would be perfect for organizing an efficient rollout. His project management skills were second to none.

Second, she wanted to play a mind game on Frieda. She planned to divulge Ahmed's identity to Frieda beforehand so that her working with Ahmed would be frustrating and agonizing, akin to mental torture. Yes, Frieda could speak to him through the muffle-altered CG mechanism, listen to him, be closer to him than she had been for the past two centuries. But how could she reach out to him? How could she embrace him? Moreover, since Ahmed would not know it was Frieda, how could either of them genuinely connect?

Gupta planned to revel in Frieda's frustration and Ahmed's ignorance. Their conversation she would closely monitor: if Frieda lent Ahmed a single hint of who she was, Gupta would terminate everything and raise a figurative sword drawn from above Frieda's head. It would be a unique mind game, Gupta joked to herself. Tantalizingly fun.

Ahmed's collaboration with the CG required him to visit a special setup located in the Authority's New York headquarters. He was met at the cavernous steel-beamed entrance to Block3, then escorted by Dr. Gupta Mantharathna along several monochrome silver metallic corridors, planes of unfinished molded concrete interrupted occasionally by large metallic mauve taupe triangular prisms, then five levels down an elevator to the basement and finally along a nondescript hallway to Room B5R0248. The room was square, pint-sized, more like a booth, with grey walls, one ceiling light, and two speakers at head level.

Gupta motioned for Ahmed to seat himself in a sizable leather chair located in the center of the room.

"Well Gupta, I must say it'll be an absolute treat to work with the CG once and for all," said Ahmed. "I hear he's an immense talent. Is he confident this is ready to roll?

Gupta was already chuckling to herself, as Ahmed was assuming that the CG was a man. "He sure is, Ahmed, the CG sure is."

"Is the CG aware he's working with me, that is, can I disclose my identity?"

"Yes."

"Also, will the CG know that I was Frieda's spouse?"

"Yes. Just don't dwell on it because you have much work to do and the CG's time is precious."

Gupta placed a one-foot diameter silver concave metallic device over Ahmed's head, tightening it as you would a bicycle helmet.

"OK, you're set to go. All the best."

"Thanks."

Gupta left the room and the lights dimmed significantly.

Frieda, immensely excited and eager, kicked things off, xxAhmed xxIftikhar, xxis xxthat xxyou?

yyYes, yythis yyis yyAhmed yyIftikhar. yyI'm yyhonored yyto yybe yyworking yywith yyyou.

Right then Frieda desired to reach out and touch his hand, hug him, kiss him, even if she could not recognize his voice. Her heart was fluttering, but she fought to control her emotions.

Gupta, listening to them talk but and also viewing Frieda on her apartment monitor, was pleasured by Frieda's obvious frustration.

xxWell, xxit's xxnice xxto xxbe xxworking xxwith xxyou, xxtoo, xxAhmed. xxWe xxhave xxa xxgood xxproduct xxthat xxis xxready xxto xxbe xxdelivered xxto xxa xxdeserving xxpeople. xxAre xxyou xxup xxto xxthe xxtask?

yyIndeed yyI yyam. yySpectre yySocieties yywe'll yymake yyuse yyof yyagain. yyI've yyalready yycalculated yythe yyper yyunit yyapplication yytime, yyassuming yythirty yyminutes yyper yyperson. yyDoes yythat yysound yyreasonable?

xxYes. xxYou'll xxneed xxabout xxfive xxminutes xxto xxsettle xxthem xxin, xxfifteen xxminutes xxto xxapply xxthe xxCRISPR xxengineering, xxfive xxminutes xxto xxadminister xxthe xxliquid xxmixture, xxand xxfive xxminutes xxto xxcheck xxthem xxout.

Ahmed, responded, yyI've yyalready yygot yythe yynumbers yyfor yytotal yyexpected yyunits, yyand yywith yythree yymonths yyto yydo yythis yywe'll yyhave yyto yyutilize yythe yySpectre yySocieties yyall yyday yyand yyall yynight.

The way he expressed himself so assuredly convinced Frieda that this conversation was authentic, that she was talking with the real Ahmed. Gupta had duped her before, but not this time.

Frieda explained, xxWell, xxthat's xxnot xxa xxproblem. xxThe xxpeople xxwill xxline xxup xxeven xxin xxthe xxmiddle xxof xxthe xxnight xxto xxget xxthis. xxI xxassure xxyou xxthey'll xxgo xxfor xxit xxas xxmuch xxas xxthey xxwent xxfor xxage-xxdecoding, xxespecially xxthose xxmiddle-xxaged xxor xxolder.

Frieda had to be honest with herself. She would never see the light of day past this rollout, no matter how successful its implementation. Would this conversation today be the closest she would ever come to reuniting with Ahmed? After so long waiting, was this it?

She continued, xxI xxunderstand xxthat xxyou xxwere xxthe xxhusband xxof xxDr. xxFrieda xxSengmeuller, xxthe xxrenowned xxscientist xxwho xxinvented xxage-xxdecoding. xxHer xxwork xxwas xxextraordinary."

Gupta was readying to send Frieda a caution signal, as the conversation was getting personal, but she held back because Frieda was not giving direct hints about herself. Besides, it was entertaining to see her desperately reaching out.

yyIndeed, yyshe yywas yymy yydear yywife, yyan yyamazing yyscientist, yya yygreat yymother. yyI yydearly yymiss yyher yyto yythis yyday.

Frieda's eyes teared up and she could not speak. She turned away from her microphone. Whether or not Gupta would punish her for her silence because it might send a signal to Ahmed would remain to be seen. But there was no way she could control herself, and in some defeated way, she didn't care. She longed to ask him directly about Ximena and Jesus, to open a small window into their current lives. But that was impossible, of course, so she purged the thought and pulled herself together.

Their tortuous silence brought much joy to Gupta. Never had silence so delighted her.

Ahmed restarted the conversation, yyI yyalways yymarveled yyat yyher yywork yyethic. yyI've yynever yyseen yyanyone yyso yydedicated, yyand yyprobably yynever yyagain yywill.

Those tender words danced across Frieda's wakened, yearning soul. She replied, xxWell, xxyou xxhave xxmy xxcondolences, xxAhmed. xxI'm xxjust xxthrilled xxto xxbe xxcarrying xxon xxand xxextending xxher xxwork xxinto xxthe xxrealm xxof xxreverse-xxaging. Her voice was cracking, but the effect was filtered by the muffle-altered system. She pressed on, xxMost xxof xxwhat xxwe've xxaccomplished xxon xxthat xxfront, xxI xxand xxmy xxteam xxof xxscientists, xxborrows xxheavily xxfrom xxher xxfindings xxand xxtechniques. xxI xxknow xxher xxwork xxbetter xxthan xxanyone xxin xxthe xxworld.

Gupta caught that last comment and did not like it. Frieda was going too far. But Gupta held back from disconnecting them, and as it turned out that was the only hint Frieda dropped for the rest of the conversation, which proved perfunctory to the end.

When the CG and Ahmed concluded their session, the microphones were disabled and the muffle-altered system wound down. Ahmed sat in his chair and contemplated. In conversing with the CG, he found that he had formed a strange bond with its voice, certainly more than could be accounted for by its role as the CG. It was an intuitive, positive bond that Ahmed could feel but not rationalize.

The room lights brightened and Gupta re-entered.

"You can get up now," she said to him.

As Ahmed rose from the chair, he said to her, "I'm curious, Gupta. Why did you and Reubers choose me to collaborate with the CG, of all the potential people within our government?"

"Because you're the best, Ahmed. You're top drawer. And this project is just too important."

Ahmed's countenance brightened, but later, when he thought about what she had said, he could not shake the suspicion that she had demeaned him. In all of his time with the Authority, not once had he held that feeling.

Frieda, seated at her window, stared out but saw nothing. She tried to calm down. To her, the conversation she just had with Ahmed made things worse, not better. In no way did it bring her closer to Ahmed. Knowing what they had done to her was enough to convince her there must be so many other wrongdoings associated with this Authority. She asked herself, what was the nature of those wrongdoings? and was Ahmed aware of them, or, worse, complicit in them?

Fifteen minutes later Gupta was standing at the doorway of her apartment, asking, "How did it go with the CG?"

"Good. We made significant progress on the rollout," said Frieda.

"You also made progress in revealing your identity. You'll pay for that."

CHAPTER 24

ONE HOUR AFTER HIS communication with the CG, Ahmed was invited to a meeting in the President's office. When he entered the conference room, Reubers was already there waiting for him along with Zhinghu and Gupta. They looked somber. Something must be up.

Reubers stood up and paced while the others waited for him to say something. Betrayal allegations were serious, and Reubers had to be convinced. Before this meeting, Gupta had done just that. Her argument was: Ahmed's visit to the Spectre Society, which she learned of a few weeks ago via a FENCODE_11 alert, indicated that Ahmed was mentally unstable, verging on killing himself. Additionally, they could never know if Ahmed had picked up on Frieda's clues today, and could not inquire about it with him directly, because that might render even more clues for him. Reubers and she had agreed that keeping the identity of the CG airtight was crucial, and Ahmed was the last person they wanted to be aware of the CG's identity. The fact that Ahmed was suicidal meant he might be open to sacrificing his life to reveal Frieda's captivity to the world, and who knows what else might he reveal about the Authority? Finally, they needed a way to punish Frieda for furnishing a hint about her identity. What better way to punish her than to torture her loved one?

Reubers finally stopped pacing, placed both hands on the table, and turned to Ahmed, clamping a piercing gaze upon him.

"It is with great regret, Dr. Iftikhar, that I inform you of a revelation made by Dr. Mantharathna, which was brought to my attention a few minutes ago. To you, however, it will not be a revelation, but an admission of betrayal to the Authority based on your recent visit to the Spectre Society as well as your conversation today with the CG."

A sinking feeling hit Ahmed. He dreaded what they knew or believed, and the consequences of these allegations. Where was the respect he deserved for his leadership on dozens of top priority Statistical Verification Agency projects? For always coming through as a crackerjack analyst? For his years of collaborative work with these people?

Ahmed quickly defended himself, "I have no idea what you're referring to, and I resent your implication that I'm betraying the Authority. In conversing with the CG, I was simply doing my duty to coordinate the near-future application of reverse-aging; that and no more."

The room fell eerily silent. The decision was already made. More talk would not change their minds.

Ahmed, becoming desperate, raised his voice, "How the hell can you accuse me of this, whatever this is?" But his pleading was met with more silence.

Nobody of Ahmed's stature within the Authority – certainly nobody in Core6 – had ever been subjected to *laserneurosplicing* torture (LNS), though it had been used effectively with a few in Apex200. Zhinghu was charged with the task of applying it to Ahmed.

Strangely, Zhinghu used this moment to divulge, "We can't afford any external evidence. LNS leaves no scars. It's all internal. We just want to send our comrade here a strong message. We don't need to know what he's been up to, where he's been, who he's seen ... we know enough of that ... we just need to see him squirm around for a while and think hard about his actions."

In making these bold statements, Zhinghu surprised even himself. The mutual respect he once held for Ahmed meant nothing now: a deep crevice had emerged that would never close up, especially after the torture.

It took four security guards to move Ahmed into the zero-gravity SI chamber. Once there, suspended in the middle of the space, he had nothing to latch onto and no way of propelling himself out.

Torture is beautiful, Zhinghu thought, since it approaches perfect control, which is a rarity in human undertakings. For perfect control, there must be perfect power, and torture has always been based on the use of power. The torturer uses power to control the pain of the victim. The stimulus is rooted in power; the response in a lack of power. Sometimes, Zhinghu reasoned, in a specific circumstance, humans assume they have achieved perfect power, smiling inwardly with self-confidence which belies their insecurities. Who of any of us has not at some time succumbed to complete self-assurance in a circumstance, to the feeling of perfect control?

These considerations by Zhinghu overlooked the fact that conquering was a charade: power and self-assurance always rendered unknown, unforeseen elements. As he watched Ahmed through the glass barrier, Zhinghu pondered more reasonably, admitting that the victim, not the torturer, might hold some power. The victim can withhold information, look the other way, refuse to divulge, and so in many ways exercise control through mustered willpower. While the torturer might be pleasured by the sufferings of the tortured, he would not enjoy the refusal of the victim to capitulate. Notwithstanding this, every tortured human had their limit, and if the torture is administered carefully, with ruthless precision through incremental, balanced episodes of pain, without offering escape – especially the escape of death – there comes a moment when the locus of control must shift to the torturer like ground shifting in a landslide. Upon that ground, Zhinghu planned to elevate himself.

He had heard claims that torture was most effective if others in society were aware of it: if everyone knows, everyone must be intimidated. However, he knew the Authority took the position that torture was most effective if conducted behind the scenes and for this reason, LNS was his method of choice.

Developed in the late 2100s, LNS used laser beams to irritate specific portions of the central nervous system. It held two key advantages compared to traditional methods of torture. First, it left no visible evidence. Though the pain was real for the victim, outward signs were nonexistent: not a scar, not a lesion, no blood, no burning, not a bump or a bruise. Second, it could be applied endlessly. For example, a male could be subjected to the rupturing of his testicles for hours on end, but the excruciating pain, real in itself, did not reflect any physical reality within the testicles themselves; it was simply the manifestation of laser bombardments of the central nervous system, usually in the brain, though sometimes lower, in the brain stem. This allowed for externally undetectable torture, for as long as needed.

The SI torture room was zero-gravity: the victim was suspended at the geometric centroid of the room, incapable of propelling themselves away from that location. Hence no need for chains, braces, or racks. Subjects were reduced to convulsing, squirming about, and flailing their limbs with nothing to hold on to except their own body parts. Three-dimensional real-time imaging of the victim's central nervous system enabled the laser to precisely bombard the victim's microanatomy. LNS focused on afferent (sensory) pathways.

In Ahmed's case, Zhinghu began with the lateral spinothalamic tract. He pressed a single control button and within seconds, a base-like humming noise permeated the room as the LNS bombarded Ahmed's lateral spinothalamic tract. The initial lasers induced general temperature reactions. Zhinghu watched as Ahmed began groaning and squirming. Ahmed felt his flesh heating, first his skin, then his deeper tissues. He tried not to move or react, but the pain built. Within a minute he was shrieking like a wild animal attacked by its worst predator.

No questions were asked by Zhinghu.

The laser then shifted to Ahmed's anterior spinothalamic tract, which brought intense pounding across all parts of Ahmed's body: calves and knees; back and groin; chest and arms; head and neck. Convulsing and clutching himself, Ahmed tried using his mind to harness something nonphysical. He witnessed his own body, as an external agent, separate from himself – proof, was it not, that he still held some control? Yet that control was brief and fleeting, outlasted by more and more and more pounding.

Finally, it stopped. Ahmed lay suspended in midair, exhausted. The room was quiet, except for the sound of labored breathing and sweat droplets hitting the floor below. He noticed his hands were still clenched.

Again, no questions were asked by Zhinghu.

Why aren't they interrogating me? Why aren't they trying to extract information? Perhaps this was just calisthenics for the main event?

He was right. Before he could think further, Zhinghu aggressively triggered Ahmed's limbic association cortex using L-9 intensity, which ushered in a myriad of vividly disturbing memories. First, a T-bone car accident when he was sixteen, which crushed the neck of his best friend Lucas. Then his grandmother's slow and painful battle with death from cervical cancer. Then Frieda's suicide, his feelings of shock and guilt. Then his breakdown and rejection of his daughter. Try as he may, dark memories and images infiltrated his limbic association cortex. He dug deep, bore everything with clenched teeth and fists, but failed to hold back the first wave of tears. His jaw ached as he worked hard to resist full-fledged wailing. He toiled to assert his will and clutch on to anything positive – anything – but his resolve was railroaded by negatives and nightmares. The tenacious LNS was unstoppable, all at the whim of Zhinghu. Ahmed's life shook and unraveled in detail. Xi lunged at him. Frieda's suicide harrowed him like a restless unnerving apparition. It all whelmed and pierced his cortex, racked his mind, cemented his despair with knife-edged harrowing: visceral, penetrating, guttural. His groans, though strong, did no justice to his agony. He was forced to replay a thousand times the unfortunate death of Frieda, whom he had never properly loved and whom he would never properly lament now. He tried in vain to control the agony, which, though he knew it to be psychological, was gristlier, tougher, more real than he could have imagined. He had done nothing in his life; worse, he had done less than nothing, working with the corrupt. Science, yes, but negative science. So many right things he could have done, furnished as he was with Frieda's example. So many right paths he could have taken by her side. Things he could have done to help her. But he had gone the other way, left his only child, lived for himself for two hundred fucking years.

Squirming and screaming now, Ahmed spied Xi looking at him from the top corner of the room, pointing, smiling, laughing, but not in a joyful way. Moments later, Jesus appeared two feet above him, floating in the Buddha position, peering down and shaking his head, repeating *apatrapya, apatrapya, apatrapya*. Guilt and agony merged into one hell for Ahmed. His pained nerves and crystallized selfishness narrowed to one clear end: Frieda had been so good; he had been so bad. He was tearing apart with agony and could imagine his shameful due. Hamlet's *dread of something after death* permeated his throbbing skull, which was undergoing a final rupture. He would never see Frieda again. Never love her again. He had no right to go where she was.

"Stop Zhinghu! What do you want from me? I'll do anything! I admit it! I was talking with Rethinking. Stop!"

That admission registered with Zhinghu, but he did not yet stop the LNS. This was worse than torture, Ahmed thought, because there was no way out, nothing more he could confess, therefore nothing he could give in to. Just torture for torture's sake. If only

I had followed through at the Spectre Society. I should have ended myself then.

One risk of LNS torture was heart failure for the victim. The isometric contraction of so many muscles can induce a strong cardiac reflex, triggering a heart attack.

Heart failure indeed came upon Ahmed. As the attack took hold, he became aware of a shift in his pain locations and guessed correctly what was happening to him. Oddly, it satisfied him as he envisioned the white suicide room in the Spectre Society, spied the alluring, androgynous robot hostess Lolita, soaked up the titillating options for inner peace ... the torture is here for me, the torture is now, the torture is worth it, the torture is done.

As Ahmed's blood flow gradually wound down, his waning mind mustered up one last thought: Frieda deserved better and I deserved this. Then his blood flow ceased and his body went limp.

Zhinghu noticed what had happened and stepped back from the controls. He was furious with himself. This death put him in jeopardy because Ahmed was a *bona fide* leader, revered by the SI Committee, Apex200, and Core6. He nervously contacted Reubers, first mentioning that Ahmed had confessed to collaborating with Rethinking, then explaining that a cardiac arrest had unfortunately taken Ahmed's life. Zhinghu expected tongue-lashing and reprisals. Surprisingly, Reubers calmly suggested that they find a way to use Ahmed's death to their advantage.

Within two minutes Reubers convened a full virtual meeting of the SI Committee, Apex200, and Core6. The virtual room quickly filled up with expectant members, as this was not a scheduled affair. Their excitement quickly turned sour when Zhinghu hammered them all for allowing a traitor to operate in their midst. He issued a threat, his piercing eyes ravaging the pictoplath, "If I get word that any of you are acting in a similar vein, I'll use LNS on you for weeks, not hours. It'll be like hell everlasting."

Zhinghu stopped, and both he and Reubers glared out across the crowd of fearful holographic faces.

The young Tavon Brooks was not the only one to recoil from their threat. But his blood was boiling more than anyone. Who the hell did these people think they were? His mind harkened back to many things at once: his growing up in the poverty-stricken areas of Detroit, living only with his mother in a rundown apartment complex known as The Mews; the grade school bullying, with few friends; his hard work through middle and high school, always at the top of his class; scholarships offers from Stanford, Harvard, Cornell, Johns Hopkins, UCLA, and MIT; hard work again through his chosen program: Statistics and Data Science at MIT. Did he persevere through all of that – for this?

The two leaders waited for someone, anyone, to respond, but that would never happen, for two reasons: the system was set on unidirectional, and, even if they could, nobody would dare.

One hour later Gupta was at Frieda's apartment informing her that Ahmed had been tortured, not for his sins, but hers. She sadistically elaborated on the LNS technique, though she neglected to share the detail that Ahmed had been killed.

CHAPTER 25

JESUS AROSE FROM BED abnormally, with a briskness and vigor that contrasted with his normal feeling of the past two centuries. His spunk was underpinned by his desire to overturn the trappings of his old frame and get something done in a meaningful way, on a grander scale. Peering through the top floor window he took in what his old eyes could: the shapes of distant trees, the glare of the sun, the immediate dew on the glass. He felt much younger, like the old days, when ideas sprung eagerly forward – buoyed by positives.

Today his soul was about to beget his true human capacity. He called out to Ximena, but she was still asleep. Walking into the bathroom, he nearly bumped into Jason, who was just coming out.

"Good morning, Jesus," said Jason. "How did the meeting go yesterday?"

"It went well. I learned something important about my family, and something vital about every eubeing in Zone1." Jesus grinned in a way that showed Jason that there was more to the story.

Pretending he had no idea who visited, Jason asked, "Who were the guests?"

Jesus answered, "I'll tell you all about it later," and went into the bathroom to brush his teeth.

At breakfast, Sarah asked Jesus, "Why haven't we seen any children? Where are the kids in Zone1?" She said that Jason had not been able to answer that question.

Jesus considered his approach carefully and replied, "Your brother could not know the answer to that. You see, Sarah, there are some children in our world, available for you to see. They don't exist as you would expect – in neighborhoods, parks, valleys, schools, etc. – but our world does have about 900,000 youngsters under sixteen years old. They are so rare that the Authority tasks itself with taking them from their lottery-lucky parents and boarding them at camp-like schools, free of charge. These children are as real as you are, Sarah. But they can only be properly raised in unique new ways since old ways such as neighborhood schools, daycares, and parks would never work. For example, because there were so few children, they would need to be transported huge distances to be educated at schools like the ones you and Jason went to. For this reason, new methods were developed, known as Authority Educational Paradigms. Remember, these children will not be age-decoded until they are twenty-five. They are just like you, but very rare. You must understand that the Authority wants to protect these children, to serve them better, not because they are needed ... no, children are not needed, and only a limited number are allowed for that reason, but because they are treasured. As I said before, less than a million children exist. With a total Zone1 population of eleven billion, that means just one out of every eleven thousand people in Zone1 are children. To summarize, Sarah: youngsters are an absolute treasure."

Sarah asked, "Can I play with some of them?"

Jesus tried to think of a positive response, but could not. He said to her, "Not yet, but eventually, yes."

Jesus then decided to address Jason, although Sarah continued to listen in. He explained, "There are some people who believe the Authority age-decoded a prepubescent group of youth known as *euchildren* in an experiment on the effects of the procedure on youngsters. It is rumored that those children *regressed* in age. Age-decoding did not freeze, but instead reversed, the aging of these subjects. But that experiment was a catastrophe because the effects were unstoppable, so the subjects reverse-aged back to infancy and even further, ultimately dying of young age. It's rumored that those kids had shriveled down to premature embryo-like entities at their last breath."

"That's awful," said Jason.

"So where are the children?" asked Sarah.

"The euchildren?" Jesus asked.

"No, the children. The normal kids."

"As I said, they're kept at camp-like schools, far from their families, where they receive excellent education and protection. These children are used to educate us, to help eubeing adults remember what it was like to be truly young. I imagine this is difficult for you to believe since the two of you are also young, but believe me, the memory of youthfulness – of irresponsibility, freedom, riskiness, etcetera – does fade away for eubeings after decades and decades. Everyone has noticed and talked about this!"

"How can you just forget about something so important?" asked Sarah.

"Well, you can't, but you can lose the inner feeling for it, slowly, over time. I can't explain why, because I don't know, but that's what people have experienced. Have you ever had an amazing dream, which, after you awake, slowly fades away, no matter how much you try to hold on to it? You want the feeling to remain with you, but the force of time works its erosion. It seems the feeling of being a young human is like that too: calibrated to a certain time frame, certainly not the eubeing time frame."

"What do you mean ... calibrated?"

"Timed naturally. So that's why eubeing adults find it so satisfying to use *neurotaps* to psychologically "tap into" children: to re-experience childhood. We pay handsomely for these neurotaps. It's all supply and demand. Supply's short, but demand's high."

"Are the children paid for this service?"

"Ah, good question," remarked Jesus. "They can't be paid. Nobody in Zone1 can be paid for any task they do before being *age*-decoded. It's illegal."

"Why not?" asked Jason.

"Because their time is deemed too valuable. It would be too expensive to pay non-eubeings to work. The moment they are successfully age-decoded, however, the value of their time decreases since their life expectancy rises. That's why eubeings are paid very low wages."

Jason asked, "How do you know they don't just deny wages to non-eubeings so they'll want to become eubeings?"

The question stumped Jesus. He had never thought about that possibility. It was hypercritical. "Well. I was just giving you the official explanation. But that's clever of you to think of it from that angle."

"Thanks."

"That's all very weird!" cried Sarah, who then asked, "How about Zone2? Do they have kids? And are they paid?"

"Yes, they do have children, evidently more than they can handle. Of course, they don't have age-decoding, so most of their people, including many millions of their children, work and get paid for it."

"I see," said Jason. "Can we go there and see some of their children?"

"No. that's forbidden. Zone1 is more or less closed off from Zone2. No official trade or travel. No visiting. Even communicating with them is illegal, though it can be done, for a cost."

Sarah headed out to the garden, leaving Jesus and Jason alone.

Jesus used this opportunity to inform Jason that Ximena's father was one of yesterday's guests and that he had tried to reunite with Ximena.

Though he already knew about the meeting, Jason reacted agitatedly, "He doesn't deserve to see her after ignoring her for so long. How do you think that makes Xi feel? Do you think she should just forgive Ahmed and love him like a normal father? What about you? What do you think? You're the one who was forced to step in as her replacement father. Aren't actions what matter? I could see Xi loving her mother, Dr. Sengmeuller, if she were to miraculously come back – but her father? How do you think Xi feels?"

Jesus chose his words diplomatically. "I understand what you're saying, Jason, and your concern for the welfare of Xi, who deserved better. But you are perhaps too young to understand the Buddhist concept of *kensho* – personal awakening, or enlightenment. I believe Ahmed has recently undergone kensho. To me that's awesome." Jesus gently clutched the boy's right hand between his own. The creases and crinkles of his fingers somehow harmonized with the whiteness and softness of the boy's. He then said, "I believe it's our responsibility to allow kensho to flow to its fullest."

Jason's eyes widened, for the wisdom and wonder of this old man had a strong positive effect. Xi, he mused, was so lucky to have Jesus as her replacement father.

He wondered if he and Sarah would ever find a replacement for their parents.

CHAPTER 26

XIMENA AND JESUS TOOK in what Tavon was telling them with stunned disbelief. Ahmed was dead. Tortured to death by the Authority. The father whom Ximena had finally seen after two centuries of resentment and self-doubt, was gone forever. The fact that Tavon was relaying this horrible news made them trust him even more. Why else would he tell them, unless he was on their side?

Ximena's first thought was that she had no hope of ever reconnecting with her dad. Though she had rejected him that day, her innermost reflections were inching toward some forgiveness. He had at least tried to reach out and redeem himself. Now, building bridges and healing meant nothing.

Jesus hugged Ximena, who hung on and wept. I don't remember the last time she cried, Jesus thought.

When she did eventually calm down, Ximena demanded more information about what happened to Ahmed.

Tavon obliged, speaking naturally: "Our most recent Authority meeting was brutally disappointing," he said. "Our leaders threatened that any one of us could be next. It reminded me of Nazi Germany's pathetic Reich Security Main Office (RSHA), the secret German Nazi Party police organization commanded by Heinrich Himmler before and during World War II. Zhinghu in particular seems to me to be another Hitler's Himmler in the making ... to think Ahmed worked for Zhinghu for so long."

Ximena exclaimed, "Didn't Ahmed see this coming? Why didn't any of us see this coming?"

Jesus answered, "Because we had so much time. Humans with so much time naturally avail themselves of it inefficiently. Anonymous once said: *The thief to be most wary of is the one who steals your time.* With age-decoding, I believe it's the opposite. I think the thief to be wary of is the one who lends you too much time. They steal your humanity."

Tavon added, "I feel bad enough having worked there for three years."

Jesus replied, "Imagine how Ahmed would feel knowing that he worked there for two centuries, and they were ready and willing to kill him. He was an amazingly dedicated worker. The Authority was lucky to have him as they did, to tap his brilliance for so long!" Jesus paused, took a big swallow, then went on: "We so much appreciate what you're doing, Tavon. It takes as much courage as what Ahmed recently showed." He shifted his glance back and forth between Tavon and Ximena, "Believe me, I'm not blaming either of you. I'm making a general comment about a misbegotten system ... misbegotten quantities of time ... misbegotten servitude to the individual rather than the species. All *dukkha*, or suffering, is due to delusions of immortality. As it is said, birth is dukkha, old age is dukkha, sickness is dukkha, and death is dukkha. We are all subjects of that suffering ..."

"Look guys," Tavon interjected, "I came here today with terrible news and, believe me, I regret very much what I've done, and I'm trying to move forward here and now. From what I know, Zhinghu found out about Ahmed's meeting with Xi at this house, though I'm not sure exactly how. I'm probably in danger too, since Ahmed and I were collaborating. In the eyes of the Authority, our actions could qualify as sedition."

"Really?" asked Ximena.

"We met two times. Once at a bar, and once, of course, here."

"Is that much evidence? Is that such a crime?"

"Not necessarily, but their connection tracking technology might make use of that. I'm worried FENCODE_11 has already alerted them to my meeting with Ahmed. And the fact that we're meeting here today makes everything more salient and suspicious in the eyes of tracking technology."

Tavon hesitated for a few seconds. He took in the view of the rock garden beyond the back porch where hundreds of insects circled and gamboled about, highlighted by the contrasting tessellated sunlight.

He then looked back at Ximena and Jesus, and said, "We're taking an enormous gamble here today. However, ironically, it's way safer for us to be here, in the raw flesh, than it is to do this virtually. Before we proceed any further, I must have your assurance that our conversations are never shared with anyone. Remember, I'm still officially in Apex200 of the Authority. Please give me your assurance." His words were meant to ease everyone's fears, but they had the reverse effect.

Ximena asked Tavon to excuse her for a moment and took Jesus by the arm and walked him into the next room. She said to Jesus, "Should he be telling me these secrets, knowing I work for Rethinking? Can we trust him to be telling the truth?"

"You'll never know for sure," said Jesus. "But my gut feel tells me that he can be trusted: working as he did with Ahmed and also trying to reunite him with you. Ahmed invested so much in collaborating with Tavon and evidently died because of it. Your father wouldn't have staked his life on a questionable connection. The fact that they killed Ahmed leads me to believe me that Tavon is trustable."

"What if that's not the case? Isn't it possible that Tavon used his inside position to set up my father, to test him out? Maybe Ahmed failed that test? What if Tavon's working for the SI group at the Authority, fabricating things, working to weed out insurgents like me? You know SI will stop at nothing. How can we even be sure Ahmed's dead?" She held back for a moment as a vortex of questions and doubts swirled through her mind. "It's also possible they used my father – our reunion and everything – to set me up, then turned on him when it looked like he was about to turn on them."

Jesus tried his best with her, "Xi, I hear what you're saying, but I think you're being paranoid. Based on how Tavon just decried the Nazi RSHA, and his overall demeanor with us all along, I believe he's genuine."

Ximena wanted to believe what he was saying and prayed he was right, while in her mind he recalled that clever saying: *just because you're paranoid doesn't mean they aren't after you.*

"Look," he said, "Why don't we at least go back in there, chat with him a bit more, and just be careful. I don't see any danger in listening to him some more."

As usual, Ximena appreciated Jesus's insights. She and Jesus decided to return to talk with Tavon, though she was still very much on her guard.

When they re-entered the room, Tavon was gone.

On the coffee table lay a scribbled note, which Ximena picked up and read to Jesus:

> *Sincerest condolences once again for your loss. I had to leave, concerned about overstaying. I do have a question for Xi: Would she like help with the Rethinking Party?*
>
> *Soon, Tavon.*

Ximena crumpled the paper into a tight mass with her good hand, rubbing her bad limb continuously along her side.

She knew that collaborating with Tavon was like spinning the Roulette wheel. Rethinking would not tolerate and did not deserve careless gambling on her part. Jesus's assurances aside, she had to be careful – extremely careful – dealing with anyone who worked for the Authority.

She also had to admit to herself that she found Tavon attractive. His intellect and brave demeanor allured her.

What she and Jesus did not know was that Tavon had become guilt-ridden about Ahmed's death and too ashamed to stay any longer. He could not erase from his mind the fact that he had been part of the team which optimized the FENCODE_11 tracking technology, which was instrumental in deciphering the doings of thousands of citizens day in and day out. How, he wondered, did he ever let this unscrupulous entity entangle him? Wasn't he smarter than that?

On his journey home Tavon mulled over the rollercoaster ride Xi had endured – the messy reunion attempt with her father, then his torture and death. He found her to be a genuinely beautiful person and wondered if she might be fond of him. He cared about her and hoped to get to know her better.

Tavon then shifted his thoughts to his favorite teacher of all time, Mr. Johnston, who properly explained to him in grade 7 the history of black slavery, especially in the United States of America, and taught him about the civil rights movement and legal reforms through the 1800s and 1900s. He despised but very much appreciated what Mr. Johnston told him about the Jim Crow laws forcing segregation in public facilities, which led to multifarious legal and nonlegal segregation and disadvantages for blacks in schools, busing, streetcars, restrooms, restaurants, and many other areas of life. He loved Mr. Johnston's stories about Dr. Martin Luther King, how he inspired the world to explore nonviolence, choose forgiveness over ignorance, and to see others not by their skin color but by their character and actions. He also loved Mr. Johnston's story about President Eisenhower calling in the National Guard to protect the first few black children trying to enroll in the all-white Central High School in Little Rock, Arkansas. These leaders, he knew, chose the right side of history.

Based on Tavon's outstanding performance in school, Mr. Johnston predicted remarkable things for him, sometimes in front of the class. Tavon, embarrassed whenever this occurred, held his pride deep in his gut.

What Mr. Johnston did not know about was the high correlation between his praising of Tavon and the bullying occurrences during and after school. Not even his mother knew how that pack of boys tormented him in the shadows. They did not bully him because he was black, since most of them were also black. They did so because he was smart.

AGE-DECODED

CHAPTER 27

TAVON FLEW IN HIS CAR from New York to Detroit to visit his mother. He had an urge to see her but also needed to save precious time. Tavon's mother, Angela Brooks, was age-decoded when she was forty-four years old in the year 2055. She married a welder named Fred Brooks at the age of thirty-three, and they had a daughter named Shaquana. Two years after they were both age-decoded, Fred abruptly left the family with no explanation. Angela completely lost contact with him and could only suspect that he had found another woman. Their only child, Shaquana, left home as a crack cocaine addict by the age of sixteen.

Angela never remarried, but she retained the last name Brooks over the next two centuries, during which she enjoyed the affections of about two dozen boyfriends, some serious, including five that involved living together. When she was fortunate enough to win the Family Rights Lottery in the year 2230, Angela surprised many by choosing not to sell those rights to someone else who might give that future child a better chance for success. Because of her failure with her daughter Shaquana, she was eager for another chance to successfully raise a child, and her boyfriend Marquis Jones professed his willingness in this regard. So they exercised her family rights and conceived Tavon. Unfortunately, Marquis died in a flying car T-Bone collision two months after Tavon was born, so he never got much opportunity to be a father. Angela was convinced he would have made a terrific one.

Tavon saw his sister Shaquana just once, when he was ten years old. By chance, his mother and he encountered a street lady on the sidewalk on Mack Avenue in Detroit one snowy Saturday afternoon. He remembers being left out of the conversation as the two of them talked for a couple of minutes. Standing there holding his mother's hand, he could not avoid staring at the lady. Her hair was a frizzled mess of grey wisps, making her appear fifty years old – twice her eubeing age and wore old, baggy clothes. His mother did not introduce the two of them.

"Who was that? He asked his mother afterward.

"That was your sister, Shaquana."

"What? I have a sister?"

"You don't, really."

She held him at his shoulders and added, "You're not to have anything to do with her, do you hear me?"

He was old enough then to know not to pursue the topic any further.

As his flying car descended to his mother's *Detroit Socio-Equity Co-Operative*, Tavon contemplated how this action was always a hoot for the neighborhood folks, and today was no exception. A group of about two dozen residents gathered in the parking lot to observe his touchdown on the front grassy area. None of them were children.

The Co-op itself was more like a complex, built just a few years ago in the low-income Warrendale neighborhood of Detroit. It encompassed four entire city blocks and butted up against the wall of the Southfield Freeway. When Tavon secured a Co-operative apartment for her two years ago, her hug almost asphyxiated him. It overjoyed her to escape the rat-infested Forest Park apartment complex where she had raised him.

Emerging from his car Tavon walked straight forward, found his mother in the group, and hugged her tenderly for a few seconds. She then motioned for him to follow her.

They walked past a series of service outlets, including massage, tutoring, health care, virtual reality therapy, psychology, music, employment and training, NIT services, and even tattoos. They then entered an unremarkable foyer, checked in with security, and took the elevator to her 6th-floor apartment.

"Take a seat on the sofa," she said, speaking naturally as she always did. "I got it second hand at the Value Place."

Tavon lowered himself into the sofa, sinking quite low. "How are things, Mom?"

"Excellent, dear. You know the saying: *If I did complain, nobody would listen. So why complain?*"

Tavon smiled.

"How's work with you, dear?".

"Well, it's fine, but I don't think I'll be working there much longer," he said, reconfirming in his mind that he was speaking naturally, without the NIT.

His mother took on a look of worry, "Why ... is something wrong? I thought you said it was the best job in the world."

"It is. But there's something brewing there – which may soon become a runaway freight train – and I won't be able to stop it. My hunch tells me I won't be there by this time next year. Please don't tell anybody else what I'm saying to you, OK, Mom?"

"If that's the case that's a darned shame. I'm always bragging to people about how you've moved so high up in the Authority."

"I used to be so proud too, but I'm just letting you know things may be changing. Don't worry, Mom – as the saying goes, *I'll land on both feet.*"

"Knowing you, I'm sure you will. Promise to keep me posted. I won't say anything to anyone."

"Thanks."

His mother then changed the subject, prodding, "Any new girlfriends?"

"No, single as ever. Too busy with work to do much about it. Though I did meet a beautiful lady not long ago that I'd like to get to know better."

"Really?" She shifted in her chair.

"Yeah, her name's Xi. That's short for Ximena."

"How'd you meet her?"

"Working for the Authority," he said, knowing full well he should have said working *against* the Authority.

"Does she work there too? Is she a statistician with them?"

"No, she works for an independent group that collaborates with the Authority," he said, knowing he should have said collaborates *against* the Authority.

"Sounds nice. When do I get to meet her?"

"Probably never," he cautioned, being realistic. "I'm not so sure Xi's attainable for me. One issue is that she's older. Two years older than me, biologically-speaking, which isn't a big deal, but *two hundred and two years older*, chronologically-speaking!"

"Oh, dear," replied his mother.

"Though there's hope in all of this. It's a fact that in two years we'll be the exact same biological age, twenty-five years old."

"Well, there you go, kid. Problem solved!"

"But there's one more issue."

His mother leaned in, curious. "What's that?"

"Well, I happen to believe she's too good for me."

She promptly retorted, "Stop that nonsense! There's no man in the world better than you, not to mention more handsome than you. You've earned your way honestly ... you've always done the right thing, your absolute best. You're a highly accomplished young man. I brag about you all the time with my friends. I know you're proud of who you are and your heritage. How could you say such a thing? Dismiss those negative demons!"

She might be right, he mused, but he was not sure, because there was much she didn't know.

For the rest of the evening, Tavon and his mother relaxed. They watched a ninety-minute documentary called *Antarctica Rebound*, describing how its vast ice pack almost completely disappeared in the 21st century due to global warming, but was rapidly recovering in the 23rd century. This was precious time for Tavon, and he savored every single moment with her. His thoughts occasionally shifted to Xi, and how horrible it must be for her to lose her mother, and now her father.

CHAPTER 28

THE NEXT AFTERNOON, sitting out on the cantilevered balcony of his New York apartment at the West end of Central Park, Tavon was summoned by Zhinghu to a Core6 e-meeting. He was given only fifteen minutes' notice, which was certainly not enough time to ready his defense in what he assumed would be an onslaught.

Tavon relocated to his family room and paced back and forth rehearsing makeshift answers to probable questions. *Question:* Why did you visit the house of Ximena Sengmeuller of the Rethinking Party? *Answer:* She wanted to meet with me to discuss a proposal for government research, and I obliged since it's my duty to enlist proposals. *Question:* Why did you meet twice with Ahmed Iftikhar of Core6? *Answer:* I'm obliged to follow orders from SI superiors, and Ahmed wanted me to talk to him about data mining techniques relating to his latest project because he was impressed with my recent Apex200 presentation and valued my interpretation. *Question*: Why did you escort the young man Jason Smith to the Rethinking leaders? *Answer*: Pardon me?

He tried to consciously control his nerves, upbraiding himself for naively ending up in this circumstance. They'll expose me, he fretted, using questions I can't anticipate, questions that'll lead me down the path of self-incrimination. One single bad answer could do me in. They have a clear advantage: access to the vast myriad of information streams of enormous complexity and extent that I'm only partially aware of, including all FENCODE_11 data. I can't begin to control my odds here. Interesting, isn't it, how my youthful talent might be destroyed by this circumstance of information imbalance?

So, this must be it, Tavon surmised. Who or what can preserve me by providing the information I now need? As a probability expert and I'm sure my odds in this scenario are extremely long. Zhinghu and others in Core6 are likely to expose me. My demise is drawing nearer by the minute. Even if I did beat the odds and survive, would it not be a fleeting victory? Could I ever succeed in the long run against the SI *château fort*? Especially with what I've done? And without Ahmed?

Tavon implored himself to rehearse a few more likely questions. But before he could ask himself another question, the call came in for the e-meeting. A minute later all Core6 members were emerging holographically in his apartment.

Zhinghu began with introductions, "Tavon, I'd like you to meet my fellow Core6 experts: Dr. Gupta Mantharathna, genomics; Dr. Randolph Rahilly, psychosociology; Dr. Suzanne Tellier, political science. And I know you've already met President Reubers."

Tavon shook virtual hands with each of them, careful to establish brief, polite eye contact. Zhinghu motioned for everyone to sit down.

"I'd like to welcome you, Tavon, on this occasion of your first meeting exclusively with Core6. We all witnessed your recent presentation for Apex200, and I'm sure I speak for everyone in saying that you're a very, very talented young man. Your statistical skills are second to none. Your *post facto hyper regression analysis* skills are exceptional. You have immense potential with the Authority. Though time is on our side in this era, we believe time should be protected, and that's why we've asked you to appear here today."

While he was speaking Tavon tried to control how he projected himself and what they might decipher.

"As you know," Zhinghu continued, "Core6 is an exclusive group. The unfortunate end of statistician Dr. Ahmed Iftikhar is the price we must pay for Core6 integrity. He was a long-serving great asset, who recently, inexplicably, made terrible decisions."

The holographic room fell silent. Tavon wondered, should I say something? No – I'll hold off. Why speak if they haven't asked me anything?

Tellier piped up, "Thus we've decided to invite you to join the ranks of Core6, to join our inner team. You have superb statistical skills and character, and we have the opening. You'll be the youngest ever member of our group."

That blindsided Tavon. He had been bracing for the worst – and now this? Presently, however, he figured it made sense. Why wouldn't they invite him? He was the perfect replacement for Ahmed. His instinct told him to accept their offer immediately.

He straightened his shoulders and responded, "I'm very flattered by your offer. Yes, I'd love to join your team."

Reubers's holographic self shifted forward and shook Tavon's hand resolutely. "That's the fastest job interview you'll ever have," he said.

Tavon replied, "Yes, that was very efficient, the way I'll strive to be in working with all of you." He then confidently shook hands with the rest of them, his face bearing a combination of humility and pride. With that, their five images dissolved and he was left standing alone in his apartment.

Tavon knew that advantage had gracefully fallen upon him from the heavens. He felt at this moment both younger and wiser than all of them. Or was he just luckier? He had now infiltrated Core6. Could this have happened as such? Just a few minutes ago he had written himself off as a dead man, and now he was more alive than ever.

CHAPTER 29

"DO YOU THINK ALL EUBEINGS lack the propensity to dissent?" Jason asked Ximena and Jesus. "I mean, wouldn't it make sense for a few key government people, just a few, to have the normal dissenting ability? Wouldn't they want to keep that, just to protect themselves?"

Ximena and Jesus had switched off their NITs. If they used them, Jason could not hear their response, and, more importantly, the Authority could.

"Nice observation," replied Jesus. "I'm guessing you're correct. Why wouldn't the government, if it knew what it was doing, retain the propensity to dissent for its leaders? On the other hand, it might be wise for them not to retain it, if only to keep their internal struggles to a minimum. I'm not sure, really ... maybe we should ask Tavon. I assume he still has the propensity. He appears younger than twenty-five, so he's probably not age-decoded. Either he has the propensity, or he's a total fake."

"I don't think he's a fake," said Jason.

"Neither do I," replied Jesus. "Anyhow, I believe we should all be capable of dissent, like the old days. You see, Jason, dissent can be a good thing, because if you don't have it, all that's left is compliance. There's something we Buddhists call *impermanence*. Without it, a bee wouldn't fly, a flower wouldn't emit fragrance, and a river wouldn't flow. Impermanence is the essence of all life. It's the *delusion of permanence* that leads to human suffering. My reason is as follows: if people can't dissent, they can't change things. They can't venture beyond the wall of permanence. Suffering will result – the prison of *dukkha*. As long as dissent exists at a natural level, that's good, for it fosters impermanence. Though the government may have curbed dissent in the masses of eubeings, I'm guessing it was wise enough not to do so in its highest ranks. What do you think, Xi?"

"I think you're just speculating. And you're making it all way too complicated for Jason."

"Hey, he's a smart boy, smarter than I was at his age," replied Jesus.

"I'm not denying that he's smart. But he needs for you to take it easy right now. Don't you think all this political and Buddhist talk is a little much for him?"

"Yes, Jesus – take it easy on me!" cried Jason.

They all chuckled.

Jesus then added, "This young man is capable of so much. I've been impressed by his maturity, his ability to listen, interpret, and offer opinions and queries. Asking questions and listening – truly engaging – are great skills." He turned towards Jason and said, "I mean it, young man. You're gifted."

Jason blushed, "Thanks, Jesus. Nobody ever told me that before."

"Maybe, but I'm sure someone knew. Recognizing tacitly is still recognizing–"

"Oh, lay off! Enough philosophizing!" cried Ximena.

"OK ... OK," said Jesus. He then quipped, "The closest I can get to dissenting these days is to disobey you!"

Ximena smiled and suggested that they all wind down and do their own thing for a few hours. Jesus went for a nap and Ximena walked out to enjoy the porch-side gardens.

Jason headed to the family room to read more of *Biodiversity Unplugged*. He had already completed about one-third of its 844 famous pages. It was proving to be an incredible journey across species and ecosystems: insects supporting plants; big island ants and reptiles; mole crickets, orangutans and other anthropoid apes, eels and sturgeons, and bundles of new species discoveries. It all entranced him. Though he had always liked science as a subject in school, this book seemed different, felt more like true science. It revealed to him a raw difference between school and reality. School taught him facts and other interesting items, but this book taught him connectivity – nature as interbeing, as Jesus had called it. By reading this book Jason sensed himself becoming more disciplined, more able to focus. That made him learn better by alternatively reading sections of Jesus's writing, then, if needed, asking Jesus to clarify things. The book also challenged him to think at a higher level – which seldom happened at school. He certainly enjoyed penetrating the hundreds of silky thin pages. Jesus joked that the book was becoming Jason's *vade mecum*. Jason, having looked up the meaning of that term, couldn't disagree that he obsessively carried it around and used it as his guide. However, Ximena made it clear to him that he was never to take it beyond their property, as that might draw unnecessary attention.

Sarah entered the room and asked Jason what he was reading.

"Oh, it's the book Jesus gave me. Remember the book about animals, plants, and other things? Pretty cool stuff. Jesus won a big prize for writing it."

"Wow. Can you read some of it to me ... just a bit?"

"Sure."

Sarah nestled up against Jason on the couch while he found the part about the red imported fire ants. She relished the chance to be physically close to her brother. He proceeded to read to her about the huge population of fire ants in Guangdong province, China. The Authority was trying to limit the fire ant population because it was causing major damage.

He read her an excerpt:

> *"Fire ants are, in groups, aggressive and potentially destructive: they devour plants, small animals, insects, alive or dead; they attack rodents, snakes, birds; they destroy bird nests, beehives, and tree branches; they have an affinity for electrical wiring and have been known to invade air conditioners and traffic lights; they attack living foe "en masse", first biting to obtain a good grip, then stinging with*

alkaloid venom, each ant doing so several times; if they attack humans they cause burning sensations (hence the name fire ants) and in the case of large-scale attacks on sensitive humans, can cause coma or even death."

"Death? How can an ant cause death?"

"It's not *an* ant, Sarah; it's *thousands* of them. They do as a group what they could never accomplish individually. The ants detect an enemy and use the sheer force of numbers to overwhelm. One colony can have up to a million ants. That's a lot of ant power!"

Sarah asked, "Is it bad for ants to be like this?"

"I don't know."

She pressed him, "What does the book say?"

"It doesn't specifically say if they're bad," Jason answered, amused but also a bit irritated by his sister's question. "But it does say the following at the end of the fire ant section: *Humans brought them in by mistake and humans made many more mistakes trying to eradicate them.*"

"What does eradicate mean?"

"It means getting rid of."

"Oh. And what mistakes did humans make trying to get rid of the ants?"

"I don't know. Maybe Jesus wrote about that somewhere else."

"Mommy once said to me that one mistake leads to another. Is that what this is all about? Is that what she meant?"

Sarah's comment struck Jason. His little sister was getting smarter by the day. He replied, "Yes, I believe that's what she meant. She sure knew about things. About humans. They say all mothers are like that."

Sarah's eyes lit up. "Yes," she said, stretching out right across Jason's lap. "I miss Mom. Don't you?

Jason nodded emphatically.

Sarah asked, "Can you tell me more about the fire ants? Please?"

"Sure. One intriguing thing is how they need water, but too much of it can kill them. It says in this book that their nests include tunnels that can reach down to the water table. But flooding from heavy rains will force them to escape and seek dry shelter, sometimes inside people's homes. After a period of heavy rain, their fire ant mounds rise above the water level to protect the larvae, pupae, and eggs of their colonies. Most mounds are usually just a few inches tall, but some can reach as high as two or three feet! As a last resort, if the mounds are not high enough and the nest becomes flooded such that the queen is threatened, workers link themselves up to form a raft-like floating structure to safely carry the queen until the water recedes or dry land is reached."

"Boy, those red fire ants are smart little guys. How do you think they got so smart?" Sarah asked.

"They got smart by dying. That's how."

"What? How can ants get smart by dying? That doesn't make sense."

"But that's what I'm trying to say. Natural selection, something Jesus taught me about, works through the survival of the fittest and death of the weakest. Without death, the ant species gene pool can't change to reflect smarter characteristics or traits. The species can't adapt to the environment. The death of individuals in the species makes the species grow stronger. It happens over many generations."

"I have no idea what you just said. Speak English!"

"Sorry. It's a little much, I know. How about I reduce it to this: if you want to get smarter, you have to try things: you have to succeed but you also have to fail in the environment in which you live. Ants have done lots of trying and succeeding and failing over millions of generations, and they've learned from that. You do know what I mean by a generation, don't you?"

"Of course I do! It's in a family. Parents and kids. When those kids grow up and have their own kids, that's a brand new generation."

"You're exactly right!" cried Jason, delighted with his sister. "You see, Jesus describes in his book how generations build up species smartness. It doesn't happen overnight or even over a few years. Some species of ants have existed for more than one hundred million years. That's a long time to become smarter and smarter! Death is the connecting border between generations. Without death, there could be no generations."

Sarah nodded, and Jason went on, "In one section of this book it explains how, without death for any given species, the population would explode, which the environment could not support, so many individuals would die, saving the rest of them, meaning death is helpful for life. It also explains why simply not producing as many new ants cannot solve the problem of overpopulation. It might control the population in the short term, but the species would suffer in the long term because there would not be enough new generations to help it adapt. So you see, Sarah, death helps ants."

Jason was pleased with his explanation. Even Jesus, he figured, might have been impressed. As Jesus once said to him, *death finds a way.* He hoped Sarah understood that now.

His sister contorted her face then unraveled it with a smile, "I think I get what you're saying. For life to get smarter, it needs death."

"Exactly. You're a good learner, sister!"

Sarah grinned, "And you're a good teacher, brother." She jabbed him playfully in the ribs. "Can we do something more fun now, rather than talk about natural selection?"

"Sure, what would you like to do?"

"Let's play with some of the gadgets."

"Alright, I know a good one. Xi showed me one called *PsychoAlien II.* One person is the innocent victim, and the other person is an alien who tries to infiltrate the victim's life, acting as an imposter guardian angel. I'll be the victim first. Show us your evil alien skills!"

"That sounds neat."

"OK. Let's do it. I stand here on this square, you stand over there on that circle. We have to put these helmets on and these bracelets. Good ... I'm pressing the start button ..."

CHAPTER 30

TAVON WOKE UP FEELING fidgety. Today was the day of his induction ceremony with Core6. His neck was stiff, and he noticed that the covers were completely off the bed. The alarm had not been set. He pulled up the corner of the drapes to see that the sun was already high.

I'm twenty-three years old, he thought, and still aging in a supposedly real way. But it never *feels* like I'm growing older. Aggravations such as muscle erosion, arthritis, and memory loss are all foreign to me and will remain so if I'm age-decoded in a couple of years.

He fixed himself a piece of toast with peanut butter and carved up a grapefruit. When the coffee was ready he carried his breakfast to the sunroom and looked out through the screen window. The sun was behind him, shining in the direction he was looking, which intensified the green and yellow hues of the willow trees that stood motionless.

Tavon contemplated AACT. In 2251, after so long in limbo, legal barriers to AACT which had been erected by the Authority were finally overturned by its own Ministry of Justice. He knew that Jason and Sarah were two of the many successful AACT cases held and supported by the Rethinking Party in cooperation with HF Capital. He went over it in his mind: AACT could challenge the Authority in a few ways. It could compete directly with the Authority's age-decoding technology; such an assault would be underpinned by two advantages of the private sector: strong marketing and nimbleness. That would directly threaten the "monopoly" of age-decoding as a means for avoiding death. Second, since AACT did not involve genetic decoding, its adoption could end the clandestine control of the propensity to dissent. This would challenge the Authority's popularity and could be enhanced if AACT offspring favored AACT versus age-decoding. The fact that AACT humans were fertile, while eubeings were not (unless they won the Family Rights Lottery) would factor in on this threat. Still, it would require a long period for AACT to be adopted by many young people. Many of these challenges, Tavon figured, were long-term in nature and not an immediate threat to the Authority. But what if eubeings were convinced *en masse* to undo their age-decoding, re-install their propensity to dissent, then adopt AACT?

Tavon washed up and put on his best suit. He left his apartment and took the subway downtown for his Core6 induction ceremony. His edginess reminded him of how he felt just before his MIT thesis defense. The only difference was that his mother could not attend this time – it was a closed event.

The ceremony itself was simple and brief. The six of them sat positioned along each edge of a large glass hexagonal table. At the center of the table stood a statue known as the Vertical Infinity: a blue-green semi-gloss marble structure standing almost two feet tall and mounted on a Swedish ebony granite base.

Zhinghu handed a small leather pouch to Tavon and said, "With these, we entrust your talents, your teamwork. It contains keys to this building, the parking lot, your personal computer, and the computer system. You must return your minor key to FENCODE_11 and your Apex200 key. Now please, young man, pick up the statue."

Tavon did so. Its heaviness surprised him.

Zhinghu announced, "Let us all state our motto, in unison."

Everyone held hands and slowly emitted the words, which flowed like sapid lava from an eternal volcano: *"The four avoidable physical sufferings are birth, old age, sickness, and death."*

The ceremony now complete, they served themselves coffee and took their seats at the conference table to talk strategy.

Zhinghu began by asking Tavon, "Are you ready for your first Core6 project?"

"Yes. Definitely."

Gupta elaborated, "Allow me to fill you in. You'll be working with the Authority's Chief Genomicist (CG), whose identity is kept secret from everyone except Reubers and me. Nobody else is privy to the CG's name or face. All others in Core6 must communicate blind-blind with the CG using the muffle-altered system. To those beyond Core6, including all scientists collaborating with the CG, the CG is thought to be nonhuman, an artificial superintelligence entity."

Tavon asked, "Is there a reason that CG's identity is kept secret?"

"Yes," answered Gupta. "It's to protect the integrity of the scientific mission, as well as to protect the CG themself." She paused, and her eyebrows moved further up into to strong forehead. "I should add one more thing, which is a very recent development: we've gotten word that the CG has, remarkably, discovered the means for reverse-aging."

Tavon blushed with astonishment, "Reverse-aging? Are you kidding me?"

"Believe us, it's going to happen," affirmed Zhinghu.

"Wow ... that's ... bloody incredible!" Tavon cried. "I never imagined we'd see that mystery solved so soon. Most people I've talked to thought it would take another fifty years ... or five hundred!"

Gupta explained, "Well we learned to eliminate the word *never* from our Core6 vocabulary a long time ago. Reverse-aging technology is upon us, here and now! Specifically, we'd like you to oversee its implementation, to ensure the timing and integrity of the rollout. You'll need to collaborate closely with the CG."

Tellier added, "The timing of this implementation is crucial. Reverse-aging is the culmination of two centuries of research. It's as profound an accomplishment as age-decoding. We think practically all eubeings significantly older than twenty-five will choose to take advantage of it. What older eubeing wouldn't want to be twenty-five again? To revel in the gradual disappearance of grey hair, wrinkles, and arthritis? Can you imagine? Reverse-aging should be an absolute hit! Its implementation, decreed by Reubers, will take place over the three months before the next election, to maximize the impact on the Authority's popularity. That means we must get moving with the rollout."

"This isn't simply a political move," said Zhinghu. "With reverse-aging, we expect to lower health care costs by over 90% over the next century. It's funny, you know, when most forms of cancer were conquered about one hundred years ago, we thought health care costs would plummet, but they didn't. Other diseases just filled the void. But that shouldn't be the case with reverse-aging. Based on the premise that aging is itself a disease that triggers many other diseases, reverse-aging should eradicate all conditions associated with old age, including many remaining forms of cancer, Alzheimer's disease, diabetes, hearing and vision loss, muscular atrophy, cardiovascular disease, hypertension, osteoarthritis, and dementia. It's the blanket antidote we've dreamed of! It should also resolve the bias against those who were age-decoded at older ages: those unfortunate eubeings who got locked into older bodies. They'll gradually grow younger and healthier, evidently at a rate comparable to normal biological progression, except reversed."

Rahilly then spoke for the first time, "Reverse-aging will create a more equitable distribution of age-decoding. In time, all older eubeings will be reverse-aged until they too are twenty-five years old. All of this will be accomplished in less than one hundred years, since the oldest person in Zone1 is, biologically speaking, 125 years old. It—"

"Reverse-aging should further entrench the Fundamental Platform," added Zhinghu. He then reached out over the center of the table and grasped the base of the vertical infinity with both hands. Fixing his eyes on it, he stated, "The Fundamental Platform is strong now, no doubt, though perhaps a bit prone on the political front. With reverse-aging, the Platform should become as solid as the marble of this statue."

Zhinghu gleefully lifted the Vertical Infinity to eye level. "Are you ready to accept your mission, Tavon? Just so we understand ... I'm offering you the lead role of implementing the grandest genetic engineering breakthrough since age-decoding. Your main challenge will be to get the timing right, *vis-à-vis* the general election. Do you accept the challenge, Tavon? We won't settle for *dos-a-dos*."

"Yes. I'm ready to get to work."

"Excellent," said Zhinghu. He slowly lowered the statue back onto the table, then added, "Now we'll need to get you up to speed as soon as possible regarding coordination logistics and deadlines. Tomorrow Dr. Mantharathna – please, call her Gupta – will set you up for initial communication with the Chief Genomicist."

Zhinghu extended his arm to shake hands with Tavon. The remaining four members followed suit. The Core6 was complete again.

CHAPTER 31

XIMENA LOCKED HERSELF in the downstairs bathroom. The kids did not know her whereabouts or her doings. If they had, the abnormality of it would have shocked and saddened them. They would never understand how she could not help herself, that her left arm was her salvation. With Ahmed now dead, everything was ramped up, even worse. She held her arm up like a crucifix and proceeded to sacrifice a small part of herself, her flesh, once again. The ritual was familiar and vital to her. The gnawing meant life, not death, to her sanity.

This moment brought her closer to her concerns. Why do I not have a mother? Should I accept finally that she's dead? Why do I not have a father? Could it ever have worked out with Ahmed? Why do I not have a sister? A brother? A daughter? A son?

Here I sit, gnawing pathetically, a sliver of one generation, isolated, infertile, unable to relate or reach out. I'm stuck in one egotistical dimension, alone. I'll never experience the primary bonds of bloodlines, and the stories that go with them. Never care for youngsters. Never know children or grandchildren. I'll never share or grow older with the love of a younger person. Never be obliged. Never have to stand by, help, protect, enable, or challenge. I feel like the heavy head of an ax forever marooned in a thick tree trunk.

Not having the opportunity to be a mother haunts me. What's it like to nurture a baby, to bring up a child, to see it walk and talk for the very first time? What's it like to listen to a son or daughter tell stories about school and friendships, and to grow old witnessing them mature into adults, companions, and caregivers? What's it like to fully experience the cycle of life with loved ones? I'll never know the joy of being a real mother, like women were in the old days. If I did come to know it, it would be in some artificial way, not naturally.

Such musings preoccupied Ximena's tender mind while her soul physically satiated herself on her left arm. Using her good hand, she held her left limb up by the elbow, at mouth level. She licked the fresh blood from her limb onto her lips, then peered at it uncommonly, like it was foreign to her.

As beautiful as others thought she was, Ximena believed she was dysmorphic. Not a person, really; just some unloving entity in Zone1.

She pierced her blood-drenched lips for a moment while trying to recall a saying she had once heard. What was it? Oh yes, she thought, muttering it softly so it would not be heard beyond the walls: *Children are love made visible.*

Not quite satiated, she moved in with her lips and teeth for a bit more.

CHAPTER 32

TODAY TAVON WAS MEETING with the Chief Genomicist (CG) in Block3. He was escorted to Room B5R0248 by Dr. Gupta Mantharathna. Gupta motioned for Tavon to take a seat in the one chair. Strangely, he thought, this is not unlike my mother's LazyBoy. Gupta stood at the doorway and explained how his conversation with the CG would be a certified blind-blind encounter, guaranteeing no possibility of tracking from either side. She told him it was set up that way to ensure an airtight bond between Tavon and the CG, to protect the CG's identity from potentially unscrupulous outside entities such as the Rethinking Party or even potential conspirators within the Authority.

Tavon assumed correctly that Gupta would be eavesdropping.

"Remember," Mantharathna said, "no one in Core6 except Reubers and I are privy to the identity of the CG. When you converse, your voices will be muffle-altered to mask your age, gender, and voice patterns. The important thing is to glean the information you need from the CG to plan the implementation of reverse-aging, which will be a massive undertaking with a tight time frame. Good luck. And ... welcome aboard, Tavon."

With that, she closed the door and Tavon was alone in the square booth.

Presently the muffle-altered system kicked in.

Frieda spoke first, xxGreetings xxTavon. xxI xxam xxthe xxChief xxGenomicist. xxCall xxme xxCG xxfor xxshort. xxHow xxare xxyou?

yyFine, yythanks, yyand yyyou?

xxCould xxbe xxbetter, xxcould xxbe xxworse. xxAnyway xxit's xxnice xxmeeting xxyou xxeven xxthough xxwe xxaren't xxmeeting xxface-xxto-xxface xxor xxreal xxvoice-xxto-xxvoice. xxStill, xxI've xxheard xxtremendous xxthings xxabout xxyou, as I'm xxtold xxby xxGupta xxthat xxyou're xxa xxstatistical xxgenius. xxI xxlook xxforward xxto xxworking xxwith xxyou xxon xxthis xxproject.

yyThanks. yyI'm yyexcited yyto yyget yystarted. yyI yymust yysay yyI'm yyhonored yyto yywork yywith yythe yylead yyscientist yywho yyinvented yyreverse-yyaging.

xxThank xxyou. xxI xxshould xxbegin xxby xxnoting xxan xximportant xxfact xxwhich xxyou xxmay xxalready xxknow: xx60.998% xxof xxeubeings xxare xxof xxa xxbiological xxage xxgreater xxthan xxtwenty-xxfive, xxthat xxis, xxthey xxwere xxolder xxthan xxtwenty-xxfive xxwhen xxthey xxwere xxage-decoded. xxThat's xxa xxkey xxpiece xxof xxinformation. xxIf xxthe xxneeds xxof xxthose xxindividuals xxcan xxbe xxaddressed xxby xxreverse-aging, xxthe xxresult xxwill xxbe xxa xxfurther xxgrand xxenhancement xxof xxthe xxFundamental xxPlatform, xxas xxI'm xxsure xxDr. xxZhinghu xxhas xxexplained xxto xxyou.

yyYes, yyhe yyhas. yyThat's yywhy yytiming yyis yyso yycrucial yyleading yyup yyto yythe yyelection. yyIs yythe yyreverse-yyaging yyprocedure yyvery yycomplicated yyor yytime yyconsuming? yyDo yywe yyhave yythe yyinfrastructure yyin yyplace yyto yydo yythis?

xxWe xxdo. xxThe xxinfrastructure xxto xxcarry xxit xxout xxalready xxexists xxin xxthe xxSpectre xxSocieties, xxwhich xxwere xxalso xxused xxfor xxage-xxdecoding.

yyGreat, yyso yyare yythere yyany yylarge-yyscale yyissues?

xxYes. xxThere xxwill xxbe xxsome xxtiming xxchallenges xxfrom xxwhat xxI xxcan xxsee. xxWe xximplemented xxage-decoding xxover xxa xxperiod xxof xxabout xxeleven xxmonths, xxwhereas xxyou xxonly xxhave xxabout xxthree xxmonths xxto xximplement xxreverse-xxaging; xxmind xxyou xxthe xxlatter xxinvolves xxless xxthan xxtwo-thirds xxof xxthe xxpopulation xxwhile xxthe xxformer xxinvolved xxalmost xxeveryone. xxStill, xxwe'll xxneed xxto xxprocess xxmore xxpeople xxper xxunit xxtime. xxThe xxinfrastructure xxwill xxbe xxpushed xxto xxthe xxlimit. xxYou xxwill xxneed xxto xxutilise xxit xxaround-xxthe-xxclock.

Frieda stopped for a few seconds, then added, xxMay xxI xxask xxwhen xxyou xxwere xxhired? xxI xxdon't xxremember xxhearing xxof xxyou xxbefore. xxI xxused xxto xxwork xxwith xxDr. xxAhmed xxIftikhar.

Listening in, Gupta had no problem with what Frieda was asking Tavon, so she allowed the conversation to continue. This accommodation may have been the single biggest mistake in her career with the Authority.

yyI yywas yyjust yyhired yyinto yymy yycurrent yyposition. yyI yyreplaced yyDr. yyIftikhar, yywho yywas yythe yyformer yychief yystatistician, yya yytop-yydrawer yymathematician yyand yydedicated yylong-yyserving yymember yyof yythe yyCore6. yyUnfortunately yyhe yyturned yyagainst yythe yyAuthority yyand yywas yytortured yyfor yythat. yyI yywas yyshocked. yyHe yywas yya yymentor yyof yymine, yya yyproud yyYarsani yyIranian, yynobody yysaw yythis yycoming.

Hearing Tavon talk about her husband's downfall and torture ripped at Frieda's heart, and she reflexively uttered, xxPoor xxCrunchy.

That went over Gupta's head.

But Tavon processed it. Did the CG just use the term *Crunchy?* It took a few seconds for it to sink in, but it did so profoundly. Only one person in the world could have referred to Ahmed by that nickname.

He withstood the foolish urge to immediately ask the CG if she was Dr. Sengmeuller. Was this the legend herself? Or was this some kind of trick? A test by Gupta? His emotions waggled about. Could he trust what he heard?

These questions paralyzed Tavon, but he could not stall any longer, as it could make Gupta suspicious.

So he asked a pedantic question to restart the conversation. yyHow yylong yywill yyityy yytake yyto yyreverse-yyage, yycompared yyto yyage-yydecoding? yyIs yyit yytime-yyconsuming yyto yydo yythis yyto yypeople?

xxIt xxrequires xxabout xxthe xxsame xxamount xxof xxtime, xxthirty xxminutes xxper xxsubject.

yyOK, yythat's yygood. yyAnd yyshould yywe yyagain yyuse yythe yySpectre yySocieties yyas yythe yyvenue?

xxYes, xxthat's xxstill xxa xxvery xxgood xxadministrative xxchoice. xxI'm xxguessing xxthose xxunits xxwon't xxbe xxin xxas xxmuch xxdemand xxwhen xxreverse-xxaging xxcomes xxout.

yyWell, yyyou're yyprobably yyright yyon yythat, yysince yymany yyof yytheir yyclients yyare yyeubeings yytrapped yyin yyold yybodies.

Tavon found it almost impossible to concentrate as he dealt with the reality of who he might be talking to. He wished he could see her real face and hear her actual voice. It was too much for him; so he found a way to abort the conversation early and sign out.

When he left the room, Gupta asked him how it went.

"Very well. The CG and I think we can get this implemented within the tight time frame. Reverse-aging will be an unprecedented blessing for humanity."

"And for the Fundamental Platform," Gupta added with a smirk.

She neglected to tell him about her plan to take full credit for inventing reverse-aging. *The CG would be unveiled as her.* Only she and Reubers knew that.

After Gupta escorted him out of the facility, Tavon sat on a sidewalk bench, inhaled deeply, and pondered, had he truly been speaking with Dr. Sengmeuller? Was her suicide, so famously reported, just a sham? All this time her death was accepted, a tragedy suffered by so many. Even Ahmed, though not so much Xi, believed it. Could the Authority have faked her suicide and used her as the CG? He could not come to accept it, but the idea was germinating within him.

I can't believe it, he thought. When I first met Ahmed, he told me about the propensity to dissent manipulation. What kind of a government does that? Given that, would it be unreasonable to believe they could have done these horrid things to Dr. Sengmeuller? What distresses me most is knowing that, if I implement reverse-aging to the best of my abilities, I will contribute to this government. And if I contribute, and Dr. Sengmeuller is the CG, they'll probably kill her after reverse-aging is launched. Who would know they killed her if they didn't know she was still alive? Everything would happen far from the eyes and ears of mindful citizens. If that was her that I spoke with today, she needs my help. I'll have to be extremely careful. I can't imagine the retribution if they found out.

CHAPTER 33

AVOIDING THE USE OF his NIT, Tavon left a note at Ximena's house asking her and Jesus to meet him in person at 10:00 am at Bayou Ridge Trail trail just east of Lake Pontchartrain. The day was already warm, with the usual humidity, but the steady onshore breeze off the Gulf of Mexico kept things bearable.

As Tavon shook both of their hands in the parking lot, Ximena's allure did not escape him, though he vowed to shut it out as best he could, as there was important business to tend to this morning.

Tavon said to them, "Thanks for meeting with me. Remember to speak naturally, no NITs. I need to tell you both about something weird that happened during my first meeting with the CG at the Authority."

"OK let's start along the trail," said Jesus, who, despite his frailness, was eager to walk.

They began working their way along the well-maintained, tranquil trail, a combination of gravel path and boardwalk bordered by a river swamp, interrupted by shorelines of towering cypress trees draped beautifully with hanging Spanish moss. Ximena positioned herself between the two men. Jesus made use of two hiking poles.

"You said CG," said Ximena. "What do you mean by CG?"

"CG stands for Chief Genomicist. As you know the Authority has been working for decades trying to unlock the secret for reverse-aging. The CG is the scientific leader for that undertaking. The identity of the CG is kept under wraps for security reasons. I had my first meeting with the CG just yesterday."

"Sorry, but how can you meet with someone if their identity is secret?" asked Ximena.

"Oh, I forgot to mention. We used a special blind-blind muffle altered system, so I never actually saw the CG or heard their real voice."

"That's interesting," said Ximena.

Their trail was nearing a boardwalk lookout overseeing an expansive marsh. Several golden-crowned kinglets fluttered in the shrubs, while in the distance Ximena spotted two great blue herons.

"Look at the herons. Gorgeous!" she cried.

They all stopped and peered in the direction she was pointing, taking in the sight of the majestic birds.

Jesus explained, "Notice their drooped wings. That's because it's hot and they're trying to increase air circulation across their body. That serves as great air conditioning when there's a breeze like this morning."

"Intersting," said Tavon.

They began walking again and Tavon went back to his account of his meeting with the CG. "Anyhow, we had a good discussion, planning the rollout for reverse-aging."

Jesus stopped and touched Tavon on his lower arm. "What? Are you serious? Reverse-aging?"

"I'm dead serious. Everyone in Zone1 will be made aware of this in the next few days, and the actual rollout will start right after that. I'm telling you, this new science is about to happen. They want it all done before the election."

"Of course they do," said Ximena.

"That's truly incredible," remarked Jesus. "Age-decoding and now reverse-aging. It's all too much if you asked me. My first reaction is: What would Nature think? Or God, if you believe in Him or Her?"

Ximena gave her grandfather a short jab in the ribs. "You're an old and frail eubeing. You should be jumping for joy!"

"I guess I should," he said.

"Please keep this quiet," Tavon urged them. "Don't talk to anyone about this, not even Rethinking. We must save that discussion until just before it's officially announced, which, as I said, should be in a few days."

"You have our word," Ximena said. The high-pitched ascending notes of the tiny golden-crowned kinglets rang out just a few feet away from the boardwalk, from the direction of the duckweed, salvinia, and spider lilies.

Ximena added, "Then why are you telling us about this now, if we can't talk about it?"

"Because, while conversing with the CG, Ahmed's name came up. I told the CG about how I replaced him, how Ahmed had run afoul of the Authority. The CG's reaction was strange: she mysteriously said, *Poor Crunchy*. At least that's what I think I heard. She almost whispered it. So I must ask you, does that mean anything to either of you?"

To his surprise, they both shook their heads.

Tavon stood baffled. He was certain Ahmed had told him that Crunchy was the nickname Frieda used with him. Why didn't Ximena and Jesus recognize it? Had he been misled by Ahmed? Duped by the CG? Had he merely imagined the CG using the word?

He explained further, "Look, I better tell you something more, because this could be incredible and I can't hold back. When I first met Ahmed, he was reminiscing about Frieda and told me she used the nickname *Crunchy* with him, a cute play on the term *data cruncher*."

Jesus and Ximena glanced at each other, then back to Tavon, still uncertain as to where he was going with this. Tavon could see that this was still not sinking in. The cicadas fizzed electricity from the cypress trees as the hot sun exerted itself.

He explained further, "Don't you see? Ahmed's nickname with Frieda was Crunchy. The CG used that same term when I brought up Ahmed. Why the heck would the CG do that? Call me crazy, but I think the CG is Frieda herself!"

"Holy shit!" cried Ximena. "Are you kidding?" Her mouth opened wide and her face turned off-white. Ximena bent down from the waist, covering her face with her hands as a broad smile took hold that nobody could see. She gradually lowered herself to her knees. Above her, a large flock of the brown pelicans, the Louisiana state bird, sailed across the sky towards the breezy ocean shores.

Exalted, Ximena cried out, "I knew it! Nothing made sense ..."

Jesus stood stunned. His daughter Frieda? Alive? "That's the most profound thing I've heard in my eubeing lifetime. If it's true, it means the world. *Vimutti*!"

CHAPTER 34

RETHINKING MEETINGS were fairly informal affairs: no appointed leader, no detailed agenda or electronics; candid exchanges all around. The Authority knew of the meetings and did not interfere, since it was important to have official opposition, however weak, for adherents of The Fundamental Platform to scoff at.

Tavon had waited until today, the last possible moment, to make his announcement to the Rethinking Party because tomorrow the Authority would announce the breakthrough of reverse-aging. He felt compelled to notify the Rethinking group beforehand, but he also knew the risk of leaking information.

Tavon was escorted to the meeting by Ximena and Jesus. The three of them were received at the side door of an indistinct warehouse, located off East 85th Street in Brooklyn, not far from the Jacqueline Kennedy Onassis Reservoir. Tom Stephenson greeted them and guided them across the floor of a dimly-lit hanger structure, through a large rusty metal door, along a hallway, and into a room which appeared to be a spacious old office. A group of about thirty Rethinkers quietly observed as they seated themselves at the front of the room, adjacent to a large desk. Several of the onlookers sat in card table chairs, while the rest stood along the walls. Attendance was higher than average because the word was out that something big was about to happen.

Tom wasted no time getting started. "Hello everyone. Please be reminded that you must communicate naturally with each other, whether addressing the entire group or conversing with the person beside you. No NIT usage whatsoever. Now, Xi, would you like to present our guest?"

Ximena rose from her chair. "Good evening. Tavon Brooks, from the Authority, has chosen to visit us and share some valuable information. While we are taking some risk in doing this, we believe that risk justifies listening to what he has to share with us, then building on that relationship moving forward."

Tavon then stood and addressed the group. He meticulously detailed his meeting with the CG, stating he thought it could be Dr. Sengmeuller. If that was true, he surmised, she had somehow been confined for two hundred years to work on reverse-aging and would likely be killed once it was rolled out. He admitted that there was no way for him to completely verify this because he could not ask her directly in a conversation monitored by Gupta or others in the Authority. Finally, he explained how the propensity to dissent had been genetically deactivated in all eubeings.

They absorbed every word he said, dumbfounded and dead silent.

As it sunk in they became aghast and disgusted with the alleged maneuvers of the Authority – confining Dr. Sengmeuller, tampering genetically, and hiding the truth for so long. In contrast, the possibility that Dr. Sengmeuller could still be alive was awesome news. Jesus clung to Ximena's good hand, and he spied tears on her cheeks. They hoped in their hearts that Tavon was telling the truth.

Tom Stephenson spoke up, "I'd like to believe she's alive, that what you are telling us is true, Tavon. How fantastic that news of Dr. Sengmeuller would be! But can we be sure it's not an elaborate setup? After all, Tavon, you never even saw Dr. Sengmeuller. Couldn't someone in the Authority have set this up? Where does this leave us now?"

"I can't prove anything, Tom," replied Tavon, "but if I'm wrong then I'm the one who's endangered. I'm out on a limb here, on my own. If this was a setup, they'll undoubtedly do to me what they did to Ahmed, and they'll do it sooner rather than later."

He paused for a few seconds to project his solemnity around the room, then cast a striking glare toward Tom, "If my intuition turns out to be mistaken, I'm jeopardized and probably dead; but if I'm right, billions could benefit. By dying at their hands, Ahmed may have done us a tremendous favor. He caused my promotion to Core6 and gave us this one chance to infiltrate them. Despite the risk, I think it's obvious what we need to do."

Tom nodded but stayed silent like the others.

Tavon waited a few seconds, then continued, "Now, let's look at the facts: 61% of eubeings have a biological age greater than twenty-five; assuming 90% of them opt for reverse-aging, and, of those, 90% change their allegiance to Rethinking once they are made aware of the truth, that would shift about 49% more support to your Party. If you add this to the 9% popular support you had in the last election in 2224, it seems you have a realistic shot at a majority in the upcoming election."

Tom had doubts, "But I thought you said eubeings lacked the propensity to dissent?"

"True, but I believe that when they discover they've been genetically manipulated on the propensity to dissent, they'll be livid. The raw rationalization of what happened to them, and the horrors inflicted on Dr. Sengmeuller, will drive their allegiance away from the Authority with a fervor that overrides their loss of the propensity to dissent. We must remember: *propensity is a propensity, not a certainty*. At least let's hope that's the case. My belief is that's how Ahmed, who was a eubeing, turned against the Authority."

Tom responded, "Even I can appreciate that nine plus forty-nine equals fifty-eight, which is more than fifty. But those are optimistic assumptions, Tavon, although there's some room for error in them, too, which I like. Look, if we do proceed with this, what role can we have at Rethinking? How can we help you in getting there?"

"Rethinking can do, must do, three things from what I can see," Tavon replied. "First, you must remain close-lipped but ready to act at the appropriate moment. Second, you must find a way to communicate the truth to everyone in Zone1. Informing people will be a tricky step, however, because we don't have control of broadcast media and I can't see a way to acquire it, at least not yet. Also, why would eubeings even trust our message if we did get it out? Finally, you must stand ready to provide leadership. I'd recommend you start formulating your shadow cabinet as soon as possible. When the Authority relents–"

"If the Authority relents," Ximena interjected.

Tavon explained, "Look, when people discover the truth, the Fundamental Platform will take a major blow. Hopefully a lethal one. Actions like mass dissent and civil disobedience can be potent. And maybe Frieda herself would be willing to step up to the plate politically if we can recover her alive. She'd be perfectly positioned for leadership. The natural one. In the meantime, you must set up a shadow cabinet as soon as possible. Tom, can you take charge of that?"

"I'll do it, of course," he said.

From the back of the room, someone shouted, "If the Authority falls, let's make sure Reubers and Zhinghu are tarred and feathered!"

Others shouted their approval, and a few began applauding.

"Now let's be careful, everyone!" cried Jesus, who had been silent to this point. He rose from where he was seated beside Ximena. Clinging to the edge of his chair with both hands, he stated, "We're a civilized group, and if this Authority topples, there'll be enough instability already without us engaging in retribution. It'll be fascinating to see how people react, especially as a disorganized, decentralized group up against a centralized controlling Authority. With their eyes opened, who knows how they'll react? The only thought that comes to mind is anger. I'm guessing they'll be teeming with anger. But how can mass anger make amends? How can anger mend two centuries of deception? I do worry. It'll already be a *Midsummer Moon*." He scanned the faces and could see many did not understand, so he added, "By that I mean it'll be a natural time for madness. So let's not add to the madness. We're basing our strategy on the knowledge and will of the masses, so we must be careful to attend to their rational sensitivities, no matter what, and to avoid the sensual temptations of revenge and extremism. We must take the right approach, the way of moderation, the *Middle Way*. That will lend us respect when we most need it."

Jesus had spoken so cogently that nobody could challenge him.

Ximena then put forward, "Everything now requires our togetherness. We have no way to tell the world what's going on ... that Frieda's alive ... not just yet. We'll have to find a way to make that revelation."

Tavon went on, "Be aware that I won't be able to attend these meetings after today, because SI and other parts of the Authority may be tracking me. So I'll need a surrogate, someone who can relay non-digital handwritten information back and forth between me and this group. I'll leave that for you as a group to decide. Also, I'll need a person to help me with the details. A double-check person. We can't afford a mistake. We'll need to be more vigilant than ever. These people are unscrupulous bastards and FENCODE_11 is hawk-like the way it sees so acutely then pounces. I think Ximena would be excellent as my double-check person."

Heads nodded. Everyone understood the gravity of the situation. They were in a different mode now: imperative, risky, real. What they had done thus far as a Party had always been conducted in the harmless realm of the hypothetical. What they were about to do was potentially treacherous, yet also potentially glorious.

Tavon examined the people around the room. They appeared somber. That was good. There could be no other emotion. He scanned their faces one more time, past their mouths, past their eyes, into their minds and their souls. Some may have sensed what he was thinking – that they might never see him alive again.

Tom thanked everyone for coming. They left silently, their heads so full and energized that there was no room for small talk. Tavon, Jesus, and Ximena were the last to leave.

When Tavon got back to his apartment that evening, he settled into his latest book, Gregor Dentalisus' recently published *Deviations*, a bestselling exposé of criminal minds in the 22nd century. He read the case about Dr.[5] Norman Ferster, who had systematically swindled over $500 million from dozens of seniors by e-posing as their loved ones. Too clever to ever be caught, he simply turned himself in. The most intriguing question was: Why would he give up? The author theorized that Ferster had been trying all along to be incarcerated, but when he realized he could not be caught, he arrested himself: a rational final move toward an irrational goal.

Tavon put the book down and pushed his ponytail off his neck and over his back. He worried. Were his own goals rational, or irrational? Would his moves toward those goals be rational, or irrational? He knew he was in over his head, but who else was in his unique position? Why was he the one thrust into this vortex? The coincidences were strong: his secret meetings with Ahmed; his recent promotion to Core6; his encounter with Dr. Sengmeuller if indeed that was her. No doubt the Authority must be challenged because the Fundamental Platform is based on the deception of billions. Only a few weeks ago his life was sane, straightforward, based on statistics, and moving up in the ranks. True, the mathematics he did was complex, but it aligned with talents. He had no political experience, no record of rebellion, no training. Did he have the ability to drop everything and do what he was now compelled to do?

Grasping *Deviations* once again, Tavon considered the contrasts: the criminal Ferster wanted to do something he should not do; Tavon did not want to do something he should do. Ferster did it so well; Tavon wondered if he could do it at all.

Yet forces of change were in motion, and he knew that turning back was not an option. Whatever transpired going forward, Tavon told himself, he would need to remain rational, because rational was his *forte*, and it could help him as much as it helped Ferster the criminal. Yet he worried to what extent rational could protect him. Ahmed's *forte* had been his rational thinking, and he ended up dead.

Tavon went to the kitchen to open a bottle of Coonawarra Cabernet Sauvignon. He poured a glass to the brim, took an aggressive sip, then returned to the family room. Placing the glass on the night table, he settled into his favorite 5% gravity setting on the virtual bed. The pressure on his back dissolved as he stretched his legs and arms as far as possible. Contrary to habit, he did not set any music, for tonight he was satisfied with just lying and thinking.

Many questions pervaded his mind. What about my fears? What is it that makes me fearful? Does it have anything to do with time lived? If I was a eubeing, with a long past and a vast future, would I less fearful?

Such ruminations absorbed Tavon that evening; an earnest, solitary stand before what he knew would be a mad rush managing the reverse-aging rollout and collaborating with Rethinking. He knew that billions of eubeings were depending on him, Rethinking, Ximena, and Frieda, in ways that they could not even imagine. His mother, bless her soul, would be extremely proud when he finally told her the whole story. If he ever got the chance.

Tavon's eyes finally grew heavy and his breathing shifted to shallow and regular as he fell into a much-needed sleep.

CHAPTER 35

FRIEDA WALLOWED IN disbelief and anger as Gupta departed her apartment. She paced erratically on the scruffy blue carpet and screamed to herself: I can't believe how casual Gupta was describing the details of the LNS torture used on dear Ahmed! Her evil is subhuman!

I already knew he had been tortured. Was it not enough for her to leave it at that?

I can only pray that Ahmed somehow survived. Don't let this crack you. In my long captivity, I've held a primary credo: be patient and maintain hope. I've been confined in this place for two centuries and always known that if I waited long enough an opportunity would arise. And it will! But I still need to bide my time a while longer, to wade through the progression of obstacles that will arise as I work with Tavon. I must be cautious and careful, especially with the scientists.

Her evil is my torture, but I won't let it derail my plans. Consider the enormous patience they've instilled in me. Isn't it ironic that by abusing me for so long they've lent me the single characteristic – patience – which I need most to succeed in bringing them down? Mind you, I admit that patience is a "necessary but not sufficient" thing. But at least I can sit less wearily now, knowing there's great potential for action very soon, not the faint hope I clung to for so long. I'm giddy with anticipation. Of course, I must wait a bit longer, be patient to the end, until the day so much will happen. What a sudden and beautiful change it will be!

So I must endure a bit longer, detailing and planning. Finishing touches never cease, they just grow finer. More and more preparation will ensure my success.

True, they granted me a few accommodations over the decades, for example, gave me access to movie streaming and scientific websites. But that was one-directional. Never could I garner a genuine two-way communication, except with Core6 members as the muffle-altered Chief Genomicist, or with Gupta, who's never softened or veered off course, except that one day when she pretended. For years, I've hoped she would lower her guard. But she's hardened over time. She's tested my forbearance: stretched me, torn me, fooled me, and demeaned me. But she hasn't broken me! I'll never let her do that, and I think she knows it. Besides, I doubt she wants to break me entirely because she takes pleasure in my wanting and waiting.

My CG communication with Ahmed proved to be pure anguish. What good did it bring us to talk, without looking into each others' eyes, touching, embracing, or sharing the deepest aspirations of our souls? I know Gupta did this to torture me, just like she tortured him.

But patience finally brought me to Tavon. Perfect steps, perfectly timed, are a must here. I so look forward to working with him on the reverse-aging rollout! I'm elated by this feeling, which I've not held for so long: looking positively forward. I've played the waiting game many ways with the Authority but waiting is now anything but a game. A revolt is about to unfold. I admit I could have announced the reverse-aging discovery one or two decades ago, but only now does the announcement befit the time. An election is pending and my pNIT, after much refinement, is now at a level that pleases me.

I'm sure the Authority has no major suspicions, at least Gupta does not. It took what seems like forever – the span of two complete lifetimes before age-decoding completely altered the notion of a lifetime – to reach this point, but I'm here at last and I can't wait to start acting instead of waiting and wanting. And wondering. Wondering is the worst part. I always wondered, for instance, how the Authority explained my death to the world. Did they use a sadistic tack, such as faking my suicide, which leaves that guilt scar on all loved ones? Or did they offer faint hope to torment my family and others by telling them I was incarcerated, to be released at some future date, which they postponed time and time again? That would strain my family, decade after decade, as they did with me. But at least they'd know I'm alive, so perhaps that tack is not as cruel as the faked suicide.

Patience by one is more likely than patience by many. My solitary patience, I hope and pray, will bring me back together with my loved ones. With all my heart I pray I'll soon see Ahmed and Xi and Jesus. How I miss Ahmed! He remains my only possible soulmate. Is he even alive? If so, would he ever take me back? Jesus, too, I miss so much. He was a terrific father, but also a fine companion to me. And my daughter, Xi – what has become of her? I only knew her as a youngster. I can sense her deep in my breast, and I long for her every day. She must have grown up to become a beautiful young lady. Yet I'm jolted by her pain. I sense it acutely as it crawls inside me like a worm and circles and circles and never leaves. What is this, her pain? Soon, I'll hold Xi as a real mother should. And her pain will dissolve away.

CHAPTER 36

TAVON WAS INFORMED by Dr. Christine Hughson, one of the scientists working with the CG, that she had uncovered something curious in the liquid mixture which was to be used for reverse-aging. She noticed a portion of code on the pNIT that seemed more like an encrypted message, not a coded instruction. Instruction code was designed to coordinate timing mechanisms between the NIT and the pNIT, which for reverse-aging was a crucial function. But to Dr. Hughson, the encrypted message seemed out of place. Too embarrassed to ask the CG or other scientists about it, she decided to bring the issue to Tavon.

Tavon told her he would double-check on it right away and get back to her. He obtained a sample of the liquid mixture from her.

This development worried Tavon. He could not afford to lose time worrying about contaminants in the reverse-aging process. His gut feel was to seek immediate help outside the Authority for an independent analysis. He contacted Felix Heinstien, a brilliant electrical engineer he knew from his MIT days, and who was still there working with the Artificial Superintelligence Group. Felix was a staunch Libertarian, not generally supportive of governments, especially the Authority. Ahmed had to be careful in the way he approached him on this matter.

In reaching out to Felix, Tavon did not communicate through his NIT. He utilized a secure platform that Felix himself had shown him three years ago.

"How's it going Felix?" said Tavon.

"Couldn't be better. How about you, Champ? How ya' doing working for the big gov'?"

"Well, the Authority is truly something, that's all I can say. I certainly have my hands full with an interesting project coming up. Sorry, I can't give details, but it will be public in a few days."

"Don't know how you do it. I'd be paranoid, depressed, and self-harming if I worked there. When are you comin' to Beantown to down a few Samuel Adams lagers with me?"

"Soon, I hope, maybe after my project is done."

"Cool, So what's up?

"I need you to look at something, and to just keep it between us."

"OK ... that sounds interesting."

"It's an NIT, but a nifty micro version. Within it, there's code to communicate with a normal NIT. Most of that code looks standard, except for a small portion which seems to contain encrypted material. Can you decipher it for me?"

"I'll take a look at it. What's your timeline? I'm guessing you needed this yesterday!"

"You always were sharp. Yes, as soon as possible."

"Shit. You think I can just drop everything I'm doing in the AS lab?"

"Didn't you once tell me that one of the great advantages of working at MIT was their flexibility in work hours?"

"Well put. You always had a memory like a steel trap," Felix quipped.

"Is there any payoff for me? Even the slightest?"

"Actually, yes, and more than just a few pints of Samuel Adams. If you do this for me, you won't be helping the Authority, you'll be helping me. Get what I mean?"

"I do. I like. Send me the info."

"Sorry. I'll have to send you the actual micro-NIT. It's within a chemical fluid, but you should be able to disentangle and isolate it, as it's the only nonorganic component of the fluid. I'll fly-taxi it to you. You should have it in a couple of hours."

"OK Champ. You'll hear back from me later tonight."

Just before midnight that very same day, Felix did get back to Tavon.

Felix explained, "The *ciphertext* was quite minimal. Whoever encrypted it was using Quantum key asymmetric cryptography, stuff the NSA used eons ago, though it's formidable even today and not easy for any pleb' to crack. Still, I didn't need our Dodecabit Quantum technology. The Qubit Quantum unit sufficed. Took about five seconds. I've attached a copy of the plaintext for you."

Tavon was curious. "Did you read the *plaintext*?"

"Of course I did."

"So? Give me a hint."

"Sure. It's two audio-visual messages from the famous scientist Dr. Frieda Sengmeuller. It'll blow your fucking mind!"

CHAPTER 37

WHEN XIMENA RETURNED to the house, Jesus, Jason, and Sarah were preparing for their day trip to Camp 4544, located about one hundred miles northwest of New Orleans. Jesus had wanted to do something to get the kids out of the house. Ximena loved the idea.

"Are you sure you won't join us?" he asked Ximena.

Ximena replied, "Rethinking needs me to do my job right here at my place. I've got lots to do. That means never losing focus, waiting a lot when nothing is happening, and being ready to act if needed. I'm not going to let them down now. It's known as vigilance."

"Vigilance? That's a weird word," said Sarah. "It doesn't sound like much fun to me. You're very loyal, Xi!"

"Thank you. You're very sweet."

Ximena walked them all out to the car and gave the autopilot their destination. Through the open window, Jesus touched Ximena lightly on her good arm.

She exclaimed, "Now remember, have fun! And look after Jesus!"

"We will!" Sarah shouted.

The car glided off silently. Squeezed between the two youngsters in the back seat, Jesus thought to himself, I love the *sunyata* of these kids, their beautiful emptiness. That's something eubeings just can't hold on to growing old chronologically.

When Jesus, Sarah, and Jason arrived at Camp 4544, the soccer game was already well into the second half. Jason and Sarah noticed immediately that the kids played well: deeks, headers, crosses, and challenges – the game was very competitive. They also noticed an odd scene along the far length of the field: a standard metal fence separating the field from a cemetery filled with hundreds of old gravestones, hung at various and sometimes awkward angles due to the irregular shapes of the knolls on which they lay. The stones formed their own ungainly, yet organized whole: like a metropolis, but of grayness and dirt rather than the shininess and light of normal cities; an array of rectangular shapes each telling the story of a singular person who aged, ailed, and died. The stones were weatherbeaten and the spaces between them littered with dandelions, other weeds, and unkempt grass.

During the game, these old stones stood as one, in the background, not in opposition to the youthful game in the foreground, but as a subconscious set of spirits gathered to follow a beautiful game, to worship the litheness and exuberance of the playing children, and to earn some respect in return. That respect came in the form of furtive glances from the young girls and boys in the direction of the stones, as if to say, *We know you're there, we can see you when we want to, and we very much know what you're about.*

At this boundary between cemetery and soccer pitch, the old and the young – the two forlorn groups of Zone1 – whispered unified statements, made mutual offerings.

To Jason and Sarah, the kids seemed like normal ten-year-olds. But Jason was wise enough to know they were anything but normal because they were future eubeings, which made all the difference. Still, like normal kids, their energy seemed immense: pent up during the time out while politely listening to the instructions of the coaches, then bursting from the huddle: jostling, bouncing, and giggling. Would they at least be normal until they reached the age of twenty-five? No, that could not be the case, since even before being age-decoded their relationship with adults would be different, as evidenced by this crowd, much greater than could be justified by a simple soccer game between kids, composed of hundreds of older eubeings who yearned to bear witness to *any child*, to see first hand the youthful immaturity; to behold that rare stage of adolescence; and, most importantly, to vicariously delight in the pride and attachment exuded by their natural parents, who were seated in two special clusters near the mid-field line, one on each side of the pitch.

Jesus explained to Jason and Sarah how it all worked: during the game, a large proportion of the non-parents *adopted in their mind* a particular child, tracking their every move. They felt pride when their child made a good play, sorrow when they went did not, and fear and worry if they were hurt. What a treat it was for them to be like real parents! Joyous tears often trickled down the cheeks of these non-parents as they bonded with their adopted children.

This powerful psychological adoption effect was not explicitly encouraged by the Authority. But it was also not discouraged. There was no denying the inestimable value it added to the price of admission. Whether the Authority condoned it was a matter of minor debate. Year after year, crowds of eubeings served themselves unrepentantly in this way at Camp 4544 and all other Zone1 camps. And soccer games were not the only fodder for psychological adoption: many other sports and activities were used for the dual purpose of parental engagement and Authority revenue generation.

"Can we go down to the field after the game?" Jason asked Jesus.

"Can we? Can we?" cried Sarah.

"That's impossible," Jesus told them. "Right after the game, the crowd is ushered out, except for the natural parents, who are allowed to stay with their sons and daughters for a while longer. Besides, it looks like it's about to rain."

"How much longer?" asked Sarah.

"'Til the storm?"

"No. How much longer are the parents allowed to stay with their kids after the game?"

"Oh. I believe it's about half an hour," said Jesus.

"What? Only half an hour? That's ridiculous," said Sarah. "How can a world with oodles of time not give kids more time with their parents?"

"Good question, Sarah. It does seem ridiculous to give them only thirty minutes, but that's only while the kids are at camp, which is nine months per year. Camp kids are very busy with academics and sports, so parent visits must be restricted. During the three-month break from camp, however, kids return home and get all the time in the world to spend with their mother, father or both."

"Well that's good to hear," said Sarah. "Good for both the kids and the parents."

"Yes, but it can also be very tough on the kids because when they leave camp they now can't see their friends for twelve weeks. You see, so few kids exist in Zone1 that it would be a fluke for a child going home to live anywhere near another child of the same age. None of them have siblings to play with. Well, I shouldn't say none, because there are a few families out there who have won the Family Rights Lottery more than once. But most kids, when they go home, have no young people to play with for twelve weeks. Many become *camp-sick* when they get home, which can be very disturbing for the parents who are trying to enjoy the precious time with their children. Computer networked virtual reality camps, of course, are a popular way for kids to deal with camp-sickness. And another great source of revenue for the Authority."

Jesus stopped for a moment to make sure Sarah and Jason were taking it all in. They seemed to be, based on the distressed look on their faces. "It's a matter of numbers ... do you see what I mean?"

As Jesus, the kids, and the other spectators headed to the parking lot a lightning bolt whirred above and split the dark sky. Patchy rain began. Jesus grabbed Sarah and Jason, one in each hand, and they slowly jogged to the car. I can still jog a bit, Jesus thought. I'm not so old. And someday, if I'm reverse-aged, I'll be able to run again.

When they got back to the house Jason opened a letter from Tavon which Ximena gave to him. He had never seen a handwritten letter. Ximena sat next to him and watched as he read it to himself:

Dear Jason; Please accept my apologies for not seeing you in person, but for security purposes, I cannot. These letters will become vital to us in moving forward. You can write back as well if you want. The Rethinking Party needs you to do us a favor, which is to do nothing, to lie low, to try to relax. I know this is probably not what you want to hear, because Jesus has told me of your wish to be more involved with our group. I thank you for that offer, and assure you that I and others will need much help at some time – but now is not the time. You are aware of what happened to Xi's father, Ahmed Iftikhar, and by now I'm sure you have heard the amazing good news that Xi's mother is, we believe, alive and that I have made contact with her through my work.

It is an evil government that tortures to death a person who is trying to do good, then pretends to kill another person to trap her for the rest of her life and use her without anyone knowing. You are only just nineteen years old, Jason, which is too young to be heavily involved in politics, especially the dangerous politics of confronting the Authority.

I know you'll understand that Xi needs your support as much as you need hers, so I ask that you work to nurture your bond with her, to help her (and Jesus) when asked, but also to be yourself, for you are an amazing young man. The Authority sees you as a threat. Others see you as a miracle of science. I see you as a gift to us all.

Finally, let us not forget your sister Sarah, who deserves your attention, for you are like her father. That is an immense responsibility. You must act as both brother and father. I know you will thrive in both roles.

Please keep in contact by letter whenever you wish. And keep up your reading!

Your friend, Tavon Brooks.

Ximena could see from Jason's reaction that he was not pleased. "Interesting letter?" she asked.

"Yes, but it made me feel so ... sidelined. Tavon is saying he wants me to stay away from Rethinking and politics. Says I'm too young."

Ximena paused. "I can't disagree. Did he say anything else?"

"To keep up my reading."

Ximena figured there might be more, but left it alone.

She offered, "We have to trust what Tavon says, because he's in a unique position, and he's doing his best to take full advantage of that. He's also being careful to look after your interests. Remember, we eubeings are not used to dealing with young people. Most of us haven't had kids, so we can't borrow from personal experience."

This didn't cheer Jason up or change his mind. He was eager to bust loose and do something. He knew his special place, unique status, as a product of anti-aging cloning totipotency and cryopreservation. He knew he represented the non-genetic approach to eliminating old age, and therefore would be shunned by the Authority. Deep inside, though, Jason yearned to help Jesus, Xi, or Tavon, and do whatever he could to improve this new world which seemed so mixed up. Did these people think he couldn't help because he was just nineteen years old?

There must be something he could do. He respected Tavon, but he was not about to "do nothing and lie low". He wished he could convince Tavon, Xi, or the other Rethinking Party leaders to involve him.

Jason vowed right then to find some way to break out and help, not to prove them wrong, but to prove himself right. He had to do something since it looked like he and Sarah were in this world for good.

CHAPTER 38

JASON HANKERED TO DO something. His visit to Camp 4544, though fun, had been a marginal distraction, and the letter from Tavon dismayed him. So early the next morning, before the sun had risen or anyone else was up, he grabbed a backpack, a change of clothing, some snacks, two bottles of water, and took the ebike from the garage. He left a brief note for Ximena and Jesus, indicating that he would be gone for a bit and they need not worry.

He cycled his way across the core of the City and along Esplanade Avenue to the base of the twenty-four-mile-long Lake Pontchartrain Causeway. In the year 2089, after decades of public lobbying, bike lanes were finally added to the outer edges of this magnificent structure. The side border of the bike lane was a one-foot-high cement barrier, above which extended five feet of see-through nylon mesh. Unlike the motorists who had their view blocked by high steel guard rails, Jason's view cycling across the Causeway was spectacular. At the apex of his crossing, he stopped and took a moment to look back at the cityscape. Between the downtown buildings, through a light fog, the rising sun was noticeable and reflected over the brownish lake water.

Jason finally reached the far side of the lake and rode off the Causeway headed eastward adjacent to the shore for another four miles to his disc golf destination in Fontainebleau State Park. He arrived five minutes earlier than his goal time of 9:00 a.m. In the parking lot, he immediately guzzled down a full bottle of water, then began to mingle with those waiting to play. The organizer hooked him up with an Asian girl who looked to be around his age, as well as an older gentleman.

"Hi, I'm Shu. And this is my father, Jiang."

"Nice to meet you, I'm Jason."

Jason shook hands with each of them and they headed through a crop of trees to the first tee.

"Have you played here before?" asked Shu as she adjusted her dark long hair under her cap.

"No. My first time."

"Well, I'm sure you'll be impressed," said her father. "The best disc golf in the region, believe me."

"And some really good players," added Shu.

Jason replied, "Well I can assure you I'll bring down the level of play."

Shu chuckled and flashed him a cute smile.

She started things off on the first hole by launching her frisbee forty yards straight down the fairway. Her father followed suit, although his throw was a bit shorter. Jason's first throw veered wildly off course into the thick forest.

"We call that a DW throw!" cried Shu, "Deep woods!"

"Or don't want" quipped Jason.

"Very funny," said Jiang.

Jason eventually scored a seven on the hole, while Shu and Jiang each scored a four.

"Do you live in this area? I noticed you biked in," asked Jiang.

"Not too far away, I live in the city."

"Wow, that's a long bike."

"Yeh, but it was interesting, especially going across the Causeway for the first time."

"Are you a student?" asked Shu.

"No, I'm taking time off. But I do plan to go to university."

Shu stood on the tee for the second hole, a dogleg par four. She extended her throwing arm, squatted, rotated, and released her tee shot. The frisbee sailed straight at first, then arched just enough to round the corner and settle well down the fairway.

She said to him, "I'm looking at schooling at Peking University to study Engineering Sciences. They have the top program in Asia and are very progressive."

"That sounds amazing," said Jason. "I'm also hoping to study next year, but I'm still not sure what exactly."

Jiang threw his tee shot, then advised, "Take your time. And don't put too much pressure on yourself. It's only your first degree. Shu is tired of me telling her that, but I think it's important to remember."

"Yes, that's also what my guardian Ximena told me."

Jason drew back and released his frisbee, managing a decent throw.

"That's better!" cried Shu.

They continued to play for about an hour. Jason enjoyed their company as well as the challenge of disc golf.

On the fifteenth hole, a long par five, Jason and Shu were alone in the forest looking for one of Jason's errant throws, out of earshot of Jiang, when Shu quietly said, "Has anyone ever told you you're cute?"

Jason blushed and said nothing.

Shu smiled at him, then screamed, "Hey, I found it!"

When they finished the game and were standing in the parking lot, Shu asked Jason, "Why don't you come to our place and get some nutrients first? It's lunchtime and you have a long trip back. We live nearby." She turned to her father, "Eh Dad, is that alright?"

"Sure, we'd be pleased to treat you to lunch, Jason."

Jason trusted the situation enough, and he had to admit he was hungry.

"Sounds great," he replied.

They hitched his ebike onto the car rack and drove about six miles northwest to their house. As they distanced themselves from the park the terrain shifted. Jason noted the few large houses separated by unsettled tracts of land.

"We're almost there," said Shu. "We call areas like this *pseudo-rural.* Not city, but not rural either."

When they arrived at the house Shu's father fixed sandwiches for everyone, took one for himself, and excused himself to leave them alone. Shu and Jason remained seated at the large, glass kitchen table.

"You suck at disc golf, but I bet you do other sports."

"I did some cross country running, was fairly good at it, but I've sort of gone away from that. I'd like to get back into running. The bike ride this morning reminded me of it: getting into a nice, peaceful mantra over a long distance."

"That's nice. My sports were basketball and volleyball. Had a hoot with those in high school."

They conversed a while longer, and Shu opened up about her childhood. "In 2036 I was born in Hong Kong, and I grew up there living with my natural parents as their only child. But my mom and dad were detained in the Hong Kong uprising of 2052 when I was sixteen years old, and I never saw them again."

Jason refrained from saying anything. He was busy doing the math in his head. It seemed that Shu, too young to be a eubeing, but must be a cryo.

Shu went on, "I tried to kill myself, drove my car straight into an oncoming transport truck, but I miraculously escaped death. Because of the damage to my body and having no parents to vouch or care for me, in the eyes of the Chinese government I was a prime candidate for something called AACT, which regenerated my bad organs and saved me. However, because of legal barriers to this technology, I wasn't recognized as a person after that, can you believe it?"

"That's sick!" he replied.

"To finish my story ... I was cryopreserved in a frozen state for almost two hundred years until the legal barriers were resolved. I only emerged from that state three years ago. Therefore, I'm what's known as a cryo. I'll tell you more about it later. It's nothing bad, though the Authority would want you to think otherwise."

Jason chose not to disclose that he too was a cryo. He liked her, but they had just met, and Tom and Tavon had warned him to be careful. He said, "That's quite a story. You've certainly gone through a lot."

With that, Shu got up from the table, and Jason could not help but notice how nicely her jeans fit around her shapely hips.

She asked, "Would you like to join me on a *somatobomb*? My dad doesn't want me overdoing it, but I'm allowed to do it once a week. It supercharges the sensory pathways in your entire body. Want to give it a go?"

Jason smiled at her and said, "OK. Why not?"

She took his hand and led him down the stairs to where they entered a room that contained nothing except one ultra-plush purple mattress which covered the entire floor and even the lower half of the walls. They lay down on it.

Shu began to take off her top, and Jason noted her small firm breasts and pointy nipples.

He implored himself. What should I do?

"Don't be shy," said Shu. "Take off all of your clothes and throw them into the corner over there."

"OK," he said, sheepishly.

They both stripped down and tossed everything aside. Shu then unzipped a pocket built into the mattress and pulled out a small glass bottle.

"Here. Take a good gulp of this. Don't worry, it's non-addictive but extremely effective." She then smiled straight through him and added, "You'll find somatobombing infinitely more fun than disc golf."

They lay close to each other, and Shu rested one of her tiny hands onto his thigh.

Jason held the bottle up to his mouth, tilted his head back, and took in a moderate amount. He handed the bottle to her, and she did the same.

"That's enough. Perfect," said Shu. "Now let's enjoy everything, including each other."

Jason noticed first that although he did not think any differently he *felt* things more intensely. His neck hair tingled; his arms and legs turned buoyant and twittery; his feet tickled. Then came a strange feeling in his loins. Her effervescent sexiness floated in the air, encircled the room, and descended upon him; and her aroma – vivacious and estrogenic – whelmed and penetrated his senses. Nothing he had ever felt before compared with this. It was too much for Jason to sensate singularly, so he lost himself with Shu and they embraced and fondled *ad libitum*.

Jason's *straightedge* status was obliterated in that room. He did not return home that evening.

Xi and Sarah worried immensely through that evening and the next morning. Jason did not have an NIT, so there was no way to reach him. Jesus did his best to calm them down, explaining how adventurous a young man his age could be.

At breakfast still at Shu's house, Jason asked her to tell him more about AACT and the cryos.

Her father, who overheard Jason, poured himself a coffee and sat to join them and explain things. "Shu is a cryo. I'm Shu's adopted father. I head up the HF Capital demographics group. HF capital is the financial entity that underwrote AACT and challenged the Authority regarding it. We supported the legality of the technology, on behalf of clients such as Shu. It took a long time, but we eventually won our case. Until then Shu and all other cryos were deemed illegal people, which, as you can imagine, gave them limited human rights."

Jason was intrigued, "Can you tell me more about your demographics work?"

"Sure. Demographics is the hot area right now at HF. My background is public medicine, and my expertise in viruses and pandemics is, fortuitously, surprisingly applicable to my work at HF promoting AACT, given that the Authority tries to contain it like a virus. If we go further with that analogy and just think of AACT as a virus, then public health pandemic models serve us very well. You see, the Authority's goal is to prevent it or contain it, and our goal at HF is to promote it, as a *benevolent* virus. Now, with our legal win, they can't prevent it, so their strategy now is to contain it. It's a beautiful application of public health dynamics."

"Forgive me if I'm asking too much, but why would they view someone like Shu as a virus? What's so bad about AACT, in their minds?"

Shu looked at her father and said, "Boy, he's a clever one." She then turned to Jason to explain, "You just asked the prime question. Nobody's sure why the Authority is worried, some say paranoid, about AACT and cryos."

Her father added, "We think birth control might be a factor, as we know eubeings are infertile, which is not the case for cryos and AACT adopters. The rate of growth of non-eubeings could be a worry for them, not in the short term, but eventually. But that still begs the question, why would they worry about lower proportions of eubeings in the population?"

Jason stood up, put his backpack over his shoulder, and said, "Well, speaking of worried, I think my guardians must be wondering where I've disappeared to. I'd better head back home. It has been super fun and interesting meeting you both. Thank you so much."

He shook hands with Jiang, and Shu led him outside to his bike.

"Here." She handed him a water bottle and a banana.

Jason put the items in his backpack. "Thanks."

"By the way, I did want to ask you about what happened to your real parents, but let's do that some other time."

He reached out his hand to gently touch the back of her neck, then leaned forward to kiss her.

"Let's do that," he said.

"See ya, Jason."

"Bye, Shu."

CHAPTER 39

NOW THAT TAVON BROOKS was installed into Core6 and working to implement reverse-aging with the Chief Genomicist, Reubers felt ready to discuss election strategy with Zhinghu, whom he had summoned to meet this morning. The two normally met on the first day of the month to discuss SI progress, but this meeting was urgent and off-schedule. He chose the New Orleans office, 100th floor, not only because of its security, which was *super-rated*, but because of its incredible view of the city and southward to the vast blue of the Gulf of Mexico.

While waiting for Zhinghu, Reubers spied the seabirds circling above the nearby bay. They glided and dove with an overall effect that was coherent and beautiful.

It must have been odd, Reubers thought, for those who lived here one or two centuries ago to wait helplessly while Category 5 and 6 hurricanes bore down on the city. It made him proud to know that the Zone1 Authority could now subdue such weather monsters with their *marine cloud brightening* technique, infusing seawater into clouds to make them whiter and more sun-reflective, thus cooling the ocean below and weakening the cyclone. Proof again that science was very much about positive control.

At the sound of Zhinghu entering the room, Reubers swiveled his chair with a quick half-turn.

"Hi there Zhinghu," he said.

"Hello, Mr. President."

"Please ... call me Manfred today. I prefer that in one-on-ones."

"Sure, Manfred," Zhinghu said, taking a seat across from Reubers at the small circular table.

"OK. I hear we're setting the stage nicely on the pre-election buttressing of our popularity. Am I to understand it's all systems go with the Chief Genomicist?"

"Absolutely. According to Gupta, the CG is ready with the technology and has already had preliminary muffle-altered contact with Tavon Brooks. The timelines will be tight for medical rollout, but we believe it can be done. We're also told by our psychosociologist Tony that the effect on recipients will be awesome. Granted, for most folks, the biological effect will only be noticeable over a time scale of a few years. That's obviously too slow to help us with this election. Intriguingly, however, the psychological effect will be immediate. In Tony's words: *Reverse-aging will dance in peoples' minds and cement the Fundamental Platform.*"

Reubers loved what he heard. He then asked the question which both men knew he had to ask, "Will the immediate psychological effect bring an immediate political effect?"

"That's not my area of expertise. But Suzanne, who is, as you know, our political guru, assures me there'll be a significant impact, politically. As she likes to remind us, there's always a link between psychology and politics."

Reubers shared a reflection, "Politics is quite selfish in the end. That's what she's always told us. It sounds awful, but I can't disagree with her. Anyhow, that political effect looks encouraging. Are there any issues, Zhinghu ... any security concerns, for example, from your SI standpoint?"

Zhinghu contemplated for a moment, then said, "I can't think of any. The scenario should be very much like that in 2053, with age-decoding. Almost everyone who qualifies will go for it. Why wouldn't older people want to grow younger? But I'm currently querying FENCODE_11 to sift through communications linkages and possible surreptitious scenarios. Remember, it nailed Ahmed's Spectre Society visit on the first pass of its classified modeling."

"It did! And none of us were even suspicious. Why was the first pass run even done on him? He appeared rock solid. Who pushed for it?"

Zhinghu explained, "I'm afraid nobody can take credit for pushing it. Evidently, FENCODE_11 went on one of its "hunches" for classified modeling of Core6 and Apex200 members. Ahmed himself once described it to me as a pseudo-random internal mechanism for limiting, and in some cases triggering, classified modeling. They're hunches, not just random checks."

"He was in on that?"

Zhinghu asked, "In on its design?"

"Uhum."

"Indeed," said Zhinghu. "He was the chief mathematical advisor for the classified modeling design team. That happened many years before the creation of SI. That's one of the reasons we brought Ahmed into Core6.

"Makes sense. He had superb experience."

"Unbelievably superb," said Zhinghu, "But it's so ironic, eh? That he contributed so much to the technology that was pivotal to his downfall... a self-imposed destruction of sorts!"

They both chuckled at his clever thought.

Reubers quickly switched back to a serious tone. "Why can't we do classification modeling for all people, all of the time?"

"That's a way more demanding analysis. The input parameters and mathematical modeling soak up huge resources and get very messy. Ahmed tried to explain it to me once. It's a situation reaching orders of magnitude complexity that limits outcome accuracy, invariably missing the mark for most complex systems – such as economic, atmospheric, and biological systems. Even modeling one human being, he claimed, was more difficult than predicting the weather. And weather is tough enough: we can nail it three days out reasonably well, but not three weeks out. So it's understandable that we can't easily predict the actions of a single human being."

"Not even three days out?" asked Reubers.

"That's brutally tough, for humans. Despite the fact that, according to Ahmed, FENCODE_11 is far superior to the former Five Eyes ECHELON_B technology used by the U.S., U.K.,

Canada, New Zealand, and Australia. That old system used PLATFORM computer linkages derived from ECHELON_B satellite, telephone, fax, and other data. FENCODE_11 uses dodecabit-based quantum computing, which makes it trillions of trillions of times more powerful than Five Eyes. And in terms of nonlinear deterministic chaos ..."

"OK, you can stop, you've far exceeded my limits in IT and mathematics."

"I respect that, Manfred," said Zhinghu. He then considered what else he might talk about while he had the President's ear. After a slight pause, he put forward, "Can I ask you about the marketing approach?"

"Sure. What about it?"

"How will we promote reverse-aging? Not that I'll be involved in that side of things, but I'm interested."

"We'll market it just like we did age-decoding. Issue a standard, low-profile announcement tomorrow, then simply let it market itself through good old-fashioned word-of-mouth. Reverse-aging is a damned miracle. Period. It won't need any pumping up. It won't require normal marketing, just basic advertising on availability, locations, and times. Everyone will want it. Expect huge lineups."

"Faustian Bargain Phase 2," quipped Zhinghu.

"Exactly," Reubers replied, trying to hold back a wry grin. He was relishing how the masses would become even more locked in by this second installment of the Fundamental Platform.

"I never thought we'd see the day," said Zhinghu.

"Neither did I. The Chief Genomicist deserves full credit."

"Yes, but after this, I'm not sure if we'll have any more need the CG," Zhinghu stated soberly. He then took on a look of excitement. "I assume we're having a coming-out ceremony for the CG. Why don't you let me set that up? I can see it right now: Zone-wide unveiling of the CG, with full accolades for inventing reverse-aging, capped off with a personal speech from him or her, outlining the science, the historic challenges, and the support from the Authority. It would be a tremendous event showcasing the importance of collaboration in the Authority science circles."

As Zhinghu spoke Reubers felt sorry for him because he was not privy to the fact that the CG was Dr. Frieda Sengmeuller. Gupta and he had once considered making Zhinghu aware of the CG's identity, but they felt it was too risky to expand that knowledge to one other person.

Only Reubers knew of Gupta's devious plan to take full credit for the discovery of reverse-aging. Whenever any scientist had muffle-altered communications with the CG over the past decades, Gupta had been careful not to be present. In the end, the revelation to the world that Gupta was the CG would be believable. Reverse-aging would surpass age-decoding as the greatest scientific accomplishment in the history of humankind, and surely the Nobel would go to Gupta. Reubers and she would have to dispose of Frieda, but that would be a minor issue.

"Leave the planning for something like that to me," said Reubers. "You've got enough on your plate with the reverse-aging rollout. Just concentrate on working hard with Tavon Brooks on that."

"You're probably right. But I want a front-row seat when the CG ceremony takes place. It'll be something to behold!"

"Guaranteed."

Reubers stood up and moved to the window and Zhinghu moved alongside him. They observed the Cerulean blue water of the Gulf's Lake Borgne and took in the whitecaps whipped up by the rare easterly wind.

"Well, that meeting was good," said Reubers. "How about a game of golf. Are you up for it?"

"I'm always up for that, Manfred. Same terms as last time?"

"No – matchplay," Reubers insisted.

"Matchplay, are you kidding? I think that's to my advantage."

"Why?"

Zhinghu reasoned, "Because when I have a really bad hole, which I will, it distorts my total, which makes stroke play tougher for me to win."

"I don't care, we're going with match play, not stroke play, and for twice our normal stakes. How about it?"

"Where? When?"

"Let's go to Canada. I haven't been there in over a year. Tomorrow morning? That exclusive Authority venue near the Rockies, the one near Dead Man's Flats. Nobody bothers us there. That sound OK, Zhinghu?"

"Sounds great, Manfred! Hopefully, you'll end up the dead man!"

"One of us will, that's for sure."

"Bring it on!"

CHAPTER 40

JESUS YEARNED TO BE young again. Though he was a eubeing, he was still a frail old man.

Very soon, according to the Authority, he could set into motion his reverse-aging. But would he go through with it? He fondly remembered how it felt to be young: his energy, his zest for writing, his headlong forays into insect research in Brazil, Tanzania, Madagascar, northern India, Nepal, Bhutan, and western China; his scientific writing – always a chaotic yet invigorating act, never finished, just worked on feverishly and finally abandoned to the publisher for the rest of the world to soak up; the flexible, springy feeling in his bones and ligaments; the raw strength of his sexual desires, primordial impulses driving him to undertake wonderful and crazy ventures with more than a few women. But mostly he remembered the sharpness of his mind, his zest to learn, his enormous devotion to more and more projects without hesitation or fear – underpinned by a capacity to criticize. He wanted to be young again. It was all to his advantage.

"Should I do it?" he finally asked Ximena outright. His wrinkled hands itched his seventy-four-year-old scalp and thin grey hair.

"I certainly think so. You're the perfect candidate. You're so old you're almost dead. Anyone in that sorry state should be first in line to turn things around." She chuckled.

"Good point," Jesus said, riding her joke. "I've been almost dead for two centuries, Xi. I've lived in this steady, frail, state so long, close enough to death to reach out and touch it. I'm akin to one of those unfortunate sinners in voodooist Haiti, unknowingly drugged by the rural elders with natural substances, rendered a Zombie, then left for almost dead to roam the countryside. Like them, I'm being persecuted for my sins."

"I don't like that analogy," said Ximena. "Because you're not a sinner. Most of those zombies probably deserved it – killed people, raped women, whatever – so the Haitian elders dealt them justice. But you, what did you do wrong?"

"It's what I didn't do that's the shame."

She was confused. "Are you referring to your enabling Ahmed's abandonment of me? Is that the shame you mean? If so, let me remind you that it wasn't your fault. My father had a total breakdown when he abandoned me, and you did the noble thing in stepping up to help."

Jesus insisted, "I should have been stronger than that. I acted like an enabler." After some pained hesitation, he added, "People can't go around blaming their genetic structure for everything. At least I can't."

"You didn't even know there was genetic structure to blame. Also, you're not to blame for that structure. Anyhow, don't you just want to be young and strong again?"

Jesus replied, "It's not that simple. I'm not sure what my real self is. Is it what I would be if age-decoding had never been invented? If that's my real self, then it died a long time ago. But let's think scientifically and non-selfishly about this. Reverse-aging will prove even worse than age-decoding in terms of the effects on our species. On a one-to-one basis, however, all individuals of our species will be so tempted to do it. It's another classic case of *the tragedy of the commons*: any social group overuses and depletes its common resources because individuals benefit more from using them in the short term rather than preserving them for the long term. To solve this tragedy, society must factor in external costs that protect long-term group livelihood. The principle was important in explaining pollution and global warming in the 21st century."

"Will you cut out your scientific crap!" Ximena cried.

"It's not science, Xi, it's economics. And economics is certainly not a science."

"Whatever you say ... but can we have a moratorium on your academic shenanigans for today! Please, dear Surrogate Father ... cease and desist!"

"OK, I will. But can you handle a few words from Buddha, who, just before he died, said the following to his disciple Ananda?:

Do not lament. Have I not often told you that it is in the very nature of things that we must eventually be parted from all that is near and dear to us? ... Since everything born is subject to decay, how can it be otherwise then that a being should pass away?"

"Beautiful, as usual," Ximena quipped. "But it's a shame Buddha didn't know anything about age-decoding, reverse-aging, or the human genome. If he did, he probably wouldn't have said anything of the sort."

"I beg to differ. What the Buddha said, I believe, is timeless. Think carefully about that line, *everything born is subject to decay*. We might use technology to stem decay superficially, but who's to say the decay can't manifest itself in some other way? Physiologically? Psychologically? Socially? They say you can always alter the course of a river, but you can't halt its flow. If you think of decay as the flow itself, then decay can't be halted. In that regard, I shouldn't choose to do reverse-aging."

Ximena rolled her eyes and gave him a frustrated look. "You're overcomplicating things again. Since you chose to do age-decoding, you're already half-way to reverse-aging. I should point out one more thing, something that's a little bit weird. If you do go for reverse-aging, in forty-nine years we'll be the same biological age: twenty-five. Isn't that remarkable? You and I, granddaughter and grandfather, identical ages!"

"That would be trippy. Would you miss me being your old grandpa? I'm tired of being an old man. You should know I'm still seriously considering going through with it. It's against Buddhist principles, but ..."

"What principles? Or dare I ask?"

"Very basic stuff. For example, in *The Complete Idiot's Guide to Buddhism,* which was published just before that religion took off in North America, it was thoughtfully written: *Let the reminder of death motivate your efforts to live each moment.* That principle is vital, because, in my mind, effort is paramount to living. Nothing upsets me more than laziness. If I'm reverse-aged, I'll gradually distance myself from that reminder of death ... rendering myself less able to push. Less able to live to the fullest. It'll be different, pulling away from my end, from my reach and touch relationship with mortality; it'll be a retreat that subverts my nature or subverts something which I can't fully describe. It's bad enough that I already went for age-decoding. Do you understand what I'm saying, Xi?"

"I think so. Well, if you don't go for reverse-aging, but the Authority is overthrown, you'll at least get your propensity to dissent back. That should make life a heck of a lot more interesting for you. I'd love to see you operating with your critical faculties restored – I bet you'd be a firebrand, a rabble-rousing old fart!" She smirked at the thought, aware of the many stories of her grandfather's past. "You might even be able to get back into research, like the old days, with the dawn of a new, transparent, fair-functioning science community. Or get into politics. We could make extensive use of you at the Rethinking Party. So maybe you don't need reverse-aging, you just need a new government." Ximena paused and looked straight at him, "So, let me ask again, will you be going for reverse-aging?"

Jesus did not utter a word but instead issued a gentle, almost submissive shaking of his head from side to side, which encompassed enough meaning without words.

Ximena responded, "With you opting not to go for it, I'm thinking that in about fifty years you'll be the only old eubeing left in the world!"

"Well, we'll be a thin herd of old farts, that's for sure. No doubt reverse-aging will cause an unprecedented demographic shift. Most everyone will, I agree, end up twenty-five years old, though it will take about one century to achieve that end since our oldest are currently 125 years old. In the end, demographics will be obsolete, with a few holdouts like me. And both the death rate and the birth rate will be negligible. Everything will converge to a single number: twenty-five. Birth, youth, old age, and death will become vestigial concepts. Insurance and health care systems will change dramatically, requiring massive restructuring and government support. Anything normally involving old people will likely wane: bridge clubs, bocci ball, bingo, bird watching, lawn bowling, square dancing, mentoring, volunteerism. Crime will increase, as it has always been a manifestation of youthful aggression. So will energy usage, speeding, illegal drugs, sexual disease, etc. And natural selection, after fighting on its deathbed for the past two hundred years due to age-decoding, will go the way of the dodo bird and breathe its last breath. The process which underpins the fashioning of life will become extinct at the level of the human species."

CHAPTER 41

ELATED EUBEINGS CELEBRATED everywhere. Strangers hugged like joyous reunited loved ones; old ladies giggled and conversed at a frenzied level; men beamed, openly consumed liquor, crouched on sidewalks, and gambled like schoolboys. All were excited to be off work for the same splendiferous reason. The thrill pervaded rural, pseudo-rural, and city folk: entrepreneurs, *enviros,* artisans, independents, technophobes, retirees, and escapees.

They jam-packed sidewalks with lineups for reverse-aging at every Spectre Society. The gatherings were akin to the opening of a World Exposition camps – chaotic and buoyant, ripe with expectation. The first to join the lines emerged from their houses moments after the implementation announcement, an awakened mass, eager to surrender deeper to the Fundamental Platform for as long as required, which was now looking like forever.

It was a heady, headlong rush into reverse-aging. A truly public mania. While the Authority had planned for such excitement, even Reubers and Zhinghu were amazed as it unfolded with such magnitude.

The Authority used Spectre Societies for reverse-aging implementation because of their broad geographical coverage of Zone1, excellent reception facilities, robotic services, connectivity to FENCODE_11, blood and chemical refrigeration units, medical supplies, and capacity to handle lineups.

Suicides were banned until after the election.

The irony of using the Spectre Societies to promote suicide one day, then implement immortality the very next, escaped everyone.

Yet their triumph was not without unfortunate incidents.

For example, at a Spectre Society in the Rocky Mountains of British Columbia, Canada, a suspension bridge collapsed under the weight of the crowd, sending about three hundred eubeings to their death. Near at a Spectre Society in Cologne, Germany, a cathedral top collapsed, pouring its two spires onto the parking lot below.

The rumble sounded like a terrorist bomb and spawned panic in the nearby crowd, crushing two dozen older eubeings. It was also reported that in Hong Kong, China, a crazed twenty-five-year-old eubeing overrode his vehicle's autopilot and plowed into a Spectre Society lineup, murdering nine and injuring fifty. Unofficial suicides also spiked during the rollout. Such incidents, though sad, were inevitable, given that tens of thousands of Spectre Societies were preoccupied with reverse-aging.

On balance, however, the reverse-aging rollout went remarkably well. Participation was naturally fervent among older eubeings. Though they were not given official priority over younger ones, they were typically promoted to the front of the line, regardless of its length, without challenge. It was not unusual to witness elders high-fived and cheered as they gently guided their hover units to the front of a line. Who among more modestly aged eubeings would deny an eighty- or ninety-year-old eubeing the swiftest access to reverse-aging? Such elders could be a few heartbeats away from death, and reverse-aging might just pull them back from the brink.

The physiological process of growing younger was felt immediately in the veins and arteries of those reverse-aged. Media conducted interviews and wrote features about jubilant elders emerging from Spectre Societies walking upright, hearing and seeing with newfound acuteness, overwhelmed, bawling like babies, and promising to be better as young adults the second time around. That these were all psychological effects had no bearing on the media frenzy.

Everyone viewed reverse-aging as the greatest scientific achievement in the history of humankind. They worshipped the Authority scientists, especially Dr. Gupta Mantharathna, who became a scientific legend and folk hero.

AGE-DECODED

As the weeks passed and the rollout progressed, Tavon received accolades from fellow Core6 members for his excellent work implementing this quantum leap for humanity.

CHAPTER 42

SQUATTING INNOCENTLY in the rolling grassy fields in the remotest area of Ximena's backyard under the shade of the largest willow tree, Sarah asked Jason what he had.

"It's a Monarch butterfly," he said. He contained it softly by cupping his hands. "They're beautiful. I love the two rows of white spots around the edges. See?"

"Yes. But I like the orange color more."

"What about the black stripes?" Jason asked her. "Do you know why they are there?"

"No."

"They're veins. But they also act as supports for the wings, sort of like bones for human limbs."

"That's neat."

"Yes. But the neatest thing about Monarchs is how smart they are."

"How do you know they're smart?"

"Jesus's book describes how the North American monarchs living east of the Rocky Mountains fly south in the fall and winter, ending up in a specific part of Mexico. But how do they do it? They don't have GPS, you know!"

"Maybe they do!"

"Yeah, maybe their own secret version. We don't have all the answers. Jesus admits that in his book."

"Why do they go south?"

"To escape bad weather."

"Do they come back?"

"Yep, the next spring."

"That's a lot of energy for such a small creature."

"It sure is. And one thing about that journey is very intriguing. Apparently, one butterfly does not live long enough to survive the entire journey. The whole trip happens across several generations. Sort of like a relay race."

"That's weird! Like a relay race where only the anchor finishes the round trip alive! The rest of the team is dead before the end of the race?"

"Exactly. It's as if the Monarch species protects itself flying south through birth and death. And scientists don't even know how one generation communicates directions to the next generation during the trip."

"Maybe they don't. Maybe every single butterfly just knows."

"That's not a bad thought! Well done, sis!"

Sarah suddenly switched the topic, "Did we die?"

Jason was uncomfortable with the question and had worked hard to protect his sister from certain things, including their family's accident, their mother's death, and the use of AACT on Sarah and him.

"I really can't answer that, Sarah. From what they tell me we didn't die; we were just preserved in some sort of frozen state."

"Why did they do that?"

"Because we were in the right place at the right time, the perfect candidates for the new technology to save people's lives. Remember, there was an accident, which killed Mom, and they tried to save us."

"But didn't we have a choice? If they had asked me, I would have said no. I would have chosen to go to heaven with Mom. That's probably what was meant to be. Did they ask you?"

Her words surprised but also touched Jason. "I can't blame you for feeling that way, Sarah, but I hope you'll change your mind someday. Maybe I can help you see it differently."

"You won't change my mind. I don't really like this world we're in now."

"I understand how you feel. But maybe, eventually, that'll change for you. Look, let's stop talking about this and go find some more Monarchs to play with."

"OK, let's go!"

She and her big brother frolicked on the grounds for a good part of the afternoon. Together they chased, captured, watched, and released many Monarchs, beholding the orange-black magic of life at their fingertips.

Occasionally they cavorted and wrestled with each other. The warm light breeze mingled playfully with long wild grass, which, together with the sandy soil, cushioned their falls. The sky shone bright blue, but not cloudlessly, and several times Sarah pointed up to the cumulus clouds and proposed animal shapes, which made Jason laugh.

The two needed this afternoon, the play and freedom it offered. The monarchs and the delightful day swept them away. It had been a while since Jason had seen smiles coming from his little sister. The more Sarah giggled, the more she forgot about her mother, the accident, and the past.

He thought it might be the best time they had ever spent as brother and sister, in either world. Today they had fashioned a simple enchanting memory, which they could look fondly back at in ten, a hundred, or even a thousand years.

Ximena put aside her binoculars, which had provided a perfect view of Sarah and Jason from her location on the second floor. She hoped that someday soon they would have the freedom to venture out in the real world. It pleased her, witnessing their joy, which, at least today, lent her the strength to leave her appendage in its healing mitt.

A tiny turn for the better?

CHAPTER 43

FRIEDA WAS CONFIDENT that her pNIT would work. Her only concern was that everyone who opted for reverse-aging received one, since that was her only way into their minds, unbeknownst to the Authority, and she did not anticipate a better opportunity than this. The pNIT would be included in the liquid mixture to be ingested as part of the reverse-aging procedure, and it would not discriminate who worked for the Authority, who was sympathetic to the Authority, who might alert the Authority, who was against the Authority, or who might change their view. Anyone reverse-aged would ingest a pNIT.

A critical element in her device was the timing of its first message, which she set for the wee hours of the morning – August 1st at 3:00 a.m. Eastern Standard Time, exactly one week before the election. That she could control. Her design was the converse of the NIT's currently used by the Authority and some large corporations: rather than allowing individuals to input to a central nexus such as a pictoplath, hers allowed a central message to be activated within individuals at a specified time. It took her 150 years to develop and perfect, though if it were not for the furtive nature of her research, she could have done so much faster.

The aspect of the pNIT's design which made Frieda so self-congratulatory was its intricate *dual-targeting function*:

- Step 1: when first ingested, the pNIT immediately detects any activity emitted by that person's NIT; it then uses a micro-GPS system to locate the NIT, travel to its location, and latch itself onto the NIT's exterior shell;

- Step 2: following successful completion of Step 1, the pNIT transmits its audiovisual message to the receiving mechanism of the NIT, which eventually communicates that message to the host human at the pre-set time

Her pride in the pNIT's dual-targeting function was all self-pride, of course, because she could not share her accomplishment with anyone. She was more impressed with it than she ever was of age-decoding or reverse-aging. In her view, it was her highest achievement.

Most importantly, its use would be constructive, not destructive.

Frieda was convinced that the scientists who had assisted her at the Authority – electrical engineers, biologists, neurologists, physiologists, and bioengineers – were never fully aware of the true purpose of her pNIT, for each contributed only partially to the complicated research web that she commanded as Chief Genomicist and which only she could comprehend from a distance. Yet these scientists had been extremely helpful. In all likelihood, the fact that the pNIT device was deemed integral to the timing coordination for reverse-aging and needed to be integrated with the host human's NIT made her project appear as a logical extension of official business. It crossed her mind that a few of the scientists may have had their suspicions, but refrained from saying anything to Gupta out of respect for the artificial superintelligence entity. Or out of fear of being completely mistaken.

The pNIT's dual-targeting function, though impressive, was not her only source of pride. Frieda, and only she, knew that the billions who underwent reverse-aging would not change. The scientists behind the reverse-aging would be shocked to know that their invention, which they had labored over for so long under her command, would be debilitated by her inclusion of the anti-CRISPR protein AcrIIA14 in the liquid mixture. Reverse-aging would not take effect and would only serve as a Trojan Horse for her diametrically different purpose.

Reverse-aging was her necessary feint, and Frieda knew that Gupta and other Authority leaders would be livid when they found out what she had done – or, worse, not done. Reverse-aging would remain unimplemented. Frieda knew that would not be the case forever, as immortality and youngness were just too tempting for humans. But she wanted no part in it now. She had learned her lesson the hard way with ELSI, age-decoding, and the propensity to dissent. Her focus was on mending the present and sparing the near future.

CHAPTER 44

AGE-DECODED

IT CAME AS A DREAM on August 1, 2254, at exactly 3:00 a.m. Eastern Standard Time, staggered across other time zones so it hit all reverse-aged people simultaneously. It was not a normal dream. No, it was stronger, more vivid and colorful, sharper in purpose, and tighter in structure than a normal dream. Dr. Frieda Sengmeuller sat at a desk, hands cupped, donning brown pants and a green jacket coat. With her calm but firm voice, she revealed how the Authority faked her suicide, enslaved her to work on reverse-aging, and altered the gene that controlled people's propensity to dissent.

Her message, which lasted just ninety seconds, was simple yet powerful: the Fundamental Platform was a charade, based on two centuries of corruption. She implored people to vote against the Authority and support a new government that would be ethical in dealing with genetic technology. Her message concluded as follows:

> *Our Authority, which owns and controls genetic information, has failed us. This is not a dream. This is a communication, a direct plea. When you wake, please share this information with people who were not reverse-aged. Humanity is within you if you reach down deeply. Use your democratic power now while you have the opportunity. Again, please know that this is not a dream.*

This single communication thundered across Zone1. No government decree, catastrophe, or fantastic event had ever delivered such a shock.

Billions had the dream, and they eagerly shared it with those who had not. It did not fizzle out like a normal dream. It could be recalled, while awake, as vividly as it was experienced. Its staying power convinced every recipient that it was anything but a dream. The relatively few who were awake when it came experienced it as an overpowering conscious thought wave. All recipients, whether asleep or awake, could not deny it, shut it out, or forget even the tiniest detail. They could replay every second of it profoundly, and many felt compelled to replay it over and over. Its effect would not fade. It was a powerful, uncontrollable visual-auditory manifestation, not a normal dream. Some never spoke of it, though that did not imply they were less affected; others felt the need to reach out and share every aspect of it, to validate and reconcile. Discovering that all others had the very same dream made it a singular phenomenon, a prophecy, certainly more than a dream. It was simple, direct, linear rendering, not a *circular ruins*, as in the Jorge Luis Borges' short story; not the "incoherent and vertiginous matter of which dreams are composed"; not a regression such as dreaming about dreaming about a dream. On the contrary, Frieda's message was a linear dream-like rendering. From the eternal darkness of captivity, she had broken through the clever apparatus of the Authority and circumvented the digital guard of FENCODE_11. Her breach was brilliant: unfathomable yet unmistakable. To the billions who had the dream, to whomever it touched, it was more, so much more, than a dream.

For all, it was a raw, overwhelming realization of corruption and deception, a rational knowing, so potent and genuine that it commanded some degree of action, even for those with a deactivated propensity to dissent. Their rational awakening, as Frieda had hoped, was about to trump the genetic tampering of the Authority. They were validating what Tavon had told the Rethinking Party members: *propensity is a propensity, not a certainty.*

President Reubers himself had the dream, and when he woke, he walked quickly to the bathroom, poured cold water over his face, and examined himself, standing close to the mirror. He peered into his hallowed eyes. What's going on? Was that a nightmare? Unlike a normal dream, it had rooted and entangled itself deep inside him like weeds in an unkempt garden. He hated that feeling in the weeds.

What the hell was it? The Fundamental Platform had peoples' faith as its linchpin, a faith decimated by that dream.

Ximena did not have the dream. But when people shared it with her and filled her consciousness with its fine elements, she shed hopeful tears. It was tantalizingly possible she could see her mother again. To Ximena, so genuine were peoples' elaborations of the dream that she relived inside her soul the longstanding suffering Frieda must have borne for her, for everyone. Tavon was right all along about her mother being alive. She vowed to do everything she could to support Rethinking in defeating this Authority.

Jesus did not have the dream, for he did not choose to be reverse-aged. But the descriptions from others were so vivid that he knew the dream. It awakened critical forces within him, with his daughter Frieda, a true hero, calling out to him and lending him the rationale to act.

An almost noiseless knock came on Tavon's back door late that morning. A moth darted in as he opened the door a few inches and exchanged envelopes with an anonymous messenger. For the past four days, once a day, this had been Tavon's means of liaison with the Rethinking Party. Even this communication worried Tavon. Who knew if the messenger was tracked or followed? He also found it awkward, letter writing, exchanging hand-written soliloquies with a time lag of twenty-four hours. It was excruciating, given how urgent things were.

He opened the envelope and read the letter:

Hi Tavon: Rethinking met and celebrated the incredible event of Frieda's dream, which we can only assume was accomplished through an undetectable organic transfer mechanism she cooked up while those bastards contained her. What a coup d'état! A masterstroke of genius! We should have believed you about her being alive. Please do not begrudge our skepticism.

We are in election mode and anticipating major inroads if not an outright victory. Based on our internal polls the Fundamental Platform is in jeopardy. We don't have a great organizational structure, but volunteers are pouring in like never before, wide-eyed and enthusiastic. The Authority must be worried.

We are formulating a Rethinking shadow cabinet and many here want you to be included, as one of the Ministers. I'm going to put your name forward unless you communicate otherwise. You are most capable and deserving.

Let us know what we can do to mitigate the actions those in the Authority are taking or planning. We are, of course, most interested in the condition and fate of Dr. Sengmeuller. Nothing would give us greater satisfaction than being able to pluck her from their filthy hands and set her free.

Keep up the great work, Tavon, and best of luck holding your cards closely in the Core6. Everyone here appreciates your courage.

Your comrade, Tom Stephenson

p.s. Ximena, Jesus, Jason, and Sarah all send their regards.

Tom's note made Tavon smile. It underscored the rightness of his resolve to work against the Authority. He knew he was not alone, with positive reinforcement from other like-minded humans.

Tavon's mind wandered, as it often did, to Ahmed's sad exploration at the Spectre Society, to his emotional attempted reunification with Ximena, and his horrid, torturous end. What made Ahmed switch to our side? And what took him so long? Was he always, deep inside, a good person? Were those at the Authority, who worked side by side with Ahmed, all bad? That seemed too simple. Perhaps people are inherently good, but capable of bad actions if trapped in bad circumstances? The entire dichotomy seemed misleading. Maybe people are like technologies: neither good nor bad, just operating within circumstances? He wondered how Jesus and Ximena might interpret this.

CHAPTER 45

TAVON FEIGNED THAT he had no idea what the emergency Core6 meeting in New York was about. When he entered the room, the others were already seated and chatting. Seeing they each had a refreshment, he helped himself to a coffee with cream, then sat down at the corner furthest from Reubers and Zhinghu, who were side-by-side.

Reubers began, "OK, everyone. This is the most important agenda we've ever entertained, and I mean that."

Tavon thought he detected a slight quiver of the President's eyebrows.

Reubers continued, "So let's get to it. For starters, how many of you had that damned dream or whatever the hell it was?"

Every hand went up except Tavon's.

"You didn't have a dream involving Dr. Sengmeuller last night?" asked Zhinghu, almost annoyed with the exception.

"No. What dream?" said Tavon.

Reubers explained, "The dream that hit everyone last night, or at least every person I've talked to this morning. It featured Dr. Frieda Sengmeuller criticizing our alleged capture of her and exposing the deactivation of the propensity to dissent. Brooks, are you saying you didn't have that dream?"

"Exactly. Are you saying you all had identical dreams last night?"

"Apparently," said Rahilly.

"It sounds crazy, doesn't it?" said Tellier.

Gupta added, "According to the dream itself, it might make sense that Brooks didn't have it because he didn't undergo reverse-aging. Recall, he's not a eubeing."

"What do you mean?" said Tavon.

"In the dream, Sengmeuller urged those who were reverse-aged to share the message with those who weren't. So obviously people like you – non-eubeings – didn't have the dream."

"That's logical," said Rahilly. "I understand that Suzanne is currently checking that with our researchers as we speak. We should get a fix on that in a few minutes. But more importantly, how did this dream get broadcast? If every recently reverse-aged person had an identical dream, there must have been a singular communication source."

Reubers asked, "Is it possible someone transmitted it electronically via FENCODE_11? Does it have the communication capacity to do that sort of thing?"

"FENCODE_11 can't do that," said Tavon. "As you know, it can broadcast through any digital media, but it can't broadcast through internal organic processes such as dreams."

Zhinghu added, "Obviously, unless we all believe in divine intervention or ESP, the mechanism for broadcasting this had something to do with the reverse-aging process itself."

"That's what I'm thinking," said Reubers.

Tellier and Gupta nodded.

Gupta said, "Whoever orchestrated that broadcast must have collaborated with Dr. Sengmeuller." She stopped for a moment; she had to be careful about what she said because she and Reubers were the only two people in the room aware that Frieda was alive. "But that's impossible because Sengmeuller killed herself two centuries ago. So some virtual surrogate of her was used? How real did she seem in the dream, to all of you?"

"I knew her very well at HGP, worked with her for years," said Zhinghu, "and I was freaked out by her presence in that dream. Her face, her speech, her mannerisms – they were all so life-like. To me, it seemed like the real her. I have little doubt." He paused, surprised by the silliness of what he had said. "But, of course, we know that's impossible."

Reubers was at a crossroads, which he knew he would reach one day. Should he tell the rest of them that Sengmeuller was confined by the Authority all this time? Until now it had been expedient for him and Gupta not to share with them the CG's identity. Should he tell them now?

Zhinghu noticed Reubers's look of consternation.

Reubers pulled Gupta aside and asked to speak to her in confidence. They left the room.

"What is it?" she asked.

"There's a piece of the puzzle, you know what I mean, that I think we should finally share with the others. How can we talk strategy with them at this crucial moment ... if they're in the dark on this? It's time to tell them, don't you think?"

Gupta responded, "You know I'm dead set against revealing it to any more people."

Reubers reasoned with her, "Look, through the dream she's already revealed herself and everything that happened to her. I'm sure millions if not billions believe her ... wouldn't you?"

Gupta thought carefully about what he had said. She could not deny the veracity of his argument. "OK. I'll fill them in," she said, knowing she was jeopardizing her chances for the Nobel Prize.

When they returned to the room, Reubers sat back while Gupta revealed to everyone that the Chief Genomicist was Dr. Frieda Sengmeuller. She explained why her identity had been hidden from them. She anxiously concluded, "Therefore, what Dr. Sengmeuller stated in the dream, everything she said, is true."

Suddenly, Zhinghu slammed his fist down and rose from the table. "What the fuck's going on here?!" He glared at Gupta, who braced herself. "You two knew about this for two centuries and didn't inform us?"

"Zhinghu, let's talk this over," Reubers urged.

"To hell with talking! What you did, or I should say what you didn't do, is a violation of Core6 information disclosure code, and you know it!"

"You're right. I admit it's that," replied Reubers. "But in this case, we needed an exception to strict policy. Only two people in the world knew about Sengmeuller, and we thought it crucial to keep it that way, even within the SI Committee and Core6. Gupta was involved from the start because she's a genomics specialist. It made sense to connect her to Sengmeuller since she worked directly with Frieda in the past. She was perfect for cajoling her to work on reverse-aging. Scientist to scientist stuff."

Zhinghu chose not to respond.

Presently a technician walked into the room and handed a single sheet of paper to Tellier, who scanned it with a blank face. "It looks like our hunch was correct. The dream experience hit only by reverse-aged citizens. Yet that's a huge chunk of the population – I'm guessing over 50%. Almost all the middle-aged and older people, and many in the group closer to twenty-five years old. So we're saying at least six billion people had the dream?"

"Six billion who know the truth," said Zhinghu.

"Well, six billion who've been exposed to the truth," said Rahilly. "But we can't assume, and I don't believe, all of them fully trust the dream or even comprehend it."

Reubers had heard enough. The truth was out, and he knew it. He realized the dream was no act of magic, but he did not know much else. Clearing his throat, he stood up stern-faced, and stated emphatically, "OK, I want an action plan moving forward. First, we need to get the truth from Sengmeuller. Find out whether or how she did this, or who else might have helped her. We'll need to make full use of FENCODE_11's tentacles. Second, we need an assessment of the popular support for the party heading into the election. Is this a credible threat to our electoral supremacy? Third, we need to mobilize our Zone Guard Forces."

Reubers assigned the duties. "First action: all of us will meet with Sengmeuller, to get to the bottom of her actions. Brooks, you can get

FENCODE_11 dedicated on high priority SI mode to determine if any other scientists helped her. Coordinate that system with input from Zhinghu and Rahilly. Second action: Tellier, help Rahilly by assessing all Zone1 voting intentions, including the latest attitudes toward the Fundamental Platform; a focus on Rethinking is paramount. Third action: Gupta, help me arrange Zone Guard mobilization through Safety and Security. We'll need the Guard more in the next two weeks than we've needed them in the last two centuries."

When he had finished, Reubers peered out the window, way down to the hundreds of small moving dots of New York traffic. He worried about what might be churning in the minds of the citizens in those vehicles. In their newly loaded minds. Turning back for one last fleeting look at everyone in the room, it struck him that his team, though talented and experienced, was very green with regards to truly serious challenges.

He returned to the table, remained standing, and stated solemnly, "The eternal honeymoon's over folks. This dream, or whatever the hell it was, is a genuine threat. However – and this is vital – it's officially to be regarded as nothing, a non-event. No acknowledgment of it, or Dr. Sengmeuller, in any external communications. Officially, this dream thing never happened."

He surveyed everyone in the room, then concluded "Alright, we'll meet back here in exactly forty-eight hours. Remember, I want action."

Reubers asked Zhinghu to stay behind. When the others had left, he told him that he understood why he was disappointed about not being privy to Sengmeuller's existence. To make amends, and because Zhinghu had done a fantastic job at the helm of the SI Committee, he told him there may be a position for him as Deputy President of the Authority if he continued his strong leadership through the current crisis. Zhinghu tried his best to contain his glee.

CHAPTER 46

AFTER THE RELEASE OF her dream, Frieda expected this interrogation. In some masochistic way, she had been looking forward to it. Her job was done. Her actions, which she had worked so hard to safeguard to the very last moment, were now transparent to all, with ramifications beyond her control. Fate, that marvelous adjudicator who rides over time and bypasses all judgment and purpose, could take it from here. Based on the line of questioning from Zhinghu and Rahilly, with the rest of the Core6 watching, she assumed operational success of her pNIT. The effect must have been potent, and she wanted to scream with joy. But she had this interrogation to tend to.

Near the end of the questioning, Frieda said, "People, I've told you the truth, the complete truth. Why don't you just accept the demise of your so-called Fundamental Platform? I can arrange to have you and the others safely exiled from Zone1. There exist many beautiful getaways in Zone2. Please, we can keep it simple and civil. I'll assist you."

Zhinghu was barely aware of what she was saying. He could not stop disbelieving how much they had been duped. How could this have happened? Didn't anyone see it coming? Why hadn't Gupta, who had worked so closely with Sengmeuller all these years, caught wind? The ploy, amidst such tight security, so many eyes, hundreds of scientists, was unfathomable to him. Did it prove Dr. Sengmeuller's brilliance? Or their incompetence?

Rahilly asked, "What other surprises do you have in store for us through the pNIT?"

"None. It's done its job – it's broadcast the truth to as many as possible."

"How can we trust you when you say it's done?"

"You can't." She then let loose on them, "Trust went out the window two hundred years ago, with your marginalization of ELSI, tampering with peoples' propensity to dissent, faking my suicide, and torturing my husband. You don't remember all of that? Trust is a non-starter." She paused, looked at them sternly, "But you'd better believe me on this."

Zhinghu jumped in, "Who worked with you inside the Authority? There must've been others."

"Many scientists worked with me, but none collaborated."

"Why don't I believe you?" said Zhinghu.

"Why not? Consider the principle of *piecemeal construction*, used by the central government during the building of the Wall of China. The decrees of the High Command, as Kafka called them in his short story, *The Great Wall of China,* came from afar, from the Emperor in Peking. A group of about twenty workers followed the decrees and labored on a 500-yard section of the wall, completing it in about five years. Other groups labored on other sections, independently. When a singular section of the wall was completed, that group was transferred to another faraway region to begin building another section. In this way, through piecemeal construction, the Wall gradually came together over about twenty years. Many have wondered why the central government chose this method. Would it not have been easier to work on the wall linearly, from one end to the other, or from each end and meeting in the middle? Resources could have been employed more efficiently. Surely it would have been the better way."

"What the hell are you talking about?" asked Rahilly, echoing the thoughts of everyone else.

Frieda answered, "I'm saying The Wall came together without the actors knowing about anything except their little part, which they could work on proudly. Look, Gupta, none of your scientists knew. Like the builders of the Wall, they worked well, worked hard, but never had the big picture. Only I, the Chief Genomicist, had the bird's-eye view. You ensured it by making me anonymous. Does any of this make sense to you folks? Why do there have to be collaborators? To suit your fancy and fit your paranoia?" Frieda couldn't hold herself back, "Are you and Zhinghu looking for an excuse to rev up your LNS torture machine? Is that why you're itching for collaborators?"

Tavon was beyond impressed with how Frieda toyed with them. It was a front-row display of brilliance.

Zhinghu withheld himself. *She's taunting me openly now.* But he had no choice but to proceed to the next planned question. He asked, "Did you reactivate the propensity to dissent in these people?"

Frieda answered, "Frankly, the technology entailing deactivation of the propensity to dissent is old, and it would have been easy to reactivate it. As you know, I was one of the original experts in that area. But that extra step was too risky. I do hope the world follows through with reactivation once your Authority removes itself from power. It would give me immense pleasure to reactivate all eubeings myself. As Kafka wrote about the building of the Wall of China, *feebleness of faith ... prevents them from raising the Empire out of its stagnation.* I'm sure the new wisdom of eubeings will quash all feebleness. You and the others had it too good for so long. You've now lost the wherewithal to control. It looks like you'll have a competitive election this time. The propensity to dissent is just a tendency trait. You're about to learn that."

Her barrage of insults stung. Zhinghu withheld the urge to whack Frieda right then. But they had to move along. He served up the final question, "Did you actually reverse-age those people?"

For the first time in the interrogation, Frieda considered telling a lie. But she decided it would not hurt her and would irritate them even more if she told the truth. "Of course I didn't. Reverse-aging was my Trojan Horse, the temptation used on you and the others. I never endorsed the implementation of age-decoding, and I would never implement reverse-aging."

Zhinghu looked at Reubers for tacit approval on some matter, apparently got it, then turned his gaze back upon Frieda, "O.K. I've heard enough from you. We all have. But I'm going to have the last word now. I have the pleasure of informing you that your partner, Ahmed Iftikhar, is dead. We discovered he was collaborating with an enemy to the government, so we tortured him to death."

With a hideous smirk, Gupta added, "Laserneurosplicing technology was just too brutal for him to survive. It worked like a charm."

Frieda looked down to her lap and pressed her hands deeper into her jacket pockets as a defense. The news devastated her, but she refused to let them see that. Inside, her guts heaved about. Tavon, witnessing this, suffered vicariously to his core. Yet her marvelous strength mesmerized him.

Reubers knew Frieda was of little use to the Authority now. She was a liability, in fact, capable of motivating the minds and hearts of the reactivated public. Yet he spared her, at least for the time being. Zhinghu mused to himself that if LNS torture was to be used on Frieda, he would have to wait. But when that day came, the fact that Frieda was a woman and a Nobel Laureate would not deter him from using it full force.

Two days later, just forty-eight hours before the election, Tellier gave Zhinghu the updates regarding popular opinion, which pointed to a potential defeat of the Authority at the hands of the Rethinking Party. The data were immediately relayed to Reubers and others in Core6, who mulled over the situation.

Tavon spoke up, "It's dour, numbers-wise. There's no way we can win this one, not at this eleventh hour."

There had to be a way to stop this train wreck, Reubers thought. After remaining silent for most of their deliberations, he suddenly cried out: "We're going to cancel the election!"

One hour later the Authority issued a declaration which rang out across all media: *the general election is postponed indefinitely.* The reason given: a FENCODE_11 electoral system malfunction.

CHAPTER 47

AGE-DECODED

THE SECOND DREAM CAME at 3:00 a.m. Eastern Stand Time on August 7, 2254, which would have been one day before the scheduled election. Again, it was delivered to all reverse-aged people, simultaneously, regardless of their location. Frieda appeared, still strong and confident, her voice sharp with purpose:

Again, this message is not a dream. This is Dr. Frieda Sengmeuller and I have a second message. I anticipate that by this time the Authority will have done nothing except "strategic optics" in reaction to my first message. If so, they have failed you, and have not solved the problem. If that is the case, and your voice of democracy is not respected, this is a second plea, a plea for a united civil action, showing that you, good citizens, will not cooperate with a government that abuses genetic technology and human dignity. Just ask yourselves one simple question: have you been allowed authentic democracy?

To all eubeings and non-eubeings alike: I urge you not to riot or act violently. That is the course of fools. I call on you to engage in civil action, to become Kafka "hunger artists": to live on water alone – except the young and the elderly, who you must nurture as usual – until the Authority capitulates from the effects of your action. You will succeed if you are strong, and in fasting, you will need to be extraordinarily strong. While doing this, avoid all productive activity, except for the maintenance of nutrition and health of the young and old. Show the unworthy Authority that Zone1 cannot function without you. Be hunger artists for the sake of humanity. Show them that the nutrients you yearn for are the nutrients of democracy. Your vigilance and sacrifice will be rewarded. Remember, this is not a dream.

The message, which lasted just seventy-five seconds, caused a frenzy across Zone1, as much as the first dream.

In an instant, billions of eubeings, equipped with insight into the cancellation of the election, resolved to become *hunger artists*. No longer would they idle away, superficially satiated. Gale force winds of change were about to vanquish their perpetual doldrums of complacency.

Few knew anything about Frieda's reference to the short story, *A Hunger Artist,* by Franz Kafka, depicting the intriguing psychology of individuals who fasted for several weeks, usually within a cage in the public square of a small town, for everyone to marvel at; who survived as professionals by collecting monies from sympathetic passersby; who made their living by nearly dying. Billions purchased Kafka's ebook, *The Complete Stories of Franz Kafka.*

Ximena immediately began to fast. When people relayed her mother's second message, it mesmerized her. She shook nervously through much of the first day; she grasped Jesus's hand with anticipatory vigor, knowing her restraint would be part of a much bigger action, a grand dissent unprecedented in age-decoded times. It all made sense to her: Frieda was in her blood. She tried to imagine: what it would be like to go ten days, twenty, thirty, or more? For the first time in almost two centuries, she would refrain from eating anything, including her hand, making her sacrifice even greater.

Jason was thrilled to be a hunger artist. He was borderline in terms of allowable age, but he would not deny himself this tremendous chance to finally get involved. His friend Shu joined the cause, and they encouraged each other along the way. As a growing young man, Jason found fasting harsh, but the pain and the weakness did not deter his ambition to be the best hunger artist in all of Zone1. His sister Sarah, not old enough to join them, did restrict her eating at times to support what they were doing. He encouraged her, but he also protected her from fasting too much.

Jesus was deemed too old to be a hunger artist, but he immersed himself in the dedication of Jason and Ximena; he taught them to meditate, conserve energy, and interpret bodily signs. "Interestingly," he noted, "once you're into the fasting, once you truly experience serious starvation, you won't fear death at all." He then surprised himself in bypassing Buddhism and recounting a popular Hindu saying from the sacred text *Brihadāranyaka Upanishad*:

> *From delusion lead me to truth,*
> *From darkness lead me to light,*
> *From death lead me to immortality.*

"After the first dream," Jesus told Jason and Ximena, "eubeings knew they had been deluded ... the golden ratio of accountability skewed. After the second dream, they understood the path to the light, as unified hunger artists. And with both dreams combined, they grasped the real difference between mortality and immortality."

Tavon was torn about being a hunger artist. He yearned to join all the others, but should he? What would Frieda want him to do if he could talk to her? He decided not to engage in hunger artistry, for he had to maintain his infiltration of Core6.

Billions of hunger artists arose from Frieda's plea. None doubted the veracity of the second dream, which they knew, like the first, was much more than a dream. Like Kafka's hunger artists, they fasted introspectively, due to the basal and individual nature of the challenge. Yet their fast was different from traditional hunger artists of days gone by; not solitary, as Kafka described, performing as one person for a small village; but alongside billions, performing for the salvation of the entire Zone1. They fasted in America, Europe, and large tracts of South America, Africa, and Asia; in cities, towns, and the remote regions; in houses and on the streets. Religious and non-religious; rich, modest, or poor. All day and all night. In unison, they did not eat, and they drank only water. They fended off hunger like a deadly plague. For the first time in their lives, nothing else mattered. Even those who did not experience the two dreams trusted their neighbors and friends and joined in as hunger artists. They all dug in fervently.

True, not every individual was successful in their fasting: some pretended and cheated; others broke down and abandoned the challenge. As anonymous wrote: *The belly talks but doesn't listen.* But billions were mad for the cause, ripe for dissent, thick with anger. They fought through the early stages of fasting: hunger pangs, listlessness, temptation, fear, second-guessing, hallucination, and sleep deprivation. They persisted and broke through to the later stages, which, ironically, were easier to bear. They learned what Kafka meant in writing of the long-term hunger artist, "For he alone knew what no other initiate knew, how easy it was to fast. It was the easiest thing in the world".

As hunger artists, they were more than mere hunger strikers. True, like strikers, their intent was political. But they were artists as well. Artists, who sought to create an indelible image, crafted in unison. Their brush was human resolve. Their colors were supplied by the palette of Frieda's exhortation and lifelong example. Their subject was freedom. Nothing could tarnish their work. A final magnificent image was implanted in the back of their eyes, etched handsomely into their souls. A single, ultimate rendering, a grand positive illustration, coming to light. Their quest for human justice hinged on artistic talent possessed by all. Their fasting, though physiologically undeniable, was artistically deep. Like artists, they forwent materiality for the numinous, the untapped, the lasting. If their hero Frieda could suffer locked away for two centuries, they could be hunger artists.

CHAPTER 48

AS REUBERS REQUESTED, Dr. Mantharathna arranged Zone Guard mobilization through Safety and Security. But the Guard was not battle-tested, because the Authority had never been challenged since the inception of the Fundamental Platform. Moreover, the Guard was not a large force, numbering only about 100,000, which could never effectively cover a region as vast and scattered as Zone1. It was armed with short-range LT's (laser/tasers), ideal for quelling disturbances, though that had never been an issue for the Authority.

The real threat was the raw zeal of the hunger artists and the commensurate breakdown of the economy and society. As a defense against that, the Guard was as useless as a fly swatter in the dark.

By August 29, 2254, three weeks of fasting had severely weighed down Zone1. People rested and cocooned in their homes, did not go to work, only occasionally headed out to check on a neighbor or to drop in on a local fasting support group. Commercial trade and public services, including public transit, were at a standstill. Travel was nonexistent. Cities were reduced to hushed remnants of their former bustling selves. The Zone1 Gross Domestic Product plummeted severely on all fronts: exports, investment, consumption, and government spending. For the first time in history, the Zone2 economy outperformed Zone1. This humiliated and mortified the leaders of the Authority.

FENCODE_11 had no precedents to feed on. It spewed out listless *petitio principii*, circular reasoning. This majestic entity could not devise a way to force-feed people. Regardless of its raw power and dodecabit sophistication, it could not command the human physiological act of ingesting food. It fixated on a singular outcome: people should just eat, people should just eat, people should just eat. But that was an outcome, not a solution.

President Reubers and the inner cabinet met each day to strategize. But a suitable strategy was unattainable. They could only hope – with increasing desperation – that the resolve of the people would weaken. But the resolve of the hunger artists flowed further each day and hardened each night like lava after multiple eruptions. How could the Guard help? What could FENCODE_11 do? What could the cabinet strategize? The President made emergency public speeches urging people to stop fasting, warning of the negative long-term effects of starvation. But it was a desperate, wasted effort, as people saw through his conflict of interest. Besides, they now loathed Reubers, the man responsible for capturing and containing Dr. Frieda Sengmeuller, and tampering with their propensity to dissent. Their loathing was widespread, rationally based, and entrenched.

By September 19, 2254, after six weeks of mass hunger artistry afforded by the will of the people, Zone1 had spiraled into mass starvation and economic plague, wobbling at the precipice of anarchy. Leaks abounded of panic within the Authority, internal defections, and a government apparatus in shambles.

Billions of emaciated hunger artists desperately turned their minds away from hunger. Many died, and many more came perilously close to death. The rest bore on, weary but resolute in perpetual inhibition and thinking – especially the thinking, which they found to be more robust than normal, a compensation for the frailness of their bodies. As for the dead, funerals were avoided through a tacit mutual understanding to preserve people's energy, which was precious. Obituaries withheld the truth: *she died suddenly in her sleep from unknown causes.* Volunteers gathered up corpses and witnessed the sorrow of loved ones who, despite their bony cheeks and sunken eyes, remained passionate.

The leaders in the Authority knew their run of power was over. Though they figured correctly that many machinations of their government, such as FENCODE_11, could continue functioning no matter how many people starved, the fact is that food would not be delivered or sold, nor shelves stocked, garbage collected, houses and offices cleaned, drugs administered, medicine and drugs distributed, people and neighborhoods protected, or sick tended to if people refused to eat or function. While robots still provided some of these products and services, humans were still the primary providers of most essential services.

Were these hunger artists mere sycophants to two strange dreams? No, because those dreams were much more than dreams. They were a historic clarion call to humanity, from a most unlikely source, the reborn Dr. Frieda Sengmeuller.

The hunger artists were prevailing. Nothing was left to govern, so continuing to govern was out of the question. The Authority was rendered obsolete.

The Zone1 Authority had emerged innocently from the cooperative seeds of genetic engineering to formulate the historic, some would say mesmeric, Fundamental Platform. It had made great progress over the past two centuries, including solving climate change. In the minds of its leaders, its most incredible accomplishment was the whittling down the four avoidable human physical sufferings – birth, old age, sickness, and death. Yet it is said that all governments, competent or corrupt, eventually implode. The two-hundred-year reign of the Authority had been substantial in terms of political history, but relative to the lifespan of a eubeing it was slight, just another political shooting star in the corner of humanity's eye.

The Authority's first act of capitulation was to dismantle FENCODE_11, its dodecabit subcomponents, cross-connections, data analyses, cross-correlations (personal or non-personal), digital backups, video and voice data, NIT recordings, pictoplath records, and any information linked to classified modeling and analysis by the SI group. The bizarre number used for its access code, the total possible genetic codings for chromosome 13, namely $4^{113113113}$, became a trivial relic, a number few needed in the past and nobody would need in the future. Statistician Tavon Brooks was appointed to oversee the great dismantling, a task he would relish.

The second act of capitulation was to contact Jesus and Tom Stephenson at the Rethinking Party to negotiate terms for the transfer of power and exile of key Authority members. Jesus made sure Rethinking leader Tom Stephenson was grounded in fairness, so the terms of the transfer were not vengeful, demonstrating compassion for those who had not operated with the same principles. All former leaders of Authority were ensured *marga*: their paths forward oblique but not tortuous, with the potential for personal enlightenment. Jesus even suggested that someday, perhaps a few centuries from now, they might be invited back to Zone1.

The final and most difficult act of capitulation was the release of Dr. Frieda Sengmeuller. This did not come as a unanimous Core6 decision, as some hawks – Zhinghu and Mantharathna in particular – wanted her executed for the vast trouble she had caused. Zhinghu even called for LNS torture before her execution. For the first time in his new position in Core6, Tavon took a stand. He argued that Frieda had suffered enough under the Authority, from what they had done to her and her family. Rahilly and Tellier backed him on this. With that, Reubers chose to liberate Frieda. Overjoyed but suppressing his emotions, Tavon could hardly wait to tell Ximena and Jesus.

Core6 members gained safe passage to the aquamarine getaway island of Phuket, Thailand. As they boarded the aircraft to leave, Tavon revealed that he would not be accompanying them – that his exile was nonsensical because he had been working with the Rethinking Party. He promptly turned around and walked away, freed from working with these people ever again. Ambling through the deserted airport hallway, he fired up his NIT and contacted Ximena to share the great news about Frieda. Ximena was ecstatic. Tavon's eyes watered up as he thought about how much he loved his own mother. He told Ximena that Frieda would be returning to her house in New Orleans within a day or two. When he suggested that he might visit Jason and Sarah sometime soon she smiled inside, knowing there was more to it.

Upon her release, the diminutive Dr. Sengmeuller, truly a giant in this world with new hope, requested her scientific digitals, reading glasses, and directions to her daughter Ximena's house, which to her surprise was still at the same location. She could truly call it home again. From the hub where she was deposited by order of Reubers, she ebiked the remaining distance alongside the Mississippi River. She marveled at how the moderate wind kicked up tiny whitecaps while the sun reflected their seafoam green towards her. Continuing along Riverside Drive, through the neighborhood, she finally reached the top of a driveway.

Frieda stood with her bike at the edge of the sidewalk under the shade of the pink Japanese magnolia. This moment was her long-awaited living dream. Two figures emerged from the house and slowly descended the bluestone slab steps, passing dozens of fully bloomed limelight hydrangeas. She struggled for her next breath and her heart jittered as the overjoyed faces of Ximena and Jesus came into focus, basking in the honeycomb-yellow sunlight.

Frieda dropped her bike and sprang forward. The three of them locked into a long-awaited, joyous embrace.

Don't miss out!

Visit the website below and you can sign up to receive emails whenever Mark P Ryall publishes a new book. There's no charge and no obligation.

https://books2read.com/r/B-A-IBTN-WPQMB

BOOKS 2 READ

Connecting independent readers to independent writers.

About the Author

Mark Ryall taught economics and mathematics at Royal St. George's College, Toronto and Hillfield Strathallan College, Hamilton for a combined twenty-two years. *Age-Decoded* is Mark's first novel. He wrote it to educate himself and the world about the imminent tsunami of genetic engineering. He believes this technology will fundamentally alter human nature, and that it must be carefully controlled and applied to serve humanity well. Mark competes in triathlons and is also an avid golfer. He enjoys acrylic art, painting historic structures and sports portraits. Mark currently serves as a volunteer cross country coach for Westdale Secondary School, Hamilton. His education is eclectic, including BSc, MBA, and PhD (University of Toronto, Education).

Lightning Source UK Ltd.
Milton Keynes UK
UKHW040941160223
417122UK00002B/315